A *Queen* Besieged

A LUKE TREMAYNE ADVENTURE

A Queen Besieged

A PORTUGUESE LIAISON
1658

GEOFF QUAIFE

ARPress
ILLUMINATING IDEAS,
EMPOWERING VOICES

ARPress
45 Dan Road Suite 36
Canton MA 02021

Hotline: 1(800) 220-7660
Fax: 1(855) 752-6001

Ordering Information:
Quantity sales. Special discounts are available on quantity purchases by corporations, associations, and others. For details, contact the publisher at the address above.

Printed in the United States of America.

ISBN-13:   Softcover   979-8-89389-193-5
           eBook   979-8-89389-192-8
           Hardback   979-8-89389-963-4

Library of Congress Control Number: 2024914535

THE LUKE TREMAYNE ADVENTURES

(In chronological order of the events portrayed)

MAJOR CHARACTERS

Cromwell's Men

Sir Luke Tremayne	Major general, special envoy
Capt. Peter Frost	Luke's equerry and interpreter

The Queen's Party

Count Rodrigo da Costa	Member of the royal council, husband to Micaela
Countess Micaela da Costa	Senior lady-in-waiting to Queen Luisa
Col. Alvaro da Costa	Head of Portuguese military intelligence, brother of Rodrigo
Marquess Pero da Silva	Minister of war
Marchioness Beatrix da Silva	His wife
Baron Diego de Albuquerque	Member of the royal council
Baroness Madalena de Albuquerque	His wife
Aileen Murphy	Servant to Madalena

The Clergy

Fr. Antonio Mendes	Franciscan priest, chaplain to the royal council
Fr. Eduardo Zarco	Inquisitor
Fr. Nicodemo Oliveira	Portuguese priest in Spanish-occupied territory
Fr. Francisco Diaz	Chaplain to the Marquess of Estrela

Others Present at Castle Estrela

Paolo, Marquess of Estrela	Nobleman, cousin to Rodrigo
Joana, Marchioness of Estrela	His wife, cousin of Queen Luisa
Baron Carlos de Cipriano	Chamberlain to Paolo, castellan of the castle
Baroness Ana de Cipriano	His wife
Maj. Alfredo Matos	Carlos's deputy, former army surgeon
Vitor Abrega	Acting chamberlain
Lord Manuel Caro	General
Viscount Gaspar de Mota	General
Viscountess Camilla de Mota	His wife
Count Baltasar Pinto	General
Countess Teresa Pinto	His wife
Lord Ramiro de Lima	Frontier warlord

The Spaniards

Lord Jorge Zoritas	Spanish landowner imposed on Portuguese villagers
Mendo Zoritas	His degenerate son
Federico Sanchez	Spanish general, governor of Castle Passos
Col. Marcos Barbosa	Spanish spy, troubleshooter, envoy

Others

Viscount Roberto Delgado	Commander of Portuguese militia regiment, heir to a powerful and wealthy duchy
Marabella Gomes	Accused witch

Real Historical Personages

John, Duke of Braganza	King of Portugal (1640–56) as John IV
Luisa de Guzman	Queen of Portugal and consort to John (1640–56), regent (1656–62)
Baltasar Sandoval	Cardinal archbishop of Toledo (1646–65)
Gaspar Alfonso de Guzman	Ninth Duke of Medina-Sidonia (1602–64), brother to Luisa, led failed rebellion against Felipe IV in 1640
Antonio de la Cerda	Seventh Duke of Medinaceli, commander of Spain's Western defenses
Felipe IV (III)	King of Spain (1621–64) and Portugal (1621–40)
Oliver Cromwell	Lord Protector of England, Scotland, and Ireland
Thomas Maynard	English consul to Lisbon

Spanish and Portuguese names have been simplified and titles anglicized.

PROLOGUE

In 1640, the Duke of Braganza rebelled against Spain, which had ruled Portugal since 1580. Proclaimed King John IV, he achieved Portuguese independence but died in 1656, leaving as regent for his young son Afonso his wife Luisa de Guzman. She was the Spanish-born granddaughter of the Duke of Medina-Sidonia, who led the Spanish armada against England in 1588.

As regent, she was besieged on all sides as she battled to maintain Portuguese independence. Her Spanish birth led many ultranationalists to distrust her, yet conversely, one-third of her nobility wanted the restoration of Spanish rule. The Catholic Church, led by the Inquisition and the pope, refused to accept Portuguese independence and in turn whipped up popular sentiment against the two allies that Luisa cultivated—England and France.

Spanish troops, concentrated on three areas along the frontier, indulged in constant border raids that, at any time, could escalate into major invasions. The Dutch had destroyed the Portuguese Empire in the East Indies, capturing most of Indonesia and Ceylon. They had initially captured Brazil, but the Portuguese successfully regained most of that colony. The Dutch, however, continued to harass Portuguese shipping and made several attempts to capture the valuable sugar fleet on which the Portuguese economy now depended. The French sent an army into Catalonia to divert Spanish troops from the Portuguese frontier, while the English fleet made Lisbon their base to protect Portuguese trade against the Dutch.

Queen Luisa faced trouble within her family as the young King Afonso for whom she ruled was both mentally and physically weak and the subject of unscrupulous politicians determined to turn him against his mother. Of immediate concern was evidence that one or more members of the queen's government who sat in the council of war were traitors.

Anxious to assist the Portuguese queen against her many enemies, England and France combined to send Luke Tremayne to assess the situation.

RETURNING HOME FROM HIS mission in North Africa, Luke and the *Cromwell* put into Lisbon, now a major supply base for the English Mediterranean and Atlantic fleets. Soon after they had docked, the ship's navigator, Capt. Ralph Croft, announced that the English consul to Portugal had come aboard with an urgent message for Major General Tremayne.

The envoy introduced himself. "I am Thomas Maynard. My instructions are to give you this sealed letter and to invite you to have dinner with me this evening, where a representative of Queen Luisa will give you details of a special mission."

"Am I not to continue to England with the *Cromwell*?" asked an apprehensive Luke.

"All will be made clear in this letter."

It was. The personal directive from Cromwell was clear.

> After a request from Queen Luisa—conveyed to me through the French ambassador, with Cardinal Mazarin, the French chief minister's support—you are seconded to the Portuguese court to assist the queen as part of her alliance with France and England. You will act overtly in your role as a soldier sent to assess how many troops England should commit to the defense of Portugal. Your real mission will be conveyed to you by the queen soon after your arrival. Maynard knows your cover story but

is to be kept ignorant of anything that the Portuguese crown reveals to you. He will second one of the Portuguese speaking officers attached to the consulate as your equerry, interpreter, and deputy.

As Luke watched the consul's coach disappear into the city, he was glad that the dockside was filled with heavily armed Portuguese troops. They formed a barrier between the *Cromwell* and a growing group of local agitators, who were methodically tossing rocks in the direction of the English vessel.

Later that day, the coach, with a large escort of Portuguese cavalry, returned to collect Luke. He arrived at the consul's residence at the appointed time and was concerned to note another large deployment of soldiers surrounding the consul's home. He remarked on the widespread need for Portuguese protection and received a disturbing explanation from Maynard.

"General, the public hate the English. Although the government has signed a treaty seeking our help in return for trading concessions, the populace, lied to by the Inquisition, sees us as heretics who should be driven from the land. Last week, I survived an assassination attempt. Our sailors, who are protecting Portuguese trade from the Dutch and preserving the local economy, can no longer come ashore without armed guards. The locals set upon them, and several have been killed. The troops out the front are a mixture of the Portuguese royal guard and our own men, who do not wear any distinguishing clothes. If the mob knew they were English, it would just provoke further outrage."

"Why troops from the royal guard?" asked Luke.

"Put bluntly, as you will discover, the only person in Portugal whom the English can trust and who has sent some of her best men to protect us is the queen. In fact, her representative has already arrived and awaits you through that door. After you have finished your discussion, please join the rest of us in the banqueting hall."

Luke entered the antechamber to be greeted by a petite woman in her mid-thirties with dark brown hair and surprisingly bright blue eyes. Her facial appearance was immediately familiar. Luke wracked his brain trying to remember where they had met. The woman held out her hand, which he formally kissed. She beckoned him to join her on a lavishly cushioned bench, where she addressed him in perfect English—with a slight accent that Luke immediately placed as French.

"General, I am Micaela da Costa, Countess of Cacella, senior lady-in-waiting and confidante to the queen. Welcome to Portugal. Her Majesty wishes to thank you for coming. I am to outline your covert mission."

"Before you do so, I am sure we have met before—but I cannot place where," admitted Luke.

The countess smiled. "No, we have never met, but I do resemble people whom you know. Before I married the count, I was a member of the French court as Michele St. Michel and am a cousin of the Marquess des Anges, whose honor, estates, and life you saved during your time in France five years ago. At that time, my cousin and the chief minister of France, Cardinal Mazarin, were both full of your praises. I look a lot like the St. Michel women you met at my cousin's chateau. It was my memory of your efforts on his behalf then that led to your invitation here."

"I can blame you for delaying my return to England," Luke half-joked.

"Yes. When the queen expressed concern that she could trust very few of her military officers, I suggested that she invite a French, English or Spanish hating-Italian general to assist her. On reflection, I suggested you, whom I believed would have both French and English support. Her Majesty wrote to Cardinal Mazarin to use his influence with the Lord Protector of England to send you here to carry out a special mission for the queen."

"And what is this special mission?"

"The queen is besieged on all sides. The Spaniards threaten invasion along three key areas of the frontier. The Dutch patrol the seas off our shore, waiting to capture the country's lifeblood—the sugar fleet from the West Indies. The nobility is divided, with probably a third of them preferring the return of Spanish Habsburg rule to that of an independent Portugal The populace is violently opposed to the government seeking French and especially English Protestant help. The pope refuses to recognize our Portuguese bishops. Even within her family, there are dangers. Some extreme nationalist nobles, suspicious of the queen's Spanish birth, want King Afonso, a mentally and physically weak child, to replace his mother as regent with one of their own ambitious leaders."

"Countess, even if I were the most powerful and influential man in Europe, I could not solve any of the problems you list."

"Don't worry, Tremayne, we do not expect the impossible. Your mission is simple. The queen's immediate problem is the unknown number of leading soldiers and nobles who openly support her, but are secretly on the Spanish payroll. This problem goes to the highest level. Part of the queen's council meets as a council of war. Recently, the generals devised a plan to attack a Spanish border town that had poor defenses and had no idea that our forces were in their area. When we made our supposed surprise attack, the town was heavily fortified with troops that outnumbered ours three to one. We suffered massive losses. Someone on the council had forewarned the Spaniards."

"So how can I help on this issue?"

"You have been seconded to the council of war. Your role, as far as its members are concerned, is to assess the Portuguese military situation to recommend to your government how many English troops could be sent to assist us. Your real task is to uncover the Spanish agent or agents within the council and military high command."

"Even this limited mission seems overwhelming," replied Luke.

"To make it easier for you, the next meeting of the council of war will convene near the Spanish border in the mountainous midwest of the country, in the castle of my husband's cousin, Paolo da Costa, Marquess of Estrela. There is a chance, if heavy rains continue or if there is an early snowfall, that you may be isolated there for some time, which will help your investigation."

"Another Da Costa! This does appear to be a family affair."

"More so than you think. The queen has placed at your disposal the head of her military intelligence, my husband's younger brother, Col. Alvaro da Costa. He speaks English and Dutch and will act as your interpreter. Your move to Castle Estrela needs to be kept a secret until you are well out of Lisbon. Colonel da Costa will be here at the consul's residence in the morning, and you will depart in disguise and on horseback for the frontier. You and your deputy, Captain Frost, who will be provided by Maynard, will have to dispense with your red jackets. It immediately identifies you as the hated English, which can send a mob into an uncontrollable frenzy."

"My lady, let us move into the reception," said Luke, assuming the briefing had ended.

"One last piece of advice—no one, including the Marquess of Estrela, must know this real reason for your visit. If it was ever revealed, it could seriously weaken the queen's position. None of the royal councillors or any of the generals must ever know. The truth is limited to the queen, myself, and Colonel da Costa. You will remain popular with the generals if they think you are here to provide them with English troops. Cromwell's army has a very high reputation."

Luke and the countess entered the banqueting hall and were soon partaking in the feast that the consul Maynard had provided. During the meal, the countess quietly slipped away.

Two hours later, as Luke was about to return to the *Cromwell,* Maynard drew him aside. "Tremayne, I understand from the gossip that you are here to pave the way for the arrival of English troops to assist the Portuguese military. Do not agree. The Portuguese army is not united. Each general, even each colonel, does his own thing. They are a rabble. Portuguese garrisons surrender easily to the Spaniards and vice versa. Let the French provide the military assistance needed. We should concentrate on what we can do well and to our advantage—protect the Portuguese merchant fleet and our own trade against the Dutch and the Spaniards. Let our navy alone contribute to Portuguese independence."

"Thank you, Consul. I shall consider your advice. Can you send me clothing to disguise my appearance—and horses? I am to leave Lisbon first thing in the morning."

"Yes. I am also ordered to make available to you one of my Portuguese-speaking officers to act as equerry, but more importantly to be your translator and interpreter. I strongly suggest that you conceal this officer's ability to speak Portuguese as long as you can. I would not trust the government's official interpreter to always translate correctly. Keep this officer's ability secret, and he will prove to be a great asset."

"You do not trust the current administration?"

"It speaks with too many voices."

"When do I meet this officer?"

Maynard spoke to a servant, who left the room and returned with a tall, well-built, light-brown-haired young man.

"Capt. Peter Frost reporting for duty, sir," stated the newcomer as he saluted Luke.

"Relax, Captain. Are you ready to return to the *Cromwell* with me now and then depart for the hinterland in the morning?"

"Yes, sir! I am delighted to serve under you, General, but also to renew my acquaintance with Miles Oxenbridge before he sails on to England. Three years ago, we were both lieutenants of the troops aboard General Blake's flagship on his first adventure into the Mediterranean."

Maynard cut the introductions short. "Return to your ship now in my coach and under escort. The authorities have already increased the cordon of troops dockside. The locals may attempt to board your vessel. I will send with you the clothing you need to leave Lisbon safely."

Luke experienced the strength of anti-English feeling as the coach made its way back to the docks. Several missiles hit the vehicle despite the Portuguese cavalry and its aggressive action against the mob. Troopers rode straight at the gathering groups of would-be assailants who lined the road, scattering them with dramatic swings of their swords. Others had their horses rise on their hind legs and attack the mob with their front feet.

Miles greeted Luke as he disembarked from the coach, both just avoiding a barrage of well-aimed missiles. He was delighted to see his former comrade, Peter Frost, and muttered, "Ungrateful swine! Don't the Portuguese realize we English are protecting them from invasion and the devastation that such an event brings to everybody?"

"Are they motivated by a genuine hatred of us, nurtured by the Inquisition, or are they a paid mob recruited by the deep purses of pro-Spanish nobility?" asked Luke to no one in particular.

"A bit of both. The populace finds it hard to accept that a strong Catholic nation has to stoop so low as to plead with extreme Protestant heretics for assistance, especially as the Protestant Dutch continue to threaten Portuguese survival by attacking their lifeblood, the sugar fleet from Brazil," answered Peter.

"Did you discover the details of your mission from the mysterious agent of the queen?" asked the curious Miles.

"Yes, from a beautiful French noblewoman whose relatives I knew quite well. I have to be ready to leave for midwestern Portugal at eight in the morning. I am to attend the council of war and meet most of the Portuguese generals in an isolated castle in the mountains. We are to be accompanied by the head of their military intelligence, a Col. Alvaro da Costa. He is my official interpreter. Peter, you will conceal your ability to speak and understand Portuguese. We may not be able to trust this Da Costa."

Captain Croft joined them and indicated that he would feel safer if he moved the ship out into the harbor. "Despite the efforts of the Portuguese troops, missiles are still hitting the ship. If any of them is an explosive device, it could do considerable damage. I don't need to raise sail. The current tide should allow us to drift into a safer position."

Luke agreed but cautioned, "We will also be well away from the Portuguese protective net, and our opponents might endeavor to approach our new position by boat. Miles, your men must keep watch throughout the night."

2

LUKE HAD LITTLE SLEEP. He was awakened from time to time by musket fire from the English watch as it kept at a distance hostile boats attempting to approach the *Cromwell*. Early the next morning, Luke bid his companions of the North African adventure farewell, especially the sailors Ralph Croft and John Neville and his military deputy, Miles Oxenbridge. They would sail for England on the next high tide.

At eight, Luke and Peter, his new deputy, prepared to board the ship's longboat and be taken ashore.

Ralph stopped them. "Wait until your coach and, hopefully, an effective escort arrives. There is a large unfriendly crowd gathered near the dock. The constant fire by the Portuguese troops suggest that it is considered dangerous. I have been watching through the telescope. The demonstrators are being urged on by two priests."

Half an hour passed, and the promised coach did not arrive. The noise from the growing mob increased, and one could make out many abusive anti-English phrases. Around nine o'clock, the beat of a drum was heard, which became louder by the minute. The crowd also heard it. The Portuguese protecting the English ship took advantage of it and fired above the heads of the mob. Within minutes, a full company of infantry wearing the queen's own livery joined the dockside guards, augmented soon afterward by a large troop of heavy cavalry. One of the horsemen dismounted and waved toward the *Cromwell*.

Ralph put down his telescope. "It's Maynard. He is indicating that it is safe for you to leave."

Maynard was apologetic. "Sorry, Tremayne. Our plans had to be changed. My coach was vandalized overnight, and when I became aware of the size of the anti-English mob gathering between my residence and here, I sent a message to the queen, who responded by sending me part of the household guard to disperse the rioters. Colonel da Costa has sent a troop of his own men to escort you directly from here to the Three Crosses, a *taberna* several miles out of town, where he will meet you."

A young officer cantered toward them, leading three horses, two already saddled and a third ready to carry their meagre belongings. Luke and Peter mounted their new steeds, and the former thanked Maynard for his assistance.

The consul was blunt. "Frankly, I do not know why the protector wants to help this Papist-infected country. I would not waste a single English soldier defending them against Spain. I cannot see how the queen can withstand the widespread opposition to her rule. The Spanish Habsburgs will be back in power within the year. Persuade the Portuguese to make peace with Spain!"

Luke, well aware of the mercantile bias of the English consuls throughout southern Europe, commented, "But you are still happy that the navy risks life and limb to defend Portuguese shipping?"

"Of course. In defending Portuguese shipping, you are assisting English trade. It is in England's economic and political interests to defend Portugal at sea—but not on land. Our merchants in the Netherlands desperately want peace with Spain, as do we here."

Before Luke could respond, the young officer from military intelligence signaled for them to depart.

The unit soon left Lisbon far behind as they progressed in a northwesterly direction beside the River Tagus. Around noon, with Luke beginning to feel hungry, the troop stopped. Its leader signaled for a ferry, then on the other side of the river, to return to the southern bank. He indicated to Luke that they should board the vessel as soon as it arrived and pointed out a *taberna* on the opposite bank, where they would meet Da Costa. He saluted, turned, and led his men back toward Lisbon.

Across the river, the English officers tied their horses to the railings outside the Three Crosses and entered the establishment. They were immediately accosted by weasel of a man who led them into a back room, where they were greeted by a well-built officer with long black hair, a short black beard, and clear signs of wounds obtained in battle—or through dueling. There was a large scar across his left cheek, and he was missing the three middle fingers of his right hand.

He saluted and announced, "Col. Alvaro da Costa at your service. My sister-in-law has briefed me on your past, and I am honored to work with someone of your eminence."

Luke, always uncomfortable when praised, responded, "Colonel, I am sure your history is as illustrious as mine. Intelligence in a complex society such as Portugal must be an incredibly difficult task."

Alvaro smiled but otherwise ignored the comment. "You must be famished. Let us enjoy a meal, during which I will inform you of what lies ahead."

Servants entered the room, bearing a range of dishes.

"What do we have here?" asked the cautious Peter, already a victim of Portuguese cuisine.

"Good peasant fare. Once you reach Castle Estrela, you will be spoilt with the refined tastes of the nobility. Here, that first bowl is caldo verde, a soup consisting of potatoes, shredded kale, and chunks of spicy sausage. The second is *caldeirada*, a stew of mixed seafood with potatoes, onions, and tomatoes. The third is tripe and white beans. The smaller dishes have grilled sardines or chunks of salted cod cooked in milk with potatoes and onions."

"And these carafes of wine?" asked Luke.

"Both are *vinho verde*, which means they should be drunk young. The white is slightly sparkling and the red very light. As we have a hard journey ahead, I did not think heavy mature wines would be helpful in the middle of the day."

The three soldiers enjoyed the meal, during which Alvaro outlined the situation.

"The council of war that will meet in Estrela—in the absence of the queen, who is her own chief minister—will be presided over by the minister of war, Pero da Silva. He was a favorite of the late King John, but his attitude toward the queen regent is difficult to appraise. He is very anti-Spanish, and Luisa's Spanish birth may make him open to those nobles led by Viscount Roberto Delgado, who want young King Afonso to remove his mother and appoint a new regent, presumably one of them. Only two of the leading aristocrats on the council have come with Da Silva. One is Diego de Albuquerque, whose relatives have played a major role in gaining and maintaining Portuguese independence and colonial power. I fought as a young man under his illustrious uncle Matias. The third civilian member of the council present is my brother Rodrigo da Costa, Count of Cacella."

Luke indiscreetly commented, "This is very much a family affair. Apart from any ideological and nationalistic commitment you have to Queen Luisa, your family's fortunes seem heavily dependent on her favor."

"Yes, but it does not mean that we Da Costas dance to the same tune. For example, Rodrigo is not aware of your real mission. The queen, Micaela, and myself alone are privy to that secret," replied Alvaro haughtily.

"Surely, the council is not limited to three men," said Peter.

"No, but only three permanent members of the council will go to Estrela on this occasion. And it is always augmented by five or six military men deemed most appropriate to the agenda on hand. The queen has carefully selected three generals who have pledged their absolute loyalty to her—but one of whom she suspects may be the traitor, she hopes you will uncover."

"Who are they?"

"Manuel Caro, Gaspar de Mota, and Baltasar Pinto."

"So the queen and you have helpfully limited my suspects to six—Da Silva, Albuquerque, Da Costa, Caro, De Mota, and Pinto," commented Luke with a hint of sarcasm.

"Yes. It should not be beyond us to set a trap and catch the traitor as he tries to pass on the confidential details of our next offensive—the plans for which will be devised at the coming Estrela meeting."

Peter suddenly put his finger to his mouth, demanding silence, and then pointed to the door.

Alvaro moved quickly and swung the door open, and a large fat man with a round face, a tonsure, and the habit of a Franciscan friar half-fell into the room. He immediately apologized, explaining that he was just about to enter the room, not knowing it was occupied, when the door suddenly gave way and he fell forward.

He retreated.

Alvaro shut the door. With concern written all over his face, he asked, "Was that just an accident, or was the friar trying to hear what we were discussing? The pro-Spanish sections of the church are determined to undermine even your overt mission, which is anathema to them—the provision of Protestant troops to help Catholic Portugal defend itself against Catholic Spain."

Alvaro returned to the door, opened it, and shouted. The weasel-like servant came running and, after a harangue from Alvaro, scuttled away.

Alvaro explained, "I have asked the porter to find out when the priest arrived. I hope he has been staying here for a few days."

"Which means he has not followed us here, and his intrusion was just an accident," commented Luke.

"Let's finish the wine before we move on," suggested Peter.

Ten minutes later, the weasel returned. Alvaro listened with an increasingly puzzled brow and doleful expression. "The very worst of news. The priest came on the ferry on its crossing immediately after yours. He probably followed your troop out of Lisbon. We must take precautions."

"What does that mean precisely?" queried Luke.

"My first instinct is to entice the friar back here and kill him, but the murder of a cleric would have half the province following three men who left the tavern in a hurry after his death. The last thing we want is to attract attention to ourselves. And we do not want to risk killing an innocent man of God," confessed Alvaro as he crossed himself.

"What do you suggest?" asked Peter.

"We will leave in a few minutes. The road northwest soon enters a forest. Once in the forest, I will leave you and hide beside the road. If the friar is following us, I will remove him."

"It might just be a coincidence that the priest is heading the same way as us," added Peter.

"It is not a coincidence I am willing to risk," proclaimed Alvaro.

The three soldiers left the Three Crosses and followed the main road along the northern bank of the Tagus. Half an hour later, the cultivated fields gave way to a dense, dark forest.

After they had progressed for another fifteen minutes, Alvaro spoke. "I will leave you here. Ride to the edge of the forest and wait for me there."

"I'll stay with you. If the friar is following, two of us can dispose of him more easily than one. Some clergy I have known are as good a swordsman as any of us," volunteered Luke.

"No, Tremayne. I will handle it. If I do not rejoin you in an hour, continue on to the Golden Goat, our overnight destination."

Luke and Peter cantered slowly through the forest and dismounted at its edge. After some time, they heard voices. It was a lively discussion, and Luke recognized that one of the participants was Alvaro. When he emerged from the forest, his companion, chatting loudly and amicably, was the fat friar whom Alvaro introduced as Fr. Antonio Mendes, chaplain to the queen and her council.

"He is heading for the same meeting as we are. Antonio does not speak English but is fluent in Dutch, as I believe you are, Luke," he added.

"How come you did not kill him before he had a chance to explain who he was?" asked Luke. "You intended to shoot him in the back of the head before he knew you were there, drag the body deeper into the forest, and then disappear. What changed your mind?"

"You are right. I intended to shoot him as he rode past. At the last minute, I thought that if he were an enemy agent, intensive interrogation might prove useful. I stepped out in front of him with my pistol primed. His first words surprised me and lessened my desire to dispatch him immediately."

"How can any man's words make such an impression?" asked Luke.

"Maybe it is not possible in English, but in Portuguese, the right words can alter a situation immediately."

"What were his magic words?" probed Peter.

"He said, 'Desist in the name of the queen.' Most clerics in Iberia would have used the name of God or Mother Church to explain the authority behind their statement. I told him that I too was acting for the queen. He then showed me a letter addressed to the minister of war, announcing he was the new chaplain to the council."

"Why did you not recognize him when he fell through the door at the inn?" asked a suspicious Luke.

I HAVE NEVER MET HIM. The old chaplain died only a few weeks ago. The queen has moved very quickly to replace him. Mendes is a Franciscan friar who is also a priest. Most of the clergy around the old and new king were and are Jesuits or Dominicans. This appointment is a move by the queen to use the rivalry between the orders to her advantage. The Jesuits are supporting the ultranationalist nobles and may wish to see the Spanish-born queen replaced as regent and the local Dominicans control the Inquisition, which is the strongest opponent of Portuguese independence within the church. It uses its immense religious and political power to terrorize those who support the queen with threats of eternal damnation. The Franciscans have been one of the few elements in the church to support both Portuguese independence and the current queen regent."

"What does the queen hope to achieve by sending a priest to the council of war?" asked Luke. "I could never see the point at home of our council of state having to listen to long sermons by fanatical preachers before it settled down to urgent state business."

"Queen Luisa is a very devout Catholic in that obsessive Spanish manner in which she was educated. There are two clerics very close to her. Her confessor is a very ancient Benedictine who lives within the queen's quarters and whom I have never met. Only those very close to the queen, such as my sister-in-law, have actually seen him. The other priest close to her is the royal chaplain, who acts with her on public occasions. This is now our new companion, Mendes."

"I repeat my question," reiterated Luke.

"I can only repeat what Father Mendes told me. He was told that shortly, the council of war would be meeting near the frontier to determine an issue on which Portuguese independence depended. It was so important that God's assistance must be called on to ensure its success. He was leave for Castle Estrela immediately and report his presence to the minister of war on his arrival."

"Do you believe him?" Luke asked.

"Yes, although I suspect the queen has sent him as a special agent to spy on us. She does not trust anyone—including me, her head of intelligence."

"Could Mendes be aware of my real mission?" whispered Luke.

"Not if we believe what he says. In this toxic environment, the queen probably does not trust him to that extent. He believes our mission is for you to decide whether to send English troops to our assistance and the numbers and conditions that may be involved in such a decision."

Luke was skeptical. "The priest may not be alone. I would like to assure myself that there is not a host of potential enemies on our heels. Peter and I will backtrack and see who is behind us. We will meet you at the Golden Goat."

"Don't get lost. A few miles farther upstream, along the Tagus, you will come across its confluence with the Zêzere. Turn north along the western bank of that tributary, and you will eventually reach the Golden Goat."

"I hope the name doesn't reflect its menu," muttered the culinary cynic, Peter.

Alvaro and Antonio moved on, and Peter and Luke climbed a small grassy hillock. While their horses happily grazed, they lay on the ground from where they had a good view of the road but could not be seen by the travelers upon it. Their vigil proved disappointing. There were very few travelers, most of whom Luke could not envisage as active opponents of the queen—a group of boisterous women returning from the market with the profits of their sales spent on carafes of wine, which they continued to consume as they frolicked along the road, a group of peasants leading two cartloads of dung, and a group of nuns who, in sharp contrast to the peasant women, walked in absolute silence, except for the rhythmic chant of their recited rosary.

Later that night, after the four travelers had consumed an indefinable variety of stews and soups, Luke and Peter retired to a tiny room.

An observant Peter commented, "You're unhappy, Luke. What's the problem?"

"Father Antonio. I have my doubts."

"As a true Cromwellian veteran, you simply have no time for priests, but what exactly troubles you in this case?" probed Peter.

"The countess Micaela is very close to the queen. I find it strange that she did not mention that the regent was also sending a priest to this secret and most important meeting. I am also worried that Alvaro has never met the man. The person in the next room may be a pro-Spanish imposter who has killed the real Father Antonio—and he speaks Dutch."

"So do you. Is that a crime?" joked Peter.

"It suggests that this priest was in the Netherlands—the *Spanish* Netherlands. The only Portuguese presence there are a number of wealthy merchants, most of whom are Jews. They would have no need of a priest. This man could easily be a Spanish imposter."

"Luckily, the queen did not inform the real Antonio of our real mission," added Peter.

"We only have his—or his imposter's—word that such is the case," concluded a depressed Luke.

The next morning, the four men headed into the mountains. As the valley of the Zêzere gradually narrowed, the pace of the river rapidly increased. Agrarian land gave way to pine and beech forests, and many castles and fortified houses were seen atop the various summits as they moved northwest. As the climb became steeper, the track left the cascading river and moved deeper into a dense pine forest that excluded much of the sunlight.

Suddenly, the gloom and silence was broken by gunfire. A large red-bearded character confronted them, while seven or eight of his men surrounded them—two of whom began searching their saddlebags. Redbeard introduced himself as Ramiro de Lima, Count of Prados. After a discussion with his men, who had turned up few valuables in the saddlebags, he ordered the four travelers to place any valuables they had on their person onto the ground. Little was forthcoming.

Suddenly, Alvaro exclaimed, "Don't you recognize me? We fought together in the early days of our war of independence under that great general, Matias de Albuquerque. You did not have a lavish red beard in those days."

Ramiro put his hands on either side of Alvaro's face and stared into his eyes. "Holy mother! Young Da Costa. What are you doing out of Lisbon? I thought you were a foppish courtier."

"I am visiting my cousin at Castle Estrela and have with me a Franciscan priest and two English soldiers who have come to inspect the frontier. It is our hope that they will provide troops to help us against Spain. But what are you up to? Reduced to highway robbery?"

Ramiro ignored the question and commented, "You will not reach Castle Estrela before nightfall. Stay with me overnight."

Ramiro's large country house was perched on a small plateau, which made defense relatively easy. Attached to it were large stables, which Luke estimated could cater for a company of cavalry. Ramiro was much more than a highway robber. After a satisfying meal of roasted goat and sheep, washed down with some mature heavy red wines, Ramiro and his four guests retired to a cozy antechamber in which a large fire burned huge pine logs, effectively pushing back the continuing chill of an early spring. Alvaro translated Ramiro's remarks for the Englishmen.

"I drink a toast to you English in the hope that you will help us be rid of the Spaniards. I am not a wealthy man. This is not an agrarian area and has limited grazing possibilities. My main income comes from the slate mines farther into the hills and my family's investment in the sugar plantations of Brazil. But this is not enough to maintain my private army without a little highway robbery and raids into Spanish territory."

"You are carrying on a private war with Spain?" asked Alvaro.

"Yes, someone has to. Since the death of King John, the leading generals seem to have gone into retirement or are even fighting one another. The queen must appoint an overall commander-in-chief and unify the army. We are a long way from the border, and our raids into Spanish territory have been increasingly less rewarding. The Spaniards have withdrawn from a number of villages that were once good pickings for us."

Luke asked Ramiro, "Are you a cavalry officer? I was for many years."

"My men are what you English would call dragoons. We have to move in and out of Spain as quickly as possible. Heavy cavalry would be too slow, and there is no use for the infantry other than those mounted as dragoons."

"I would like to join you on your next raid. I began my military career in the Dutch cavalry, attacking the Spaniards. It would be good to do it again under your leadership," suggested Luke to a surprised but chuffed Ramiro.

"I would be honored to have you ride with me, General. I must retire now. I am sorry I cannot find you beds or female company, but these cushions and the blazing fire should give you all a comfortable night."

As soon as Ramiro left, an indignant Alvaro turned on Luke. "Invading Spain is not part of your mission!"

"No, but it will provide support for my cover story, how best to assess the needs of the Portuguese than to join them on a raiding sortie into Spain," he replied.

The next morning, they breakfasted on ham, cheese, and freshly baked bread.

Ramiro joined them and suspiciously asked, "What is really happening at Castle Estrela?"

Alvaro looked alarmed.

Antonio asked with an air of innocence, "What makes you think something out of the ordinary is happening at Castle Estrela other than a visit by two English officers?"

"I am not a fool, priest," said Ramiro tersely. "For the last few days, the road below us to the castle has been very busy. Numerous groups of horsemen, large contingents of infantry, and the occasional carriage that either carried women or very high-ranking officials have been seen. I had to suspend any attempt at robbing these people as most groups were heavily escorted by troops that bore the insignia of the queen herself."

Alvaro, who had recovered his composure, replied, "It is no great secret. To discuss English military help, senior generals and government officials are meeting at Castle Estrela to explain the needs and difficulties that the Portuguese military face along the border. As anti-English feeling is running high in Lisbon and other seaports, it was deemed more appropriate to meet in the mountains."

"Is the queen herself to be present?" probed Ramiro.

"No comment. Spain is ever ready to send a raiding party across the frontier. Their best agent, would-be assassin, and guerrilla fighter—the notorious Chameleon, otherwise Col. Marcos Barbosa of Spanish military intelligence—is constantly roaming the borderlands, causing trouble. To capture the queen near the frontier would put an immediate end to Portuguese independence. Would we be so foolish as to risk that?" answered Alvaro without much conviction.

"I hope that is the case. I have had several brushes with the Chameleon. He is an able operator."

"Why the Chameleon?" asked Luke.

"To the local peasants, he is a master of disguise—nothing sophisticated and designed to be effective only at a distance. For example, the Marquess of Estrela is known for wearing elaborate hats with long plumes. At a distance, Barbosa wearing a similar hat has been mistaken for the marquess. He more often dresses as an innocent friar or mountain shepherd."

Ramiro indicated that should he plan a raid into Spain while Luke was still at the castle, he would be welcomed to join him and added, "You may even confront Barbosa himself."

WHEN THEY REACHED THE main road leading to Castle Estrela, Alvaro was unpleasantly surprised. It was full of people— and they were headed toward the castle. Several carts hauled produce to feed a large number of visitors. Onions, potatoes, parsnips, beans, and flour were evident. Shepherds were driving small flocks of sheep, soon to be meat for the castle's guests. In addition, several military units marching to the beat of a single drummer added to the congestion.

"Hardly the isolated and sparsely populated environment that the queen expected when she ordered her council of war to meet here," Alvaro eventually confessed with considerable annoyance.

"It looks as if the council already has plans for some immediate action given the number of troops we have seen," remarked Luke.

"I can understand the large number of soldiers and the need to have the resources to feed them, but why are there so many religious on the road? We passed a group of nuns earlier, and just ahead of us is a religious procession following priests carrying a golden cross reflecting the rays of the sun right into my eyes," muttered the irritated anti-Catholic, Peter Frost.

"And what have we here?" remarked Alvaro as they passed a group of traveling minstrels taking refreshments at the side of the road.

As the travelers drew level with small group of friars, Antonio, prompted by Alvaro, asked, "Reverend brother, where are you heading?"

"To the chapel of the Castle Estrela to celebrate the Feast of Our Lady of Estrela."

"I am not from hereabouts. Why is Our Lady of Estrela so venerated?" asked Antonio.

"Centuries ago, an ancestor of the current marquess, when a little girl, fell from the parapet of the castle and plunged headfirst toward the raging river Zêzere below. Emerging from a cloud, Our Lady intercepted the falling girl in her arms and carried her safely back to the castle. Every four years, we come to the chapel to seek the help of Our Lady through contemplating the relics of the girl she saved. Her bones are preserved in a glass coffin in a corner of the chapel," explained the friar.

"There seem to be a lot more people than devoted religious moving toward the castle," commented Alvaro.

"Over the years, the feast gradually became a day for the whole local community to celebrate. Local nobles and their tenants and servants gathered in the fields below the castle to engage in sports, dance, and listen to music but, above all, drink and eat. But in the past, there have never been any soldiers, who, this year, seem to be taking over the place," replied the friar with some bitterness.

A little later, the four travelers came in sight of the castle. It was a magnificent edifice that ran along the summit of an elongated ridge overlooking the River Zêzere. It was built on three levels of terraced courtyards. Below the castle walls, on two sides, four terraced fields led down to the main road. One side of the castle was protected by a steep ravine below which the Zêzere raged. What interested Luke was that the field closest to the castle was covered in the newly erected tents of the military, while in the field below that, there were larger tents, and the melodies from assorted minstrels drifted through the air.

The castle's administration was efficient. They were welcomed by the chamberlain of the marquess, himself a baron, and dispatched to various parts of the castle, led by servants wearing bright green-and-yellow livery. The English soldiers were led to their shared bedchamber and then to an antechamber to await an audience with the minister of war. Father Antonio was directed to the chapel and Alvaro summoned to meet with his cousin, the marquess.

After some time waiting in the antechamber, the two English soldiers were rejoined by Alvaro. He was overtly and extremely unhappy.

"What's the problem?" asked Luke.

"I have just come from a very heated family conference. My brother, speaking for the minister, is livid. The queen had sent her council, several generals, and many companies of troops to what she thought was an isolated and deserted area to indulge in highly secret military discussions, decisions, and maneuvers. My cousin claims he was never told anything other than a royal council and some troops would be billeted on him. He assumed the date chosen had been to coincide with the local festivities associated with the Feast of Our Lady of Estrela, which he, as senior aristocrat in the region, hosted every fourth year."

The meeting of the three men with the minister was short. He welcomed them and indicated that they would meet formally the next morning. He indicated that the three invited generals had been asked to devise a plan that would show the English visitors the strengths and weaknesses of the Portuguese military situation, and he hoped that this would influence them to make a favorable decision. Luke asked whether the troops gathered in the field below were those of the particular generals.

The minister replied, "No, most of the troops are from the queen's household brigade, although each of the generals has brought some of their general staff and a few troops. Pinto, as usual, has brought four times more men than the other generals. The deployment of all these soldiers will depend on decisions we make tomorrow. As we have been placed unexpectedly in the middle of a rural festival, you might as well enjoy it."

The only meal that the chamberlain had mentioned was supper at nine, half a day away. Alvaro suggested they visit the entertainment field where drink and simple fare were available. Several goats were being roasted on a spit, slices of which were being removed by a giant of a man with an equally large knife. Luke consumed the thick slices with a pulled handful of freshly baked bread. Another tent provided a drink that Luke had not yet experienced—Portuguese beer. It was clearly infused with an indistinguishable herb that dominated its flavor.

"Different but not unpleasant" was Luke's assessment.

Another stall dispensed various cheeses. Luke's attention was directed toward one of the only patches of green that had not been covered with tents or wagons. Around this verdant area, peasant youth were gathering— strong, strapping lads, each armed with a heavy long staff. Alvaro explained they were congregating for one of most popular competitions—the *jogo do pau*, a conflict between two staff-wielding opponents.

The first contest began with both parties swinging their staves with excessive vigor. Peter tried to coax Luke into participating, but the general declined. He felt instead that he might join a group of men rolling cannonballs toward a small wooden sphere. This would be more to his liking—and status.

Peter took up *the jogo do pau* challenge and proved a little too athletic for his bulkier and slower opponent. Luke was impressed.

"Don't give me too much praise, General. Our detachment at the English consulate in Lisbon regularly play the game."

The soldiers lingered, listening to the music and admiring the dancing, which was rhythmic and cheerful. Both men and women were arrayed in bright colors.

This was not the doleful music that, according to Peter, dominated Lisbon.

Luke now tried a bowl of potato-and-onion soup that contained pieces of boiled fish. They were joined by Father Antonio, who was accompanied by another cleric. He seemed delighted to meet them and recounted to Alvaro his problems since his arrival.

"They seem to believe that I am here to lead the Feast of Our Lady of Estrela. I have insisted that the honor remain with the local clergy and that I am here simply to represent the queen at the festival. None of the clergy here or their servants had any idea that the council of war was to meet in the castle. They attributed the large number of troops to an imminent Portuguese offensive across the frontier in retaliation to a Spanish raid that, a few months ago, almost reached the castle."

Alvaro asked, "Have you picked up any information that might help our cause?"

"No, but I was approached by General Caro, who discovered that I arrived with you. He wanted to glean every bit of information I had on the English officers and why a military intelligence officer was to attend the meeting of the council."

"And what did you tell him?" probed Alvaro.

"That you had been appointed by the queen herself as the official interpreter and guide for the English officers and that your presence had nothing to do with your role in intelligence."

"How did he respond to that answer?" asked Luke.

"He seemed satisfied, commenting that your closeness to your sister-in-law, the queen's senior lady-in-waiting, probably explained the choice."

Alvaro passed this information onto his English comrades.

Luke asked, "What can you tell us about General Caro?"

"Manuel Caro is a war hero. He is a tiny man, not much more than five feet tall. It was his tactics and strategy that enabled him, although heavily outnumbered, to win back several towns in Brazil from the Dutch. On his return to Portugal, he was immediately thrust into operations in the south, where he totally freed the Algarve of isolated Spanish pockets of resistance. He is the one thinker among our generals, having read extensively on the art of war, and he has certainly followed the tactics and strategy of General Cromwell over the years. He does not speak English, but he is fluent in Dutch, which served him well in the Brazilian campaign. I suggest you discuss Cromwell's tactics with him as I imagine you were present during many of the key battles. He would be the one general whom I would cultivate."

As they returned past the staff-wielding contestants, Luke stopped in disbelief. A tall red-bearded giant of a man was taking on two opponents at once.

It was Ramiro de Lima.

"He didn't tell us he was coming here when we left him this morning," added Peter.

The men were leaving the area when Alvaro grabbed Luke's sleeve and pointed in the direction of the staff-wielding battle. Ramiro had dispatched his two young opponents and was now being challenged by a tiny wiry figure whose staff was much longer than his height.

"This should be interesting. That challenger is General Caro. This will be a battle between brawn and brains."

And so it developed. Caro sidestepped, backpedaled, ducked his head, and encouraged Ramiro to take powerful swings, which, from time to time, put him off balance. Taking advantage of such a moment, Caro smashed the staff from Ramiro's hand as he stumbled and lost his footing. The watching crowd, including the Englishmen, cheered at the result. Ramiro was generous in defeat, lifting his vanquisher above his head as the spectators applauded.

Luke turned to Alvaro. "This is the perfect time to meet General Caro."

As Ramiro placed the general back on the ground, Alvaro approached and introduced the two English officers. Luke immediately addressed Caro in Dutch, praising his staff-wielding—and his brilliant military career.

Caro cut the discussion short. "I must talk to you before the council meets. After supper, I will seek you out."

Alvaro, Antonio, and Peter were surprised at Caro's curt comments and sudden departure.

Luke put their minds at rest. "He wishes to see me urgently but not here. I wonder what he has to say."

A S THEY ENTERED THE great hall for supper, the English soldiers were astounded at its size. Alvaro explained that centuries earlier, Castle Estrela was the most southerly outpost of the Christian advance into the territory of the Moslem state of Córdoba. Its great hall was extremely large because it originally had to house and feed hundreds of troops desperately either defending Christian Portugal from Islamic raiders or ready to embark on the further reconquest of infidel territory.

Today it was once again buzzing with activity. There were at least fifty tables, which were smaller than those Luke had experienced in the great halls of English manor houses. Each table seated sixteen people, three at each end and five on each side. A servant led Luke and Alvaro to the far end of the hall to the high table, which was elevated above floor level on a broad platform. Peter was taken to another table befitting his lower status.

At the high table, fourteen places were already occupied. The marquess indicated that Luke should take his place in the vacant seat on the top corner of the lower side of the table. Alvaro was placed next to him at the head of the table beside his cousin.

Once the two late arrivals were seated, the marquess began a short speech of welcome, which Alvaro translated, emphasizing that the marquess had placed Alvaro between himself and Luke so that he could interpret proceedings for Luke. The marquess also pointed out that the lady seated next to Luke was Madalena, wife of Diego de Albuquerque, who was of Irish birth and fluent in English. With the help of Madalena and Alvaro,

Luke should not be at too much of a disadvantage in understanding any discussion.

Luke looked around the table and, with the help of his two English-speaking neighbors, quickly identified his fellow guests. At the head of the table was the marquess, on his right, Alvaro, and on his left, Pero da Silva, the minister of war. On the top side of the table nearest Pero were his wife, Beatrix, Rodrigo da Costa, Ana, wife of the chamberlain Cipriano, Baltasar Pinto, and his wife, Teresa. At the far end of the table were Manuel Caro, Joana, Marchioness of Estrela, and Gaspar de Mota. On the bottom side of the table next to Gaspar was his wife, Camilla, Carlos Cipriano, the chamberlain, Diego de Albuquerque, his wife, Madalena, and Luke Tremayne.

Luke decided that his time could best be spent by concentrating on obtaining an insight into the six males around the table who would be attending the meeting of council in the morning. What could he find out during the course of the meal about councillors Da Silva, Da Costa, and Albuquerque and Generals Caro, De Mota, and Pinto?

He started with the easiest. He asked Alvaro about his brother. The siblings did not look similar in any way. Rodrigo was over ten years Alvaro's senior, and his short cropped hair had turned gray, and his short beard was a mixture of gray and black. He dressed the most soberly of the aristocrats—his clothes were black with the smallest of lace cuffs and collar. The only splash of color was a bright blue ribbon that he wore around his neck, attached to which was a golden medal, indicating an order of knighthood to which he had been elevated. Luke could not fail to notice his outstanding facial feature—an exceedingly large nose.

Alvaro picked up on Luke's focus and explained, "The Da Costa family, during the Christian reconquest of Portugal from the Moslems, were Jewish merchants. When the Christians were victorious, they gave the Jews an ultimatum—convert to Christianity or leave Portugal. The Da Costas did both. One branch of the family left for northern Europe, and their descendants today dominate the Portuguese Jewish merchant community in Amsterdam. Our branch of the family converted to Christianity and, over the last two centuries, have slowly climbed the aristocratic ladder. The original facial traits of our ancestors sometimes reasserts itself, much to the delight of the Inquisition, which is still trying to prove we are clandestine Jews."

"Did your brother take a lead in the fight for Portuguese independence?"

"No. He was not one of the original forty conspirators who plotted to overthrow Habsburg Spain and restore a Portuguese king, but he quickly became a trusted adviser to King John. He was never a soldier but spent most of his time negotiating with the leading nobles to join and remain supporters of John against Spain. When King John died, Queen Luisa kept him on the council because of his past loyalty to her husband and because he was the husband of the one person she trusts implicitly, his wife, Micaela."

Luke now turned to the woman next to him, Madalena. "How is it that an Irish woman finds herself a member of the Portuguese aristocracy, married into such a famous family as the Albuquerques?"

"When your lord protector, then an English general, conquered Ireland in 1648, I was sent by my father to the safety of a relative in Paris who was part of the royal court. Diego's father was sent by King John as the new Portuguese envoy to that court. The rest is history."

"What has Diego done that warrants his membership of the royal council?" asked Luke somewhat undiplomatically.

"Nothing. It's his name, General. Nothing else."

Luke was taken aback by the frank admission of her husband's lack of achievement.

She continued, "Diego, unlike his ancestors and siblings, is not a soldier nor an explorer nor a colonial administrator. I suspect King John—and now Queen Luisa—placed Diego on the council to indicate to his illustrious and powerful relatives that the royal house of Braganza viewed them favorably and relied on their continued loyalty."

Diego was a sickly looking man of medium build and a long thin face, with eyes that seemed too close together. He wore his deep brown hair long and had no other facial hairs. His clothing was sumptuous and gaudily colored—a combination of burgundy and golden silks with large white silk cuffs and collar.

"Does Diego discuss council business with you?"

"No. In Portugal, wives do not have opinions and therefore cannot assist their husbands in anything, especially matters of state."

Luke changed the direction of his questioning. "Does your husband have strong opinions on the matters currently before the council?"

"As I do not know what matters are before the council, I cannot answer your direct question. But I know where your questioning is heading. Diego is a follower. Unless he has orders from his family, he will follow the directions of Minister da Silva."

"And what can you tell me about that minister?"

"As the wife of a royal councillor, I am a member of the Portuguese court. Therefore, what I tell you is essentially court gossip. I have had little personal contact with Pero da Silva. He had a brilliant career as a soldier and rose to command the whole Portuguese army back in the days when it was under one effective general."

"His political career has not been so successful?"

"No, everybody is aware that Portugal needs a united army, well led and well resourced. Under Da Silva, this has not happened."

"Why not?"

"His enemies say that it is because Da Silva does not want to give anybody a position that could rival that of the monarch or his own and who might emulate your own leader Oliver Cromwell—move from commanding general to ruler in his own right. His friends say he has failed because of the opposition of other members of the council who prefer to divert resources to the navy because it is vital to the economic survival of the country—and to the bickering of the generals. The main culprits for this lack of progress are sitting around this table. They each want the top position, and failing that, they refuse to unite in a common cause."

"That will be my message to them tomorrow. Without a unified field command and clear direction of purpose, there will be no English troops," announced Luke.

"Da Silva may see you as his salvation," replied Madalena with a smile.

"What is the court gossip regarding General Pinto?" asked Luke.

Alvaro interrupted. "Is it wise to discuss these matters within the hearing of others? None of them claim to understand English, but I would not be so sure."

"I have perfect hearing, and in the din of this room with its hundreds of guests, I can hardly hear you or Madalena, let along voices across the table," replied Luke.

"And you don't need to worry about Diego on my right. He is completely deaf in his left ear and would have trouble hearing anything, unless it was shouted into his right ear." Madalena continued, "Pinto is a bully and martinet. The Spaniards claim his troops have killed innocent women and children and that he massacred a garrison that had surrendered to him. He has kept mobilized a large segment of the royal army at his own expense. Most of troops here, if not those of the royal household, belong to Pinto. He is the most overt in pledging his loyalty to the queen regent and has shown his disdain for the disabled boy king. If the king were suddenly to die, I would suspect that Pinto had a hand in it. His loyalty to the queen is cemented by the relationship of his wife Teresa to Her Majesty. She is the most senior lady-in-waiting next to Micaela da Costa. He would like his wife to replace Micaela. There is no love lost between the Da Costas and Pinto. He openly campaigns to be commander-in-chief."

"Manuel Caro?" continued the inquisitive Luke.

"The most popular general with the common people and among the troops. He is the ablest and most experienced, a soldier of fortune who has served the Austrian Habsburgs, the French rebels under the Duke of Conde, and, more recently, the French government, being deputy to the great French general Turenne. If Portugal wanted French troops rather than English, the first move of the Portuguese government would be to appoint Caro as commander-in-chief. He is not popular among the other generals nor among members of the council, whom he considers incompetents and backward in their thinking. He does not hesitate to tell them so. He is probably looked down upon by the aristocracy because he comes from a small impoverished landowning family in the Algarve and is of suspected Jewish ancestry."

"Where does he stand regarding the queen regent and the current state of Portuguese politics?"

"He prefers power to be exercised by the queen regent rather than the boy king or the Spanish Habsburgs, but he has little time for the current government and particularly the minister of war. He considers both the politicians and the generals as do-nothing leeches. He will certainly create an exciting meeting tomorrow."

"Is he not married, or has he left his wife at home?"

"You can sympathize with him. He has been about to marry on at least three occasions when circumstances changed dramatically, and the planned nuptials did not occur. He has a reputation as a womanizer—despite his tiny physique."

"Yes," replied Luke nostalgically. "A professional soldier finds it difficult to marry, although after this mission, I hope to do so."

"Oh, I'm sorry to hear that. I thought we might become more closely acquainted," whispered Madalena as her knees pushed hard against Luke's.

Luke replied as he squeezed her hand, "This is not the French court, madam."

Madalena turned to Alvaro, "Are you a bachelor like Generals Caro and Tremayne?"

Alvaro's answer surprised Luke. "Yes. My one true love is forbidden fruit."

It suddenly dawned on Luke—Alvaro was a homosexual.

"I AM SORRY, MADALENA," SAID Luke, slowly withdrawing his hand. "You remind me of my first true love, a young Irish girl like yourself, who was murdered by the Irish Confederates. That was ten years ago. It has taken me a long time to consider marriage with anybody else."

"That explains your reputation as a womanizer," replied Madalena as she reinserted her hand into Luke's.

"The remaining general, Gaspar de Mota?" asked Luke, anxious to change the topic.

"The most traditional and conservative of the three. His position reflects his status as one of the high nobility rather than his reputation as a soldier. He is only a viscount but was the second son and now is the brother of a duke. His family was well favored under Spanish rule, and with the onset of Portuguese independence, they were slow to leave the Spanish camp. During a series of unsuccessful campaigns against Spanish border towns, the frequent accusation against De Mota was that his heart was not in it and that he was loath to kill Spaniards. His wife, Camilla, is a Spanish-born noblewoman related to Antonio de la Cerda, Duke of Medinaceli, who is responsible for protecting the Spanish border from raids by the Portuguese. Her Cerda heritage places her at odds with Queen Luisa, who blames the Cerda family for the poor treatment of her own Guzman dynasty by successive Spanish monarchs. The Cerdas never forgave her grandfather, the Duke of Medina-Sidonia, for his loss of the armada against England seventy years ago, and her brother, the current duke, for his failed rebellion against the Spanish crown in 1640."

The next morning, Luke, Peter, and Alvaro were led through a maze of corridors and up several flights of stairs into a large room where seven men were seated. At the head of the table, Pero da Silva sat alone, on one side, the generals—Caro, De Mota, and Pinto—and opposite them, Father Antonio, Diego de Albuquerque, and Rodrigo da Costa. The Englishmen and Alvaro were directed to the end of the table facing the minister.

Father Antonio found his main role as chaplain to the council was not to evoke God's blessing on the meeting but to record proceedings. The minister welcomed the English officers and set out what he hoped to achieve from the meeting.

"We wish to demonstrate to you that Portugal needs English help with as many troops as you can spare. To convince you of this need and to show you the difficulties we face in this frontier war of attrition, we plan a major offensive to occur while you are here. I have asked each of the generals to submit a plan for such an offensive, which we shall shortly discuss."

Luke's response was blunt. "Minister, even if my report is positive, I cannot guarantee that the government will free up any troops for service in Portugal. Our army is fully employed in keeping Scotland and Ireland pacified, and the recent agreement to assist France in its offensive in the Spanish Netherlands required us to raise an entirely new army. The cost of this military establishment is crippling, and Cromwell is attempting to reduce it. Many feel that England is already helping Portugal significantly by basing its Atlantic and Mediterranean fleet in Portuguese waters. England helps at sea, and France helps on land."

The minister quickly responded, "Our first choice for military assistance is France as aid from a Protestant nation is very unpopular with the people. However, Cardinal Mazarin pointed out that he already maintains a large French army in the eastern half of this peninsula, forcing a large part of the Spanish army to defend Catalonia. This prevents Spain sending many troops against Portugal."

Rodrigo da Costa commented, "Sending troops will cost you nothing. They will be paid and resourced entirely from Portuguese funds, provided your navy can ensure the safe arrival of our sugar fleets from Brazil."

Luke added, "There is one precondition that the English government would insist upon before English troops were sent. The Portuguese army must be united under a single command, with its commander-in-chief having absolute power, subject only to the directions of this council."

"You may understand some of the difficulties in achieving that after you have been with us a little longer," the minister concluded with an ironic smile in Luke's direction.

The generals presented their similar plans suggesting a raid on a border town that was known to be undefended and the establishment of a Portuguese garrison in the conquered town, from which further advances could be made inland at a later date. The method of attack, not having the luxury of artillery, was a short cavalry charge to establish the depth of Spanish opposition and then a quick advance by the infantry.

Luke queried how such an enterprise could be achieved by the number of troops he had seen in the area of Castle Estrela. The minister explained that a larger body of infantry was making its way along the Tagus and would meet up with the troops from Estrela near the border at the newly built barracks, Magellan. This was within striking distance of all the projected targets.

After considerable discussion, progress was halted by two issues of contention—which of the three generals should lead the assault and which of several villages should be attacked. Luke saw an opportunity to advance his real mission of identifying a traitor in their midst.

He commented, "Gentlemen, you must resolve the question of an overall commander sooner rather than later, but can I suggest that, for this enterprise, you allow me to command the campaign—of course, relying on your expert advice?"

Pinto and De Mota were not impressed. But the minister could see this as an easy temporary solution to the enduring problem.

"Continue, Tremayne."

"After you draw up details of the advantages and disadvantages of attacking particular towns and villages, leave the final decision as to the actual targets to me. Cromwell never let even his senior officers know where he would attack. It made it even more difficult for the enemy to prepare any defense. If Spanish troops are thinly deployed along this part of the frontier, let's make their task harder. Let's start rumors now that we are about to attack places that we have no intention of invading. Sow confusion and doubt!"

The minister was relieved, and Manuel Caro strongly supported the idea of Luke's temporary command and hoped that if he would introduce some of Cromwell's successful strategy and tactics, it would be greatly to Portugal's advantage.

The minister and the two civilian members of the council withdrew and left it to the three Portuguese generals, Luke, Peter, and Alvaro to finalize the plans. The soldiers adjourned two hours later as the expected intelligence from Alvaro's officers in Lisbon concerning the concentration of Spanish troops in each village and town had not arrived. It was expected within the hour. It came not long after the two Englishmen had returned to their room with Alvaro.

Luke acted. "As commander-in-chief designate for this operation, I will keep the information to myself and use it in some way to smoke out our traitor."

"How are you going to do that?" asked Peter.

"At the moment, I do not know."

There was a knock on the door. A liveried servant entered and handed Luke a note.

Alvaro translated, "Luke, you are invited to join General Pinto and his wife, Teresa, for a meal immediately—if you are not otherwise committed. I am specifically excluded from the invitation."

"How then will I communicate with our hosts?" asked Luke.

"Pinto will have thought about it. Whatever his other weaknesses, he is a thorough organizer," commented a very peeved Alvaro.

"Tell the servant I accept and will be with the general and his wife within half an hour," Luke replied.

"This will be interesting. How will Pinto try to influence you, Luke? It could be quite revealing," said Peter.

"What do we know about Teresa Pinto?" Luke asked of Alvaro.

"Didn't Madalena de Albuquerque fill you in on this powerful woman?"

"No, I didn't ask about the women."

"She administers her husband's large estates, most of which she brought to the marriage. She is of ancient Portuguese heritage. She agrees with her husband in their detestation of the young king Afonso, which stems from the fact that in her eyes, her lineage deserves the Portuguese throne instead of the Braganzas, especially in their current deformed manifestation."

"If she is such a senior woman at court, why is she allowed to absent herself for several weeks or more to accompany her husband here?" asked Luke.

"To spy on the Da Costas!" suggested Alvaro with a hollow laugh. "The Pintos hate us. That is why I have not been invited to your meal."

Luke was received at the Pinto quarters and led by a servant through French doors onto a large balcony overlooking the courtyard below.

Pinto welcomed him and explained the lack of an invitation of Alvaro immediately. "Forgive me, General, but I believe I must save you from the insidious influence of the Da Costas. You have been given a warped picture of our society through the eyes of Jewish upstarts. Rodrigo keeps the family interests to the fore on the royal council, while his wife, Micaela, manipulates access to the queen and sifts all information being fed to her and brother Alvaro controls the flow of so-called intelligence that governs our military activities. Father Antonio is here to translate my words into Dutch, which I believe you understand."

Antonio appeared slightly embarrassed as he explained to Luke Pinto's tirade against the Da Costas. He also explained, as if to justify his presence, that early in his career, he had been chaplain to Teresa Pinto, whom he referred to by a series of family names that included the most illustrious in Portugal.

Luke was not unhappy to receive an alternative point of view on the state of the nation. From the beginning of his mission, the predominance of the Da Costas had troubled him. He asked Pinto directly, "Where have I been misled by the Da Costa family?"

"The Da Costas rule Portugal through our beloved queen regent, who is separated from her real supporters by this clan. They strongly support the queen as regent as it currently protects their family interests. But unless we act quickly and have the king declared incapable of ever ruling, we will be in trouble. The Da Costas ignore—to their peril—a group of dangerous nobles led by Delgado who seek to remove the queen regent and have one of them rule instead in the name of the weak and mentally disturbed king."

"Is there anybody currently at Estrela whom you suspect belongs to such a group?"

"Nobody on the royal council or among the generals, but there are three persons here that I have my doubts about. Gaspar de Mota's wife has brought to Portugal her family's feud with Queen Luisa's family, the Guzmans. She hates her fellow Spanish-born noblewoman intensely. She could be influenced to act against the queen. The Da Costa chamberlain, Cipriano, is related to the more extreme of the pro-Afonso party, and as equally worrying is that his cousin is the Spanish commander across the border, Federico Sanchez. I saw Ramiro de Lima in the crowd yesterday. He is a loose cannon. I saw him cavorting with General Caro, which is worrying. They are three misfits who could endanger our cause."

Teresa suddenly entered the discussion and, smiling broadly at Luke, issued a warning that Antonio was hesitant to translate.

"Madam wishes to warn you that your role here could also be compromised if you become too friendly with Madalena de Albuquerque. She noticed you both at last night's dinner in intimate discussion. Madalena has used her charms in the past to manipulate men in her and her family's interest."

Luke nodded a thank-you for the advice but was surprised that it was thought necessary. Did Madalena have a reputation? What exactly was Teresa Pinto trying to achieve?

She was an impressive woman. She was very tall with dark olive skin, which suggested some Moorish blood in her distant ancestry. She wore her jet-black hair long and loose. Her clothing was a well-balanced mixture of bright yellow and orange silks.

Luke had noticed an interesting habit. As she listened to the conversation of others, she pulled her flowing black locks partly across her face. As Luke left, she did exactly that, and he would have sworn she winked at him from behind the protection of her tresses.

THE COUNCIL OF WAR gathered for its late afternoon session. Pero da Silva was agitated. A member was missing.

He turned to one of the guards. "Find General Caro!" He then asked the other members, "Did any of you see Caro during the break?"

De Mota surprised everybody with a positive response. "I spoke to him as he rode out of the castle."

"Did he say where he was going?" asked Da Silva.

"No, but he did ask me a strange question."

"Which was?" continued Da Silva.

"He asked if I had received a note from any member of the council suggesting a clandestine meeting."

Luke became very interested. "That suggests that two or more of this group tried to arrange a secret meeting outside the authorized forum. Who were they? And why is Caro the only person missing?"

De Mota interjected, "I can add one more piece of relevant information. As he rode out of the castle, he was joined by that local red-haired renegade, Ramiro de Lima."

Da Silva began to interrogate the group, asking, "Where were you all during the break?"

"I spent it in the company of Father Antonio, General Pinto, and his wife," confessed Luke.

"That accounts for three of you. The three civilian members of the council dined with the Marquess of Estrela, which leaves only Colonel da

Costa, General Mota, and Captain Frost unaccounted for," continued Da Silva.

"Minister, I was within the castle courtyard for most of the period, discussing the forthcoming hostilities with the small troop of cavalry I have brought with me. We obtained our steeds from the stables and took a few canters and gallops around the lower field. Hundreds of people saw us," replied an annoyed De Mota.

Frost reported that he had gone to the lower fields to consume the country fare, where he had seen both General de Mota and Colonel da Costa.

"Is that so, Colonel da Costa?" continued Da Silva.

Rodrigo, Count of Cacella, intervened. "I cannot vouch for Alvaro during the period I ate with you, minister, but I left early, and when I returned to my apartment, Alvaro was waiting for me. We spent the two hours before the meeting reconvened discussing family business."

"Have you anything to add?" Da Silva asked Alvaro.

"Yes. After our meeting finished and I did not receive an invitation to dine with General Pinto, I took myself to the lower field where festivities and feasting were continuing. I bought myself a meal of a hybrid stew, which allegedly contained goat, sheep, and rabbit. The stallholder will remember me. The English captain waved to me from afar."

"I suspend this meeting while we embark on a full-scale search for General Caro," announced Da Silva.

"Minister, if you can allocate me six troopers, Frost and I, with Colonel da Costa, would like to participate in the search," requested Luke.

Ten minutes later, Luke and Alvaro, at the head of a small troop of cavalry, left through the main gate of the castle. As they descended through the terraces, Alvaro saw someone he recognized drinking in one of the fairground stalls. It was one of Ramiro de Lima's men.

He asked, "Is you master still here?"

"Not now. He was until about half an hour ago when he rounded up six of my comrades. They all rode off in a great hurry."

"Why have you been left behind?" persisted Alvaro.

"My horse has gone lame and needs to be rested."

"Did Ramiro say where he was going?" asked Peter hopefully.

"Yes, he said he had to reach the Bridge of Angels as quickly as possible."

"Did he say why?" probed Alvaro.

"Yes, to save someone's life."

Alvaro explained that the bridge in question was some three or four miles farther up the river valley.

As they galloped toward their destination, spasmodic gunfire was heard. It suddenly stopped. About a mile away from the bridge, a group of men hurtled around a corner of the treacherous mountain road, riding directly at Luke's troop.

Before Luke could issue an order to prime their weapons and block the passage of the oncoming riders, everybody relaxed. It was Caro, Ramiro, and several of his men.

After a brief discussion, it was decided that Caro would explain what happened to him directly to the council, which Da Silva immediately reconvened on their return to the castle. Given the circumstances, Ramiro de Lima was asked to attend.

Caro explained, "After our meeting finished around noon, I was accosted by a servant who placed in my hand a scrawled note that indicated that General Tremayne would like to meet me alone on the Bridge of Angels. At first, I thought that the note was genuine as I had indicated to the general that I wished to see him after last night's banquet. For a number of reasons, I was not able to follow up on my intention. I thought the general might have wanted to find out what I had intended to discuss with him. Then I had second thoughts. Why would an English envoy want to talk to me alone in a place unknown to him and miles from anywhere? As I left the castle, I fortunately met Ramiro and raised the issue with him."

Ramiro intervened, "My immediate reaction was this was a trap, probably to assassinate or at least kidnap Caro. I suggested he dawdle toward the bridge while I and my men race ahead and conceal ourselves—which we did. Caro arrived and waited as instructed in the unprotected middle of the bridge. Without warning, a group of horsemen appeared from the far side of the crossing and galloped toward the general. I recognized their leader immediately. It was Col. Marcos Barbosa, the notorious Spanish troubleshooter and right-hand man to the local Spanish military command. My men moved in from the other side and began to fire at the advancing opponents. Both sides exchanged carefully directed shots. Barbosa quickly assessed the situation. He was outnumbered and Caro now well protected. He withdrew his men and disappeared into the adjacent forest."

Caro continued the story. "Minister, this attempt to kill me is the start of a concerted campaign of assassination. This was a known Spanish assassination squad led by one of their most effective and ruthless officers. The Spaniards have probably sent a squad of assassins into Portugal to take out as many generals and councillors as they can, knowing that so many of us are concentrated here at Estrela. And these men are disguised in the uniforms of our queen's household cavalry."

"In addition, Barbosa was wearing an elaborate hat that, at a distance, appeared identical to that worn constantly by the Marquess of Estrela. The Chameleon is up to his old tricks," said Ramiro.

"We have been betrayed," uttered Pinto, suddenly absorbing the possible threat to his own life.

"But not by anyone here," declared the minister. "There has not been time to get a message from here to the Spanish headquarters and for them to send a squad so far inland from their frontier."

"No, the traitors are in Lisbon," concluded De Mota gleefully.

"Not necessarily. The Spaniards are not fools, and there are many pro-Spanish landowners in this region. Troop movements in this direction could have been noted as Castle Estrela is the traditional staging post for Portuguese raids into Spanish territory. It is simple deduction to conclude there would be a few generals in the area," suggested Alvaro.

Luke could not resist a comment. "I agree that the original information to the Spaniards was sent from somewhere other than Castle Estrela and sometime before we gathered here. What is alarming is that someone in this castle targeted General Caro just this morning. Manuel, can you remember anything about the person who gave you the note purporting to come from me?"

"He was not a liveried retainer nor a soldier. He had the build of one of those tumblers from the lower fields."

"But the men who attacked Manuel were heavily built, not the lithe, athletic types," Ramiro retorted.

"These Spanish assassins may be living off the land and nowhere near Castle Estrela," suggested Pinto.

"Or conversely, they are being harbored within Castle Estrela by traitors," remarked Ramiro. "There are a number of travelers visiting the festival who might hide the Spaniards. I will have my men investigate first thing tomorrow."

Da Silva thanked Ramiro for his assistance to Caro and his offer to search the lower fields. He continued, "Gentlemen, it has begun to rain. It may continue for weeks. I am ordering all troops to leave Estrela first thing in the morning before our direct route to the Spanish border is cut. These men and those marching up the Tagus from Lisbon will muster just this side of the border at the new Magellan barracks. We can follow in a few days after we clarify a number of issues relevant to the plan that Tremayne has devised and the execution of which he will control."

"When will we have details of the plan?" asked Pinto.

Luke's reply surprised the gathering. "Never!" He waited until the sighs of surprise subsided and then explained, "Only I will know the whole plan. Each of you will be allotted separate parts of the campaign and be entirely responsible for the implementation of that section."

What Luke did not explain to his military comrades was that he was devising a plan where he would give different information to each of the generals in the hope of isolating which information found its way into Spanish hands—and thus isolating the traitor among them.

Caro asked Da Silva, "Are all the troops to leave for the border in the morning? Given what I experienced today with the threat of a Spanish murder squad out to assassinate all of us, is it not foolish to denude the castle of protection?"

Da Silva replied, "Ramiro and his men will take over the protection of the council of war and its associated military officials until you move to Magellan. In addition, we have the local militia mobilized by the castle's castellan, Carlos de Cipriano."

At supper, the high table was occupied by the same people as the previous night, except that Diego de Albuquerque was missing. Rodrigo was explaining his support of Silva's decision to move all troops out in the morning and suggesting that those that remained had three to four days at the most before the road to the border would be cut. Cipriano advised that his men would continue to provide security within the castle walls, while

Ramiro's troops would protect officials if they left the castle—even to visit the lower fields.

Luke was more interested in the flirtatious Madalena and asked, "Your husband deliberately missing supper?"

"No. He went for a walk after your meeting ended, and I expected him back. Maybe he was delayed by the rain."

Luke enjoyed the freedom of being able to speak English with Madalena and not have to rely on interpreters. She exuded a sensuality that was hard to mistake. Maybe it was the absence of her husband. She was a petite strawberry blonde with the greenest of eyes, which were quite large compared to her tiny mouth and chin. Her hair was pulled back, raised, and covered by a green fabric square that matched her eyes.

The couple were so engrossed in their mutual flirtation that they did not notice an anxious servant run into the great hall and engage in a serious discussion with the chamberlain. Cipriano immediately left the table without the usual obeisance to the host. A few minutes later, he returned and spoke to the marquess.

Paolo rose from his seat and moved around the table to Madalena. He spoke seriously to her in Portuguese, little of which Luke understood. She momentarily seemed to lose consciousness and slumped forward but regained her composure before her head hit the table.

She rose and took Luke's hand. "Please come with me. Something has happened to Diego!"

Cipriano led Madalena and Luke from the hall, and on the way, the chamberlain advised the marchioness of the situation. Joana da Costa followed them. Luke expected that they were being taken to the body of Diego de Albuquerque.

T HE GROUP WERE LED to the roof of a low tower. Heavy rain was still falling. Cipriano led Madalena, protected from the rain by his large cloak, to an area against the parapet, where a large cloth covered whatever lay underneath. Luke and Joana followed Madalena.

There was a great sigh of relief when the covering was removed. Lying against the parapet was a cloak and a silver shoe buckle in the shape of an A, which Madalena immediately identified as belonging to her husband. She faltered momentarily when Cipriano pointed to a pool of blood beside part of the wall that had been sheltered from the rain. She squeezed Luke's hand. Joana came forward to comfort her.

Alvaro arrived, having been sent by Paolo, and quickly translated Cipriano's comments for Luke. "The chamberlain surmises that Diego was attacked and probably tossed over the parapet to the courtyard below. The courtyard has been searched, but no body has been found. The rain would have removed any trace of a body having hit the courtyard."

"Which means one of two things—someone was waiting below the tower to collect the body, dead or alive, or this scenario has been staged, and Diego has been abducted," replied a suspicious Luke.

"Or chooses to disappear," added Alvaro, to Luke's surprise.

"Do you know something I do not?" asked Luke.

"No, but Diego is a timid nobleman. He is a scholar rather than a soldier or politician. Hearing that there is a team of Spanish assassins in the area out to kill you, what better way to save yourself from their clutches than to disappear?"

"Maybe. Although I did not get the impression he was a milk sop or a coward. Let's examine the surrounding area for any evidence as to what may have happened," suggested Luke.

After searching the corridors that led to the exit to the tower, they found an intricate pattern of blood splashed against the wall of a hallway and, on the floor nearby, a shoe with a buckle in the form of an A.

Luke was delighted with the evidence. "Diego was hit from behind, and as he fell to the ground, the blood sprayed the wall with the pattern we see. He lost this shoe as he was hauled toward the tower. Either dead or alive, he was dragged from here to the tower and thrown over. We are missing one shoe—and a body."

"We are in luck. Since this afternoon, when we returned with General Caro, Cipriano and Ramiro's men have blockaded the castle and its precincts, including the lower fields, with their profusion of stallholders, entertainers, and religious. No one is permitted to leave until our troops have left for the frontier. This means that Diego or his body must still be here. Tomorrow we search every inch of the castle and its surrounding fields," advised Alvaro. "Are you returning to the banqueting hall?"

"No, I will visit Madalena," Luke replied.

"Is that appropriate in the circumstances?"

"This is not a liaison. Madalena will be able to tell me about Diego's state of mind and his activities prior to his disappearance."

Luke was ushered into Madalena's apartment by an English-speaking Irish servant. He apologized for his intrusion but explained succinctly the reason for his visit. Madalena turned to her servant. "Aileen, leave the room. And do not eavesdrop at the door."

Once alone with Luke, Madalena outlined Diego's whereabouts earlier in the day. "While most people were looking for General Caro, Diego attended mass at the shrine of Our Lady of Estrela. He then told me he chatted with several of the religious until well after noon. After that, he went to the lower fields to obtain a meal and where he listened to the folk music until the meeting of the council was reconvened. I do not know what he did between the end of that meeting and the time he was attacked."

"What about his state of mind? Was there anything bothering him in recent days?"

"Only me."

Luke waited patiently for Madalena to expound on her enigmatic comment. She seemed hesitant to continue. Luke took her hand as tears began to run down her cheeks. Eventually, she regained her composure.

"Diego and I have been married for some time and have no children. As you know, the main purpose of an aristocratic wife is to produce an heir so that the family dynasty may continue. In all these cases, the experts, medical and clerical, place the blame on the woman involved. Diego's family have put pressure on him to seek an annulment of our marriage on the alleged grounds that I am infertile."

"While traumatic for you, I cannot see how it would contribute to an attempt on his life."

"There is a political aspect to it. Diego is a great supporter of Portuguese independence. However, the pope refuses to recognize the Portuguese church as an independent province. The pope officially sees it as part of the Spanish church. Therefore, any requests for annulment must be dealt with by the Spanish church, which would then forward its recommendation to Rome. Diego may have been told that if he wants an annulment, he must renounce his allegiance to the Portuguese royal house and support the return of the Spanish Habsburgs."

"Could his time spent in the lower fields talking to the religious have anything to do with his seeking an annulment?"

"Probably."

"But how does this relate back to a physical attack on him?"

"He is a member of the Portuguese council of war about to embark on a major attack on Spain. If anyone here heard whispers of possible pressure from Spanish clerics being put on Diego, they may have ordered his death."

"You suspect one of the Portuguese councillors or generals present in the castle to have given such an order?" asked a surprised Luke.

"What other explanation is there?" concluded Madalena.

The next morning, after an intense discussion, Luke, Peter, Antonio, and Alvaro joined Ramiro's men as they questioned the temporary residents of the lower fields. To a man, they were hostile, furious that they could not depart when the feast and festivities had ended.

Luke's interest focused on the religious who had come to venerate Our Lady of Estrela. He asked Father Antonio to question them regarding the attendance of Diego de Albuquerque at their ceremonies. Antonio remarked that most of the males were lay brothers of various orders or elderly Dominican friars. He found a single fellow Franciscan and questioned him concerning Albuquerque's visit on the previous day. After attending mass in the lower field, Diego returned to the castle with the officiating priest. Alvaro was interested in another piece of information that Antonio elicited.

"While the nuns and brothers are housed in tents erected in the fields and courtyard of the castle, the four priests—two Dominicans and two parochial clergy—are accommodated within the castle. One of these priests officiated at the mass, and Diego and he returned to the castle together in what one witness described as very earnest, if not heated, conversation."

"Let's find this priest and question him," resolved Luke.

Ramiro concentrated his attention on the traveling minstrels, tumblers, and wrestlers. The would-be assassins were physically well-built and athletic. He summed up his negative findings. "The band of assassins is not here. The wrestlers are too large, the tumblers too light, and minstrels too weak."

Luke remarked, "That is disappointing. I had hoped to find them—and Albuquerque—somewhere in these fields."

"Don't despair, Tremayne. One of the witnesses said he had seen a group that answer the description of our quarry," said Alvaro.

"Where were they?"

"In the vicinity of the marquess's stables."

"Stables would be an ideal hiding place. We must talk to Cipriano on two possible leads—the location and behavior of the priests housed in the castle and the possible use of the stable complex as a hiding place for the Spanish assassins," contributed Peter.

Cipriano reported that Diego had not been found in the castle either despite a thorough and extensive search.

"How many priests are housed in the castle?" Alvaro asked him.

Cipriano summoned his bookkeeper. The man carefully went through several pages and reported that there were four—two parochial priests who conducted the several masses that had been held during the festivities and two Dominicans.

Alvaro asked, "Why are the Dominicans here?"

The bookkeeper looked embarrassed and replied that someone had insisted that the marquess put them up.

He turned to Cipriano, and after a heated exchange, the chamberlain quietly announced, "My man believes that the Dominicans represent the Holy Inquisition—and nobody denies its request."

"Why would the Inquisition be interested in Castle Estrela or in the private affairs of Diego de Albuquerque?" asked Luke.

"The Inquisition strongly favors the Spanish interest and would be concerned about Portuguese activities so close to the Spanish frontier. They probably used the excuse that the cult of the Our Lady of Estrela might be developing heretical tendencies that needed investigating," explained Cipriano.

"Where in the castle are the priests located?" asked Alvaro.

"In the northwest wing overlooking the western courtyard" was the reply.

"Is that not the same wing in which Albuquerque was attacked?" asked Luke.

"It is. In fact, the wall on which blood was detected is almost immediately opposite the door of the parochial priests," replied the bookkeeper.

Cipriano, Antonio, Alvaro, and Luke made their way to the priests' room.

Alvaro explained to them that he was investigating the disappearance of Albuquerque, and as his blood had been found on the wall opposite their door and witnesses had reported Diego arguing with one of them earlier on the day he disappeared, they would need to answer a number of questions.

The priests were relaxed and readily complied. Yes, they had seen a lot of Diego since his arrival, both at mass and the confessional. He was seeking an annulment of his marriage, which he believed was being blocked by the Spanish-dominated Dominicans and the pope's refusal to recognize the independence of the Portuguese hierarchy. Diego had hoped that with their closeness to the archbishop of Lisbon—one was the archbishop's brother—they might be able to persuade him to push the case more aggressively with the Spanish authorities.

Luke asked when had they last seen Diego.

"After discussing the annulment with him yesterday morning and afternoon, he returned here last evening after the council meeting had ended. When we told him that my brother, the archbishop, had no influence on the Spaniards and that he should directly approach the primate, the cardinal archbishop of Toledo, he was very depressed. He was apparently attacked immediately after he left here."

"Can you tell us anything about your neighbors, the Dominicans?"

"They were not here to participate in the Feast of Our Lady of Estrela. They are agents of the Inquisition, if not inquisitors themselves, spying either on the council of war or on the clergy who participated in the cult of Our Lady of Estrela. There are members of the Inquisition who consider our cult pagan, if not heretical."

The investigators left the two priests and moved next door to question the Dominicans. After considerable knocking, which elicited no response, Cipriano pushed open the door.

The room was deserted. The Dominicans had departed.

9

CIPRIANO LED THE OTHERS to the castle gate. He asked his men enforcing the blockade, "Has anyone left the castle since you came on duty?"

"No one other than the inquisitor and his assistant."

"How did you know he was the inquisitor?"

"The man who led them through the gate carried the green cross of the Inquisition and demanded we give way to the inquisitor of the Beira province, Fr. Eduardo Zarco."

"Why did your men let them through?" asked Luke naively.

"No one defies the Inquisition. The grand inquisitor has so terrified the young king Afonso that he has forbidden his mother to act in any way against them," answered Alvaro.

Cipriano continued, "They were the only two you let pass?"

"Two men and a cart pulled by two donkeys, the contents of which were covered."

"Could there have been a body under the covering?" asked Luke in his improving Portuguese.

"Yes."

Alvaro suddenly exploded, hitting himself vigorously on the forehead. "I am a fool! I should have recognized that priest. Zarco, the inquisitor for Beira, I have met several times. He has an obsession for rooting out concealed Moslems and Jews who claim to have been converted to Christianity. Even though our branch of the Da Costas have been Christian for two and a half centuries, Fr. Eduardo Zarco, inquisitor for Beira, is determined to prove that we are still Hebrews."

"Are you suggesting that his presence here has nothing to do with the cult of Our Lady of Estrela or with pro-Spanish spying or with the personal affairs of Diego de Albuquerque but part of an anti–Da Costa vendetta?" asked a surprised Antonio.

"The presence of three Da Costas and a Caro at Estrela was probably too much of a temptation for this obsessive anti-Semitic," replied Alvaro.

This remark worried Luke. The Da Costas had an overinflated view of their importance. After all, it was an Albuquerque that had been attacked if not killed.

Cipriano continued his questioning. "When did the inquisitors leave?"

"Two hours ago."

"You did not hear or see which way they were heading? Back down the Zêzere or up the ravine and over the mountains to the Spanish border?" asked Alvaro, already prepared for a negative answer.

Cipriano's man commented, "Either way, you will catch them. If they headed east toward the border, they will be blocked by the floods. A unit of the queen's household cavalry has just returned. They were the last of the troops to leave the castle, and when they reached the Bridge of the Angels, water was rushing over it. If the Inquisition has headed toward the frontier, they are trapped. If they headed back down the Lisbon road, they will also be in trouble. The river, after this much rain, would have flooded several of the lower-lying areas, blocking any passage to the capital."

Within half an hour, two parties left the castle. One led by Baron Cipriano, including Father Antonio and Peter, headed downstream, while the other, under the command of Ramiro and assisted by Luke and Alvaro, headed upstream toward the Bridge of Angels.

After twenty minutes of riding uphill into torrential rain, which turned the track above the valley of the Zêzere into a mini river of its own, Ramiro's party was confronted by two men and cart returning downhill.

As the two parties approached each other, a voice rang out from the descending duo, "Move aside for the Holy Inquisition!"

The caller was obviously amazed when the ascending group, not only failed to move aside, but also dismounted, and while Ramiro advanced, waving his sword, his men struggled to prime their muskets in the continuing rain.

The caller threw back his cloak and hood and declaimed, "I am Eduardo Zarco, inquisitor of Beira. Move aside!"

"Forgive us, Reverend Father. We have no argument with Holy Church and its illustrious Inquisition, but the cart that you have was stolen from the Marquess of Estrela yesterday afternoon, and we are here to return it to its rightful owner."

Zarco dismounted and surveyed his opponents intensely and finally commented, "What a group of dangerous misfits, eventual fodder for the fires of hell. Ramiro de Lima, thief, robber, and supporter of heathen cults, Alvaro da Costa, Jew lover if not a Jew himself, and a heretical English soldier of the most radical kind. My superior, the inquisitor general, will be very interested in this nest of heretics roaming the Estrelas, and inhibiting me in the exercise of my duty to God."

"Enough talk, priest!" said an irate Ramiro. "My men will stand aside and allow you and your assistant to continue your descent—but without the cart. It would be a pity if you suffered from any accidental discharge of firearms. The devil might just create such an accident."

Zarco assessed the situation. He was outnumbered and covered by an array of firepower. He remounted. He turned to his pursuers and, as he galloped past, shouted, "This outrage will not be forgotten! Mother Church will be avenged on all of you!"

He and his companion continued down the slope at a dangerous pace, anxious to be well gone by the time Ramiro and his men uncovered the wagon.

Alvaro and Ramiro slowly pulled the covering off. Both crossed themselves.

"It's Diego, and he's dead," reported Alvaro.

Luke came forward and climbed into the wagon. He placed his head close to Diego's chest and then the blade of his sword to the nose and mouth of the body and eventually announced, "He lives—but just. I cannot hear any breathing, but the blade of my sword has picked up the faintest condensation. We must get him to a doctor as fast as possible."

"There are two at the castle. The marquess has a resident physician, but Cipriano's deputy as castellan and chamberlain was once an army surgeon. I served with him in the early days of our war of independence," said Alvaro.

Ramiro was cautious. "It is getting dark. The track is being washed away as we speak. To continue downhill now would be very dangerous. There is a cave just a few hundred yards farther up the track. We should stay there overnight and return to the castle at first light."

"Diego will not last that long. Even if we continue downhill, he may die before we reach the castle. But we must try," pleaded Luke in broken Portuguese.

Alvaro suggested, "The donkeys are too slow. Let's harness my horse to the wagon, and I will drive it downhill. The rest of you move to the cave until morning. This wagon has seats in its front and can be driven as if it is a coach."

Ramiro intervened, "It is risky. You cannot see what is ahead of you in the dark, and with this continued rain, there is no hope of moonlight."

Luke muttered to himself, "For Madalena's sake, he must try." Then for all to hear, he announced, "I will come with you. Even in the best of circumstances, you may need to replace a wheel."

Alvaro, with Luke beside him, drove the horse at a steady pace down the treacherous path, keeping as close to the cliff side of the track as they could. Being bogged in the little river that ran down the inside of the track was preferable to going over the edge, where much of the path on the ravine side had given way.

Suddenly, both men were hit in the chest. Luke was knocked backward off his seat onto the floor of the wagon. Alvaro, after the initial shock, managed to pull the slewing wagon back onto its course and brought it to a halt.

Luke was livid. "The Holy Inquisition does not hesitate to attempt murder. We drove into a rope stretched across the road. If we had been riding our horses at speed, it would have decapitated us. Luckily, we were seated a foot or higher in the wagon, so the rope hit across the more protected parts of our body. And we are going slower than if riding. I am going back to retrieve that rope as evidence."

"Zarco would believe he is doing God's work—ridding the world of a Protestant heretic and a Jew," commented Alvaro as he waited impatiently for Luke to untangle the rope.

They eventually reached the castle. Cipriano had already returned as there was major flooding just a few miles downstream. No one could get through. The lower fields were still full of rain-drenched visitors who were now stranded.

"We have Diego, but he does not have much time. Summon your deputy whom I know was an army surgeon and Father Antonio. The last rites may be necessary," said Alvaro.

Cipriano soon had Diego in a warm room, while his deputy, Alfredo Matos, examined the almost-lifeless body.

Matos washed the wounds and thoroughly dried the rain-soaked body. He eventually reported, "Just like many war wounds involving a heavy blow to the back of the head, you cannot tell the extent of the damage until the man regains consciousness. His parlous state up until now is because of the initial heavy loss of blood. If he comes out of his coma, he may survive, but in what condition, I cannot tell. His wife should be informed of the perilous situation."

Luke volunteered. When he knocked on Madalena's door, it was answered by a scantily dressed Aileen.

She jokingly whispered, "Are you here to see the mistress or myself?"

"Your mistress, but I want you to stay."

The Irish wench was not certain what Luke was up to. He was led into Madalena's bedchamber. "Do not arise, my lady. I come with grievous news." Luke gently explained what had happened.

"Diego was attempting to annul our marriage, but I bore him no ill will. Why would the Inquisition have attacked and abducted him? I do not understand," she said.

"According to Alvaro, the local inquisitor, an Eduardo Zarco, is an obsessed fanatic. He tried to murder us as we brought Diego back to the castle. Ramiro considers him a madman. We do not know why Diego came to be his victim."

"I must go to him immediately."

"Useless. He is in a coma. When he regains consciousness, your presence will certainly help him recover."

"Luke, stay with me tonight," Madalena unexpectedly said.

Luke looked startled.

She continued, "Not in my bed, not even in this room. If the Inquisition was after Diego, they may also be after me. After all, I was once a Protestant. Sleep in the outer room. I am sure Aileen will look after you. She is already besotted."

Madalena's concern troubled Luke. Where was Zarco and his companion? They could not get away in either direction while the rain and resultant flood continued. Zarco could use his authority to terrorize a number of people in the castle or its precincts to harbor them or even carry out their evil intentions.

Luke explained to Madalena, "I am leaving you for a few minutes to alert Cipriano of the possible presence of Zarco in the castle. Keep the door locked. Do not open it to anybody, even the marquess. I will return, and then, Aileen, you can tell me all about yourself."

Aileen giggled.

10

L UKE RETURNED TEN MINUTES later with the two armed servants to guard Madalena's apartment. He knocked gently and repeated his name loudly.

No attempt was made to open the door. He heard sobbing and then a plaintive request from Aileen. "If that is you, Luke, tell me—what color chemise am I wearing?"

"Pale green" was the reply.

The door opened, and two crying women competed for Luke's embrace.

"What happened?" he asked.

Madalena answered, "After you left, there was a loud knock, and a voice announced himself as Fr. Antonio Mendes with a message for me concerning the latest regarding Diego. I signaled Aileen to admit him, but fortunately, she defied me. She refused."

"I have heard Father Antonio take mass three or four times. He has a very distinctive voice. This was not him," Aileen explained.

"You were right. It was not Father Antonio. He is still with Diego. I have just left him."

"Was it Zarco?" asked Madalena.

"I suspect so."

Luke went back to the door, opened it, and indicated to one of the guards that he should tell the chamberlain immediately that Zarco had tried to enter Madalena de Albuquerque's chamber. He returned to the women and asked Madalena, "Is there anything that Diego told you in recent days that might have made the Inquisition desperate to silence him?"

"No, Diego and I rarely discuss matters of state. It is not the Portuguese way. Women only exist to satisfy men's lust or to produce heirs to continue their family dynasty. I did neither for Diego," uttered Madalena with a touch of sadness.

Luke continued his questioning. "Apart from being a member of the council of war, did Diego belong to any other committees of the royal council?"

"Given his family pedigree, he was a member of the council for trade and the colonies."

"There is nothing in those duties that would bring him into contact with the Inquisition."

"Possibly not, but the church in Brazil has worried the Inquisition."

"Madam, I know something that might help the general."

"Speak up, Aileen!"

"One night, just before we left Lisbon, the master came home late. You had already retired. He seemed very elated. I asked him in my poor Portuguese why he was so happy. He replied he had just had a meeting with the archbishop of Lisbon, the provincial head of the Dominicans and the grand inquisitor, and a problem upsetting the queen regent had been resolved."

"Eureka, Aileen! There lies a probable link." Luke gave Aileen a big hug, which was returned with a deep-throated kiss.

Madalena noticed her servant's obvious lust and indicated that she would leave them together, and immediately retired into the next room.

After half an hour of mutual lovemaking, the exhausted pair lay back to enjoy the afterglow of their most satisfying activity. Luke was soon sound asleep, with Aileen nestled into him.

Sometime during the night, a third party entered the bed. When Luke awoke the next morning, Aileen was nestled into the bosom of her mistress.

Luke was disconcerted.

Ramiro and the rest of his party returned to the castle before noon. He was immediately informed of the situation that it was generally believed that Zarco and his companion were trapped by the floodwaters and were still in or about the castle. He was appalled to hear that an attempt had been made to decapitate Alvaro and Luke.

"This man is no priest. I will hunt him down!" vowed a furious Ramiro.

"He is hidden by people who accept his authority as priest and inquisitor. They will innocently conceal him from us," said Luke.

"I have a plan to change that. Cipriano, summon all those within the castle walls to gather into the courtyard and those outside to the middle of lower field! I will speak to them in a language they can understand," asserted Ramiro.

Half an hour later, all the inhabitants of the castle, except for those guarding Madalena, gathered in the courtyard. Ramiro did not mince words.

"Friends, there is an evil abroad that we must eradicate. There is a man somewhere amongst you who falsely claims to be a priest, and indeed an inquisitor. He is, in fact, an agent of the devil. He has tried to kill our favorite general, Manuel Caro, and murder Baron Albuquerque, a member of the queen's council, and some of my men. He is, by God's grace, trapped here by the floods. It is our duty as good Christians to find him and consign him to the fires of hell. He goes by the name of Eduardo Zarco, dresses as a priest, and has one companion. If you have any knowledge of this monster, come forward and give me the details. I will hunt him down."

Much to Luke's surprise, Ramiro's rousing—if exaggerated and inaccurate—speech received thunderous applaud. Ramiro repeated his oration to the group in the field.

Luke, Peter, and Alvaro joined Ramiro and four of his men in the hunt for Zarco. Ramiro received vital information as a result of his appeal. The tumblers who had been up at dawn noticed two men enter the woodlands on the slope of the ravine and head downstream. This would be slow progress, but they would avoid the road for much of the way.

"But not forever. Eventually, the sides of the ravine become so steep that the only way to progress is to join the road. I will send my men to track them through the forest. The four of us will set up an ambush where they will be forced to rejoin the road," declared Ramiro.

"What do you intend to do when you confront Zarco?" asked Alvaro.

"He will be cut down by our four muskets before he knows what hit him. No prisoners will be taken."

"Are you not worried about executing an inquisitor and a second priest?" asked Peter.

"This man lost any special protection he had in my eyes when he tried to murder my friends. In any case, the Inquisition has, from time to time, had innocent people executed. I shall seek God's forgiveness from Father Antonio."

On reaching the appropriate site, Ramiro carefully deployed Alvaro, Luke, and Peter.

Luke asked Ramiro, "Why have we brought the wagon with us?"

He smiled. "How else are we to remove the two bodies without trace? They will be loaded into the wagon, which will then be pushed into the raging torrent of the river—to any outsider, a horrible accident caused by the slippery conditions."

Luke, armed with a musket, lay beside Peter and Alvaro behind a fallen tree trunk. Ramiro was lurking in the background, ready to move behind the unsuspecting quarry.

Eventually, the noise of someone cutting their way through undergrowth was heard. Ramiro had chosen his ambush location to perfection. Zarco was the second horseman to emerge into the clearing beside the track. Ramiro made the sound of a bird, the prearranged signal. At least a dozen shots were fired at the two men.

Luke was astonished to find Ramiro with his two pistols primed, turning over the bodies of the two victims. He suddenly fired into the heads of both men and repeated the performance, aiming at the heart.

"What was that all about?" asked Luke.

Ramiro later explained, "I am a superstitious man. The devil looks after his own. I had to ensure that Zarco was dead. Two shots to the heart and two to the head should be enough. Put the bodies onto the wagon!"

Half an hour later, there was no evidence that a double murder had taken place. Even the Protestants, Luke and Peter, were worried. Surely, the Inquisition would not forgive the murder of two of their own.

Ramiro already had a story fit for the consumption of outsiders. In trying to escape his party, the Inquisitional quarry went too close to the river's edge. It gave way—and both of them drowned.

On returning to the castle, Ramiro and his party were greeted with good news. Diego had regained consciousness—and with an acute memory of what had happened. Ramiro, Luke and, Alvaro wished to hear it for themselves.

Diego, who had eaten a good meal and imbibed some sweet Portuguese red wine, was surprisingly alert. "Thank you, gentlemen. I have been told you rescued me. I have a perfect memory of what happened up to the time I was hit, and since I have woken up."

"Did you see who hit you?"

"Yes, I heard a noise and half-turned before the blow hit me. It was Fr. Eduardo Zarco."

"Why did the priest and inquisitor try to kill you?"

"A few weeks ago, I was present with the grand inquisitor, the provincial of the Dominicans, and the archbishop of Lisbon when they were confronted with a dossier from the queen, outlining the crimes, including several illegal killings, carried out against innocent people by the inquisitor in Beira, Eduardo Zarco. He was summarily sacked from his office as inquisitor and suspended as priest by the Dominican provincial, and an order for his immediate arrest was issued by the archbishop and myself on behalf of the queen."

"Why didn't you denounce him and have him arrested immediately after you recognized him?" asked Alvaro.

"I didn't recognize him. I had only met him once or twice over the years. When I saw him at the table next to ours at the first supper here, I must have stared at him, trying to place him. He obviously assumed I had recognized him, and he had to remove me before I acted against him."

Ramiro was jubilant. "Zarco was neither a priest or inquisitor when he died?"

"That is correct. Why do you ask?" said Diego innocently.

"He and his assistant have met with a nasty accident. They fell to their death into the raging Zêzere while we were chasing them. I would hate to feel the guilt of causing the death of a godly priest and holy inquisitor." Ramiro turned to Alvaro and Luke and muttered, "I knew we were doing God's work."

Alvaro asked Diego, "If the purpose of the attack on you was to silence you, why didn't they kill you, and why were they trying to smuggle you into Spain, apparently dead or alive? And why did they try to kill General Caro?"

"I do not think Zarco's attack on me is related to Colonel Barbosa's attempt on General Caro, although Zarco might have thought the body of a councillor, dead or alive, would have won him kudos in Spain. I cannot answer exactly what his intention might have been because what happened after I was hit, until I recovered here, is a total loss. I also remember that some of the charges against Zarco that the queen had presented was the illegal killing of two women by the name of Caro. Zarco was obsessed with that family as he was with the Da Costas. Given he had nothing to lose, he could have embarked on the killing of three Da Costas and one Caro. He would then have been warmly welcomed in Spain. My presence dead would have been proof of his loyalty to the Spanish Habsburgs, and if alive, I would be a bargaining point in negotiations between Spain and Portugal."

Matos, who had stood by silently, now intervened. "The baron now needs rest. It is time for you to leave."

"One last question," said Luke. "After we had rescued you, Zarco sneaked into the castle and tried to confront, if not kill, your wife. Do you know why she too was on his hit list?"

"Zarco's mind had become deranged in his dealing with anybody who had a connection with Jews, Moslems, or Protestants. Although Madalena converted to Mother Church, she was born and educated as a Protestant in Ireland. In Zarco's mind, she was probably still spreading Protestant propaganda throughout the land, probably with your help, Tremayne."

THE NEXT DAY DA Silva, informed that the floods had slightly receded, ordered the council of war and its generals to leave Castle Estrela and move to the new Magellan barracks on the border with Spain. These barracks could be defended by five hundred men but were able to accommodate ten times that number as it was specifically built as a staging post for any Portuguese invasion of Spain along the midsection of the eastern frontier. Its major disadvantage was that given the extensive troop movements into the area, any element of surprise was lost. The Spaniards were alerted to an imminent major offensive.

Luke, who planned this offensive, discussed the matter with Peter on the second day of their relocation at Magellan. "My overt plan conforms to the traditional border warfare in the area. We attack those areas not well defended and avoid areas of Spanish strength. Success will depend on the accuracy of our intelligence. My innovation is that while the generals carry out these traditional activities, we, with Ramiro and his men, will carry out a mission that hopefully will seriously weaken the Spaniards."

"And what about your special mission to unearth the traitor in the council or among the generals?"

"Taken care of. I intend to attack one or more of several villages or towns near the frontier. I will tell Caro that whatever he hears from others, our real target will be village A, Pinto will be told village B, and De Mota village C. All these villages are, according to the latest intelligence, poorly defended. If one of these is suddenly reinforced, it will be an indication that the Spaniards have been told that that village was our target."

"If only it was as easy as you suggest. The Spaniards will probably gamble on where they think you will strike. They may make a lucky guess and move troops to defend the projected target without receiving any information from an alleged traitor. It is hardly firm evidence," cautioned Peter.

"I have a more serious problem. One possible network of spies could be the Da Costas—a lady-in-waiting, a member of the royal council, and the chief of military intelligence. Consequently, I need to distance myself from Alvaro without him suspecting a problem. I will then have to rely on you, Peter, as my interpreter. So far, I do not think anybody knows you understand and speak Portuguese. From what you have heard, has Alvaro correctly translated what has been said?"

"Yes, although I have not been present on all occasions," replied Peter.

"I could still keep your linguistic secret and dispense with Alvaro, if the wives are moving to the barracks with their husbands," Luke conjectured.

"No, Luke, not a practical alternative. Madalena's help would be useful in a social context, but there is no way she could accompany us on a mission," said Peter. He then quickly changed the subject before Luke could reply. "What exact role is the brigand Ramiro to play?"

"Da Silva has conscripted Ramiro and his men as an auxiliary company to serve within the Portuguese army, under my command. We will ride deep into Spanish territory, inflict as much damage as we can, and return before they know we were there."

At first light on the morning of the planned Portuguese offensive, the council of war and the generals met to receive Alvaro's newest intelligence and Luke's final instructions.

"The latest picture of Spanish troop movements is that an army of about the same size as ours has mustered some miles behind the frontier, obviously ready to move troops to the areas we attack. What is interesting is that the garrison and arsenal at Castle Passos has largely been denuded of men and presumably of ammunition and weapons. If you find the enemy is better armed than you, I would advise immediate withdrawal," reported Alvaro.

Luke was brief and direct. "Gentlemen, everything you have been told up to now, forget it!" Luke then spoke to each general privately, outlining their new targets. He concluded the briefing by confessing, "While you are attacking Spanish positions, I, with Lord Ramiro, will hit the Spaniards where they least expect it."

"May we know what you intend to do?" asked Caro.

"I don't know. It will depend on what we discover. It will be an opportunistic enterprise," answered Luke.

Da Silva, who had remained silent during the briefings, simply announced, "Let the attack begin!"

Luke's efforts to free himself of Alvaro and find another interpreter failed. Luke, Peter, Alvaro, and Ramiro gathered in front of forty well-armed horsemen. If these horsemen were English, Luke would have considered them a half company of dragoons rather than cavalry. They were all armed with muskets in addition to their pistols, swords, and daggers. Their horses were light and built for speed, unlike the heavier cavalry mounts. These factors, to some extent, limited the actions that Luke could take. They must avoid the enemy—and certainly not confront the heavy Spanish cavalry. They must move quickly onto their target and then as quickly move on.

Luke now produced his first surprise. Servants emerged carrying three large trunks. Luke, through Alvaro and Ramiro, ordered the men to dismount and select a helmet from the trunk. They were Spanish helmets, morions, that had been captured in past campaigns. In disguising themselves as Spanish horsemen, they were leaving themselves open to being charged as spies and facing summary execution, usually after torture, should they be captured.

They immediately moved north, well away from the concentration of Portuguese troops around Magellan, and eventually turned eastward, crossing a small stream that marked the frontier.

Luke asked Ramiro and Alvaro, "Which of you speaks the better Spanish?"

"My mother was Spanish. Until I was six, I was more fluent in Spanish than Portuguese," admitted Ramiro.

Alvaro did not contest the claim but asked Luke, "What do you have in mind?"

"We head for the arsenal at Passos. If your intelligence is right, it will be depleted of troops but may still contain significant amounts of ammunition, which we can detonate, and arms, which we might be able to confiscate. As we will approach the town from the east, we will claim to be a detachment sent from elsewhere in Spain to join the offensive against Portugal. Whatever happens at Passos, we will, in the end, be able to attack the Spanish front line from where they least expect it—from behind."

Ramiro endorsed the plan. "If we move in a northeasterly direction for an hour, it will be entirely through country that was originally Portuguese, the large parish of Corba. The inhabitants speak Portuguese, and our presence will be welcomed once we reveal our true identity. Such a route will bring us close to Castle Passos, which was turned into a garrison and arsenal a decade ago to keep the newly acquired surrounding territory loyal to Spain."

The group proceeded along a well-used track for about half an hour when it entered a heavily forested area. Ramiro suddenly held up his hand to stop the cavalcade and then signaled for them to get off the track and disperse quickly into the forest. An increasing amount of shouting was heard, which came closer and closer. Eventually, a group of peasants—mainly old men, women, and children—appeared, moving quickly along the path. Ramiro confronted them. After a long conversation with one of the old men, Ramiro called his men back into formation.

He explained to Alvaro, "These are the inhabitants of the village of Corba. They are fleeing the henchmen of their Spanish lord, Don Jorge Zoritas, who was imposed on them when Portugal withdrew from the area. The able-bodied men were rounded up and are being forced to erect two gibbets at the crossroads beyond the village. These people have fled, fearing for their safety."

"Why the gibbets?" asked Alvaro.

"The Spaniards are going to hang the local priest for heresy and a young woman for witchcraft."

"Are they innocent?" asked Luke.

Ramiro talked further with the village elder. "The priest apparently, in a recent sermon, declared that Christ had not died for all mankind—he had not died for the Spaniards. The elder said it was a joke, and nobody took it seriously. Apparently, one of few pro-Spanish toadies in the village reported it to Jorge Zoritas."

"And the woman?" inquired Luke.

"A trumped-up charge. The girl not only refused the advances of Zoritas's son, Mendo, but scratched his face so badly that it became infected and still has not healed. The young man has changed from an Adonis to a hideous monster. This charge of witchcraft is his revenge," Ramiro explained.

"What should we do?" asked Luke. "Any action to help the villagers may alert the Spaniards at Passos to our presence. Perhaps we should disappear, avoid Corba, and take another route to Passos."

"No! These are my people. We must help them," retorted Ramiro.

"I think we can—without giving our identity away," interjected Alvaro.

"How?" asked Ramiro and Luke in unison.

"You, Ramiro, will become an agent of the Inquisition. You will demand jurisdiction over the priest and the girl. For decades, the Inquisition has been very lenient in similar cases. They have declared that priests have acted out of ignorance and mean no harm. They must be reeducated by an officer of the Inquisition. Persons accused of witchcraft who are under twenty-five have been given a light penance and encouraged to mend their ways."

Ramiro led his men, followed by the villagers, out of the forest and through the temporarily deserted village to the crossroads where the younger male inhabitants had erected the gibbets. The two accused were tied together as Zoritas's men prepared the ropes for the hanging. The Spaniards were initially alarmed as Ramiro's large cohort ambled down the road toward them.

Ramiro immediately revealed his acting skills. "Make way for the Holy Inquisition!"

He approached the leader of Zoritas's men, who, by the disfigurement of his face, was obviously the malicious Mendo. He interrogated the young man, demanding to know what was going on, and by whose authority had gibbets been erected on the king's highway. Mendo carefully explained the misdeeds of the victims, indicating that they warranted hanging.

Alvaro whispered to Luke, "I hope Ramiro does not overplay his hand. He is clearly enjoying his role."

Ramiro continued, "In the name of Mother Church, I am taking over both these cases. It is the church and not the local lords who have jurisdiction in such matters. Free both of them, and go about your business elsewhere!"

Young Zoritas hit back. "And how are you going to enforce this ludicrous decision? The moment you leave, I will return and finish my task."

In a flash, he turned his horse around and galloped away. The soldiers watched in amazement as Peter followed, stood up in his stirrups, and launched himself through the air, knocking Mendo to the ground and landing on top of him.

Mendo was dragged back to Ramiro, who, continuing his inquisitional role, resumed his tirade. "My men will take both accused to the local church, where I will instruct them in the ways of the Lord. I will appoint two of the village elders as officers of the Inquisition, who will report to the Holy Office if you or any of your men force themselves into this village. In addition, a troop of the Inquisition's soldiers, such as this one, will pass through Corba on a regular basis. Finally, I will report your activities and those of your father to the Inquisition in Toledo and to the local secular magistrates."

The villagers broke out into spontaneous cheering.

"And finally, my young lord, any further harassment of the women of this village, and you will answer personally to the inquisitor general. Now order your men to empty out onto the ground the goods they have illegally purloined from this village during your unwelcome visit!"

Ramiro then fired his pistol into the air and ordered Zoritas and his men to leave the area immediately. The villagers collected their looted belongings, while Ramiro, Alvaro, and the two English soldiers took the priest and woman back to the church. They continued the pretense of being agents of the Inquisition and reprimanded both.

After the girl left the church, the priest confronted Ramiro, Alvaro, Luke, and Peter. "I am Fr. Nicodemo Oliveira. Thank you for saving my life and that of young Marabella, but you are not the Inquisition—Spanish or Portuguese. Who are you?"

The officers looked at each other and nodded.

Alvaro spoke for them. "We are an auxiliary company of the Portuguese army seeking to do damage behind the Spanish lines. How do you know we are not the Inquisition?"

12

"ALTHOUGH PORTUGUESE, I AM an agent of the Spanish Inquisition. If you were the Spanish Inquisition, you would have known who your officials were in this area. For a while, I thought you may have been from the Portuguese body, which has been corrupted since independence."

Ramiro was not convinced. "If you are a servant of the Spanish Inquisition, why did Zoritas risk the ire of that body by trying to hang you?"

There was a moment of silence.

Alvaro smiled and offered an explanation. "Because nobody knows of your affiliation with the Holy office. You spy on your own parishioners, including the gentry, such as Zoritas."

"Partly right, but I do not spy on my people. My link with the Inquisition protects Corba, but Zoritas is a lawless tyrant. I have sent a stream of complaints to the Inquisition and my bishop regarding his behavior. I expect them to act against him anytime. This attempt to hang me should be the impetus they need to finally act against him."

"How do you reconcile your work for the Spanish Inquisition with your Portuguese origins and professed loyalty to the queen regent of Portugal?" asked Ramiro.

"My first loyalty is to Mother Church. Whether she is dressed in Portuguese or Spanish garb is irrelevant. Living on the borders of two conflicting powers requires a balancing act. I have no argument with the Spanish Church nor with the distant power of the Spanish state, but I detest and oppose the gang of thugs and cutthroats that were imposed as local landlords on us, following your withdrawal from the area. They are a group of penurious noblemen from Estremadura who see their transfer into this rich area as a license to loot and enrich themselves at the expense of the ordinary people. For this reason alone, I pray for and work toward the return of Portuguese control to the region."

"An interesting explanation. We must be on our way," concluded Ramiro.

"If it is not a military secret, where are you going to?" asked Nicodemo.

"Eventually to the front line, but we will pass through Passos," replied Alvaro.

"May I accompany you? My bishop is in Passos. I must report this latest Zoritas atrocity before they spread their usual false rumors."

"Leave out any detailed reference to us in your report. An unknown band of horsemen moved through the village, dispersed Zoritas, and saved your life," suggested Alvaro.

Some hours later, Luke and Ramiro's party stopped on the top of a small hill and looked down on the medieval castle of Passos. In recent times, a high wall had been built to enclose the castle's massive courtyard, within which an arsenal and barracks were located. Luke asked Alvaro and Ramiro if anything could be achieved by attacking it.

Alvaro was cautious. "There is no point in capturing the arsenal. We do not have enough men to maintain control. However, if we destroy it, this would be of great value to our war effort. Spain suffers a severe shortage of ammunition. With active campaigns in the Netherlands, Catalonia, and parts of Italy, the demand is overwhelming. Their campaign against us here will probably cease when they run out of their limited supply of ammunition."

Luke asked Ramiro if he had any way of getting the group into the arsenal and into a position where damage could be caused but from where they could escape unharmed.

Again, Alvaro was worried. "These are Spanish barracks. Our men are Portuguese. As soon as they open their mouths, their true identity will be revealed. You cannot infiltrate the barracks peacefully."

Ramiro, who had warmed to his task as an impersonator, had an answer. "We can! We will become a Galician unit sent from the northern frontier to participate in this offensive against Portugal. The Galician form of Spanish is very close to Portuguese. Any local troops still in the barracks would hardly know the difference. Our language will therefore not be a problem."

"What excuse do we use to get near the arsenal?" asked Luke.

"As a Galician unit, we have traveled through the night. We are hungry and our horses exhausted. We need new steeds and a meal before we can move to the front line. Once inside the barracks, we can assess the location of the arsenal and discover what it contains," replied Ramiro.

"We need to find a way to delay any possible explosion. We do not want our cover to be blown," warned Luke.

Father Nicodemo, who had been listening intently—perhaps too intently for Luke's liking—interrupted. "I know Castle Passos very well. Once a month, I conduct mass for the Portuguese prisoners and, sadly too often, administer the last rites to those who are dying. As you can see from here, the extended castle precinct has a large central courtyard with various buildings around the walls. The old castle is in the southwestern corner, which accommodates the governor and commandant, Gen. Federico Sanchez, and his officers. The next extended rectangular building along the western side of the courtyard is the dormitory for the troops stationed there. The smaller building next to it contains the kitchens and the refectory, the eating hall for the troops. In the northwest corner is the prison, and in the northeast, the arsenal. Two-thirds of the eastern side are stables, and the remainder consists of several workshops—blacksmiths, armorers, and wheelwrights. Lord Ramiro's plan to request a meal and refresh your horses will get you very close to the arsenal."

Luke's attention was diverted in the opposite direction to that of the castle.

On the eastern horizon, he saw several herds of cattle, perhaps mustered for imminent slaughter for the frontline troops.

Ramiro read Luke's mind. "I will send some of my men to round those cattle up and drive them back into Portugal. If they move them to the north and then west, they should avoid any Spanish patrols."

As six of Ramiro's men headed for the cattle, the rest of the group wound down the hill toward the large southern gate of the military complex. Father Nicodemo left them, explaining that he would go straight to the adjacent town of Passos to see his bishop. He would then return to the castle to minister to the increasing number of Portuguese prisoners expected from the current conflict.

Peter whispered to Luke, "Can we trust that priest?"

Luke smiled. "Not all priests are like Eduardo Zarco. Father Nicodemo is certainly an interesting character—a secret agent of the Spanish Inquisition, given free run of a Spanish military base, and yet allegedly a loyal subject of the Portuguese state."

"And possibly one of my own agents for Portuguese intelligence," added Alvaro. "I know there is a very reliable source in this area."

As they approached the main gate, a sentry asked the oncoming group to identify themselves. Ramiro launched into his lies about being a Galician unit in need of food and fresh horses. The sentry relayed the request to the captain of the watch, who, after a few minutes, confronted the visitors.

"Trust the Galicians! Always late for anything important. The attack started at dawn this morning. You are in luck. Most of the troops are at the front, so there is plenty of food, but we have no horses to spare. You can pay for your meal by escorting the last wagonloads of arms and ammunition to the front. In addition, you may be able to assist in incarcerating the multitude of prisoners we expect to arrive at any minute from the front."

Ramiro, recognizing the guard commander's accent, replied jovially, "A typical Andalusian response! Very generous and tolerant but expecting something in return."

The Spaniard then invited Ramiro and his fellow officers to join General Sanchez for a meal in the castle tower. Ramiro tactfully declined, emphasizing that as his unit would soon be in battle, it was good for morale if the officers ate with the men. He led his men to the far end of the stables, next to the arsenal and across the courtyard from the refectory.

While the Portuguese unit was in the refectory, enjoying the generous meal provided by the authorities of Castle Passos, two significant events were occurring outside in the courtyard. Six large wagons were loaded with arms and ammunition, ready to be escorted to the front line. Each wagon contained a single weapon or type of ammunition—muskets, swords, grenades, gunpowder, musket balls, and cannonballs of various dimensions. As these wagons were being prepared for departure with the hostlers and drivers attaching two large horses to each, they were passed in the courtyard by a large contingent of disarmed Portuguese prisoners escorted by a few Spanish horsemen.

Ramiro and his men, oblivious to such developments, continued to eat and drink. Father Nicodemo eventually found them and whispered rather loudly that they *must be* Portuguese—who else would spend so much time eating and drinking before moving into battle? He also cautioned Ramiro against trying to explode anything in the arsenal as it was too close to the military prison, which now contained at least fifty Portuguese soldiers. Ramiro explained that the Spaniards had asked them to escort several wagons of arms and ammunition to the front, which they would divert to their own advantage. There was probably nothing left to destroy, a fact verified by the Spanish adjutant who informed Ramiro that the wagons were ready for departure.

Nicodemo said, "Lord Ramiro, before you leave, come with me. I heard a rumor before I came in here that one of the new prisoners was a high-ranking Portuguese general with a worldwide reputation. I have permission to visit them. The high-ranking officers are in a separate chamber, a dungeon. You will be able to see who is there through a sliding panel."

Luke accompanied Ramiro and Nicodemo. Nicodemo pulled back the panel. Luke and Ramiro stared into the darkened dungeon. Both were dismayed.

The high-ranking general was Manuel Caro.

"We can't break him out. Given the number of troops still left in the barracks and those specifically guarding the prisoners, our little cavalcade would be outnumbered. At the first sign of trouble, the gate would be closed, and anyone in the courtyard would be subject to constant musket fire from the walls. We would be massacred," concluded Ramiro.

Luke agreed.

Nicodemo whispered, "Don't despair. I have a plan. Stay here until I return—and keep the viewing panel closed." He called out to the guards, "Let me into the dungeon! One of the senior officers is dying and needs the last rites."

The guard crossed himself and opened the trap door that led down into the dungeon.

Ten minutes later, Nicodemo was heard calling out for the door to be opened. He, with his hood covering most of his face, rejoined Luke and

Ramiro. He whispered, "Get me out of here before someone notices that Father Nicodemo is a foot shorter than he was." It was Caro.

They rejoined the rest of the group in the rectory.

Luke was impressed. "Father Nicodemo has probably given his life to save yours."

"Not if I carry out his plan. I will change into army gear, and one of your men can return Nicodemo's habit and hood to the prison. Keep its nature concealed if possible and tell the guards that the priest is giving some of his clothes to one of the prisoners who is feeling the cold."

"How can this help Nicodemo?" asked Alvaro.

"He will redress into his clerical garb, and when the guards change in about an hour, he will call the new guards to let him come out. Unless the guards meet and discuss the behavior of the priest, he should get away unscathed. He is a very impressive man," Caro concluded.

Nicodemo had his clothes returned to him with the unknowing help of the guards who remarked on the humanity of the priest.

Fifteen minutes later, Ramiro led his group out through the main gate, followed by six heavily laden wagons, protected on both sides by his men. Alvaro, Luke, Peter, and Caro brought up the rear.

Luke was troubled. Caro's capture conjured up all sorts of unpleasant scenarios. How had Portugal's most experienced and innovative general been captured in the first morning of the campaign?

LUKE AND RAMIRO'S UNIT arrived back at Magellan as night fell. The Spanish wagon drivers had been misled by Ramiro, who told them he was taking a shortcut to the front line. As they entered the Magellan barracks, their escorts automatically became their guards, who then supervised the transfer of the arms and ammunition into the Portuguese arsenal.

Later than evening, Da Silva convened a meeting of the council of war to assess the first day of the campaign. Luke reported that the Ramiro-led auxiliary unit had had overwhelming success. They had confiscated two herds of cattle and six large wagons of arms and ammunition from the Spaniards and added both to the depleted Portuguese supplies. More importantly, they had rescued General Caro from the Spanish stockade at Castle Passos. Da Silva thanked Luke and congratulated Ramiro. His success as an impersonator of an agent of the Spanish Inquisition and later as the commander of group of Galician cavalry had already spread through the barracks.

Da Silva turned to Caro. "Let's hear your report. Your capture could have seriously undermined our campaign. It is unlike you to make such a near fatal mistake. How did you come to be captured?"

"I was captured because of my speed in taking town D, and General de Mota's success in pushing the Spaniards out of towns A and B. I took town D with a small company of my troops. The main body of my forces were still well away from the town. The Spanish forces defending towns A and B withdrew under pressure from De Mota, but instead of retreating eastward back into Spanish-held territory as expected, they moved quickly to the north and came between town D, which I was holding with a few men, and my main army, which they then contained. They reentered town D, which, given their superior numbers, I was forced to surrender."

De Mota spoke. "I can confirm what Caro has said. My companies attacking towns A and B faced little resistance, but I could see that companies of troops had already withdrawn and were heading north toward D. I immediately sent one of my companies to assist Caro. They joined the bulk of his army but were contained by a large Spanish contingent drawn from the former defenders of A and B. I could not break through to rescue him in D."

Luke asked, "Were any of the targeted villages reinforced in the last few days?"

"No," replied De Mota. "Rather, the opposite—the Spaniards had withdrawn troops from most of the villages we attacked."

Luke was troubled. There was an obvious major flaw in his plan to uncover the traitor. He had assumed that on receiving information that a town would be attacked, the Spaniards would strengthen their defenses. None had. It appeared that Spain's reaction to any knowledge of an attack was to withdraw troops, surrender territory, and save lives.

Da Silva asked Luke, "You were the commander for today's activities. What are your conclusions?"

"This type of warfare is useless. It is a waste of manpower and resources. Portugal is never going to make great inroads into Spain without an army double the size you have at the moment. Your only reason for confronting Spain militarily is to force it to recognize Portuguese independence. You do not wish to increase your territory. A military solution to achieve your basic aim is misplaced. The only way to force Spain to recognize your sovereignty is through diplomatic pressure. England and France combined could force Spain's hand. Until this is achieved, your secondary—and military—aim is to prevent Spain from recapturing the whole of Portugal. This, they cannot do as long as the bulk of their armies are engaged in Catalonia, the Netherlands, and Italy. If the French withdraw from Catalonia or the Netherlands and Spain redirects its forces against you, assistance from England will be needed urgently. I will recommend this to my government. As far as today's operations are concerned, we have not taken any towns by force. Those that we occupy were given to us by a strategic withdrawal of the enemy. Not a good result. We must achieve something spectacular, something that will be good for morale."

"Rubbish!" exclaimed an enraged Pinto. "The English general does not understand what ten years of constant border raids has achieved. We have removed thousands and thousands of sheep and cattle from the Spanish province of Estremadura and forced every town to maintain a garrison in case we attack. Spain has been forced to spread its overstressed military resources even farther. These garrison troops are desperately needed to fight Spain's battles elsewhere. In addition, we have so undermined the economy of these Spanish areas that the inhabitants are so poor that they may rise in revolt. Spain has to spend resources in the border provinces because of our unrelenting raids."

Caro eased the tension. "I agree with Pinto about our achievements to date, but currently, there does appear to be a period of stalemate, which Tremayne's suggestions may help to break."

"Tremayne, what exactly do you suggest?" asked Da Silva.

"I suggest that, first of all, you appoint one of Caro, Pinto, or De Mota as commander-in-chief and he immediately convene a meeting of his deputies to come up with a plan. I also recommend that Lord Ramiro be present. He has a very innovative mind."

It was well into the night when the generals reconvened. Da Silva appointed Caro as commander-in-chief—but only for the current operation. A final choice would be made by the queen regent. Luke, Peter, Ramiro, Alvaro, De Mota, Pinto, and Caro met to plan a spectacular operation.

Pinto was still critical. "There is nothing much more we can achieve in this central area of operation except continue our sporadic raids. But if we moved our offensive to the far north or the far south, we could attack key Spanish cities."

De Mota agreed.

Ramiro followed their line of argument. "I thoroughly agree with the generals who have just spoken. Nothing tangible can be achieved in this area in the way of military conquest. But there is a much more spectacular area of operation—abduction."

"Kidnap the Spanish king!" exclaimed Pinto sarcastically.

"Perhaps not the king, but there are many leading Spanish generals and clergy who are not far from the frontier. Alvaro, you are the intelligence expert. Can your agents find out who of high status is within striking distance?" asked Ramiro.

Caro, who had remained silent, commented, "Let's interrogate some of our prisoners. Do we even know which Spanish general is in charge of operations against us here? If he is one of the high nobility and related to the king, he would be an obvious choice."

Alvaro commented, "The commander-in-chief of all Spanish forces along the border is the Duke of Medinaceli, who is a relative of General de Mota. He was reported recently to be in the area. The local military commander is the governor of Passos Castle, Gen. Federico Sanchez."

"Sanchez is not of high enough status and could easily be replaced," noted Ramiro.

"How would you feel if we targeted your wife's relative?" asked Pinto of De Mota with unconcealed vindictive pleasure.

"I hope you are not implying that my loyalty to the queen and Portugal is lessened by my wife's family relationship to the Spanish high command!" was the reply.

"Medinaceli is not a practical target. He has an army of personal retainers as well as several companies of soldiers that guard his every move. We need a high-profile figure whom no one would expect to be abducted—what some people call a soft target," commented Caro, determined to ameliorate the friction between De Mota and Pinto.

"What about the Spanish grand inquisitor?" asked Ramiro, obviously relishing another brush with the Holy Office.

"No, he is an old man well into his seventies and no longer travels far from Madrid. His capture would hardly be missed. He would be replaced by a more efficient person immediately. Our target has to be high profile and whose abduction would seriously disrupt Spanish society," Alvaro replied.

"High profile but not necessarily high status," added Luke enigmatically.

"What do you mean?" asked Caro.

"Who causes most harm, actual and potential, to the Portuguese cause in the borderlands of this midsection of the frontier? In my brief time here, the actions of Col. Marcos Barbosa, the Chameleon, have been constantly mentioned."

"Capture the Chameleon! That would be a coup," remarked Ramiro.

Caro ended the meeting explaining, "We can take our time to determine a target. Da Silva has mobilized the militias of both the neighboring provinces, Beira and Alentejo. The militia of Beira is controlled by our old friend, the Marquess of Estrella, who will rejoin us tomorrow. I propose that when the militias arrive, which will double our forces by over a thousand men, that we march on a major town of Estremadura, either Caceres or Badajoz, and create as much destruction as we can and then withdraw before Spain can effectively mobilize against us."

"That could be a dangerous enterprise," countered Pinto. "The Duke of Feria, who dominates Estremadura, is a very able general and can probably raise his own militia very quickly. We could be cut off or forced to indulge in heavy fighting. We should not risk losing men in such an adventure, the gains from which, as you suggest, will only be temporary."

Luke intervened. "Before any divergence from the current sporadic border advances and retreats occur, we need more intelligence. Lord Ramiro could lead a small party deep into Estremadura to assess the current military situation."

Caro did not comment and left the room.

Luke and Peter, after returning to their chambers, discussed the situation.

"Will these three generals ever agree?" commented a frustrated Peter.

"No, Portugal's military future may have to depend on a new generation of leaders."

"Do you have a clearer view as to whom the traitor might be?"

Before Luke could answer, Alvaro entered the room.

"Sorry for this unannounced visit. I have just received an urgent dispatch from Lisbon—from the queen herself—or rather, from my sister-in-law, Micaela. In essence, our spies at the Spanish court in Madrid report that there are rumors that Portuguese resistance will soon crumble through an act of self-destruction."

"Portugal's about to surrender?" Luke asked.

"As good as. If true, this act could be decisive and is very pertinent to your secret agenda. The exact rumor is that a Portuguese general who has considerable support within Portugal is about to change sides and become commander-in-chief of all Spanish armies. His first priority is to restore Portugal to the Spanish throne," elaborated Alvaro.

"It can only be Caro. He has an international reputation," remarked Luke.

"Don't expect a logical selection based on experience and ability. Most appointments made in Spain and Portugal depend on family connections and balancing of the competing interests of the aristocracy. On those criteria, both Pinto and De Mota have a better claim than Caro," countered Alvaro.

After Alvaro left, Peter commented, "Spain would gain little in enticing either De Mota or Pinto into their camp. They are, at the best, mediocre. Portugal's best generals, apart from Caro, are still in Brazil. He must be the intended target—able and with an international reputation."

"Yes, and he is a professional soldier first, and his Portuguese nationalism may be well down his list of priorities," Luke commented without much evidence.

"If you are right, his surrender to the Spaniards earlier today may have been deliberate. It was his move into the Spanish camp, but we rescued him before the Spanish authorities had separated him from his men to finalize an agreement. Our rescue took place no more than ten minutes after his arrival in the dungeon," suggested Peter.

"If Caro is a traitor, our new friend Father Nicodemo might be in serious trouble," remarked Luke.

THE NEXT DAY, THERE was a noticeable lull in the fighting as neither side seemed to know what it was trying to achieve, and cautious commanders on the ground wanted to lessen the loss of ammunition and lives. Ramiro remarked to Luke that this reflected the general malaise that had engulfed the Portuguese military effort since the death of King John.

"The sooner we can devise a spectacular mission, the better. Otherwise, I will return home and attack the local travelers," he threatened.

That evening, Da Silva hosted a banquet for the councillors, the officers, and their wives. Those who had moved originally to Magellan were joined by the two militia commanders. The Marquis of Estrela was accompanied by his wife, Joana, his chamberlain, Cipriano, and his wife, Ana, and his deputy chamberlain, Alfredo Matos, who was the effective commander of the militia. The general of the Alentejo militia, Viscount Roberto Delgado, came alone.

Luke was seated once again next to Madalena de Albuquerque, either through Da Silva's attempt to promote gossip or because she was the only person at the table who spoke English—or so it was believed.

Madalena opened the conversation. "I suppose you want to know all about the new face opposite, Roberto Delgado."

"Why should I? Is his presence going change the atmosphere at the table or the events of the next few days?" replied Luke jokingly.

"It well might!" was Madalena's surprise response.

"Now you have got my interest. What is so important about our new viscount?"

"He is not a soldier. His family dominates the province to the south of here, and he nominally commands their militia on behalf of his father, the duke, who is too old to take the field. Before he returned to Portugal to effectively take over his family's estates, he was a diplomat. And where do you think he was stationed?"

Luke looked deep into Madalena's eyes and whispered, "Tell me."

"Paris."

"And what is significant about that?"

"While there he was very friendly, according to some, he had an affair with a French noblewoman whom you have met, Michele Le Michel—now Micaela, wife of Rodrigo, who sits across the table from us at this moment."

"Interesting. Husband and ex-lover in the same room," mused Luke.

"What is more interesting is why was Delgado summoned here, and who suggested it?"

"How is that significant?"

"Diego told me that Da Silva had only intended to supplement the current strength of our forces in the area by mobilizing Estrela's Beira militia. Unless a major offensive deep into Spain was intended, there is no need for Delgado's men, but Da Silva received direct orders from Lisbon to call up the Alentejo troops."

"I imagine he received his orders from the queen."

"Of course, but who persuaded the queen to give such an order?"

"Are you suggesting it could be her favorite Micaela da Costa, Delgado's ex-lover?"

"Yes."

"To what end?"

"You are the great English sleuth. Find out."

"Affairs and liaisons at the Portuguese court do not interest me," concluded Luke churlishly.

"But what if the move is the beginning of a major change within the Portuguese government, and its attitude to war with Spain?"

"In what way?"

"Viscount Delgado is one of the next generation of leaders who believes a complete break with everything Spanish is necessary—including the queen regent. He leads a group of nobles who want the boy King Afonso to remove his mother as regent and appoint a Portuguese nobleman in her place."

"I can see where you are heading. The queen's closest adviser may have rekindled her affair with a man determined to remove the queen at the earliest opportunity. Surely, Queen Luisa is aware of Delgado's position. If so, why agree? Why would Micaela betray the queen? The Costas are the most powerful family in the kingdom under Queen Luisa's regency."

"Question Micaela when you return to Lisbon."

"By then, it will be too late. My mission here will be over," Luke replied. He was depressed. Could there be any truth in Madalena's insinuation that the traitor that Micaela had asked Luke to discover was Micaela herself? If so, his secret mission was a farce. He was being used.

A hand on his knee brought him back to reality, but he could not resist one last question on the topic.

"Has Delgado been at court recently, and has he been seen in the company of Micaela?"

"In the three or four weeks before we moved to Estrela, he was at court on at least three occasions, but personally, I never saw him with Micaela or the queen. He did see a lot of the minister of war—our host, Pero da Silva. But cheer up, Luke! You seem to be depressed by the thought that Micaela is betraying the queen. She could be doing the exact opposite."

"In what way?"

"She could be seducing Delgado to win him over to the queen and the Da Costa faction."

"Enough, Madalena. Your information is confusing me. My immediate concern is how to break out of the current military stalemate and do something spectacular that will help the Portuguese cause."

After some time of idle chatter and eating, Madalena suddenly asked, "What have you been up to, Luke? The countess Teresa Pinto cannot keep her eyes off you. Perhaps she has heard of your reputation as a womanizer."

"I have never spoken to the countess, but I would like to. Could you arrange a meeting with her? You should accompany me as my interpreter—and as chaperone," said Luke with a twinkle in his eye.

"I shall not participate in your seduction of Teresa," retorted Madalena angrily.

"Madalena, I simply want to question her in terms of what you just told me about Micaela and Delgado. As Micaela's deputy, she may know more on the matter, and if your insight into her attitude to me is correct, she may be very willing to disclose what she knows."

Madalena's hand moved farther up Luke's leg. He made no attempt to obstruct it.

While this was happening, Alvaro, who sat next to him, was approached by a servant. Alvaro rose and followed the servant to the far end of the refectory, where he engaged in a long conversation with a peasant girl. He then left the hall.

On returning five minutes later, he dramatically informed Luke, "My room, as soon as the meal is over!"

Two hours later, Luke, Peter, and Ramiro found themselves outside Alvaro's room.

"What is this about?" asked Ramiro.

"We will soon know," uttered Luke as he knocked gently on the door.

On entering the room, they were confronted by Alvaro and the young woman Luke had seen in the refectory. They immediately recognized her. She was the woman accused of witchcraft whom they had rescued at Corba.

"Let Marabella repeat her message," directed Alvaro.

"Father Nicodemo asked me to get a message to Colonel da Costa as a matter of urgency. He said he had sent messages to the colonel for years, although the colonel would only know who he was if he claimed to be the Black Heron."

"Black Heron is the code name for one of our best agents in the area. I had no idea when we met Father Nicodemo that he was the Black Heron," explained Alvaro.

"An excellent agent not to reveal his cover at that time," remarked Ramiro.

"What is the message that Nicodemo thought so important that he neglected his normal method of communication to send Marabella at great risk to her own life through the lines to contact you directly, Alvaro?" asked Luke.

"Father Nicodemo, on his first visit to Castle Passos after you had left, heard in the loose talk of Spanish officials and Portuguese prisoners that at least a company of troops were to be withdrawn from the front line to protect a very high official in the Spanish government who was coming to Passos on the Feast of the Holy Infant. He also heard that all Portuguese prisoners in Castle Passos were to be taken immediately inland to the military prison in Caceres. In addition, he was banned from the castle for three weeks."

"Did Nicodemo find out why this high official was coming to Passos?"

"The deputy commandant of the castle was heard to say that it would bring the current border conflict with Portugal to a speedy end and probably lay the basis for the eventual reconquest of Portugal."

"This fits in well with your latest intelligence, Alvaro, that a senior Portuguese military figure may go over to the Spaniards," commented Luke.

The mood in the room was somber except for Ramiro, who seemed highly elated. He declared, "This is great news! The Spanish visitor must be a high-ranking nobleman, a leading general, or a member of King Philip's own council. It suggests that the Portuguese traitor is also of high rank. We could pull off a double spectacular act—capture the Spanish official and arrest the Portuguese traitor."

Luke agreed. "This does provide us with the opportunity we have been looking for, but we need to know a lot more before we can act effectively. This information should not go outside this room."

The next morning, a gentle knocking was heard on Luke's door. He opened it cautiously to be greeted by Aileen, Madalena's servant.

"General, my mistress has arranged a meeting with the countess Teresa Pinto for nine this morning. The countess and you will meet in my mistress's apartment." She gave Luke a knowing smile and departed.

Peter was slightly miffed. "Luke, we are in the middle of a major mission, and you are chasing married women across the barracks."

"Not at all, Peter. With everything that happened last night, I did not get a chance to tell you about an even more serious plot against the queen than the problem we have been asked to solve."

Luke relayed the information that Madalena had given him the night before.

After some consideration, Peter agreed.

"There may be two separate plots—the defection of a leading Portuguese general who may have been passing information to Spain for years and the removal of Queen Luisa as regent by someone close to her."

"And we know that Countess Teresa would love to replace Micaela da Costa as the queen's senior lady-in-waiting. She may be an ideal, if biased, source of information on the plot to overthrow the queen," explained Luke.

Ten minutes later, Luke was in Madalena's room and, after a gentle hug, awaited the arrival of Teresa. Exactly at the appointed time, she arrived.

She had dressed most seductively. Given the conservatism of the Portuguese court, she had gone as far as modesty would permit in adopting the French court's penchant for bare but painted breasts. Her low-cut gown revealed everything through a transparent pale green fabric.

"I am surprised that the English general sought a meeting with me without the presence of my husband," she teasingly exclaimed.

Luke was not going to lose any advantage that might stem from the countess's possible infatuation with him. He replied, "How could I resist not having an intimate conversation with the most beautiful woman I have seen since my arrival in Portugal?"

Given the look on Madalena's face, he hoped that she would translate his remarks correctly.

He continued, "However, to give a respectable cover to this visit, I need to ask you a few questions relating to a matter that your mistress the queen has asked me to investigate."

Teresa was looking at him with such uninhibited lust that he was glad Madalena was in the room. Or maybe he wasn't.

He diplomatically explained, "I have asked the baroness to act as my interpreter because my official translator, Col. Alvaro da Costa, may be part of the group I am investigating."

This reference to the Pinto's hated rivals, the Da Costas, deflected Teresa's attention from her open display of lust. "Most likely, he is the ringleader. How can I help uncover the evil these Da Costas inflict on Portugal?" she purred.

"Is your fellow lady-in-waiting, Micaela da Costa, faithful to her husband?"

'Of course not. She is French and had lovers before she married poor Rodrigo."

"Why *poor* Rodrigo?"

"Until about a year ago, he was being cuckolded by his own but much younger brother, your comrade Col. Alvaro da Costa."

"What happened a year ago to change this?"

"Micaela renewed her earlier liaison with our most recent arrival at Magellan, Roberto Delgado. He had just returned from France to assist his elderly father manage the family estates."

"I heard that Viscount Delgado is not a particular friend of the queen. He wishes the boy king to remove her as regent because of her Spanish origins and appoint an ultranationalist Portuguese in her place."

"Such as himself," replied Teresa.

"If you are aware of such plots, have you warned the queen?"

"No, the queen only deals with the outside world through Micaela. Any move against her favorite would lead to my own dismissal."

Luke thanked Teresa for her assistance. She turned to Madalena and spoke for some time.

Madalena translated her speech through gritted teeth. "The countess wishes you to know that she hopes that this is only the first of many visits. The next visit, you should come alone, and she assures you that the language problem will, in no way, inhibit your welcome."

As soon as they were outside Teresa's room, a furious Madalena gave Luke a slap across the face and walked off.

AS LUKE LEFT HIS confrontation with Madalena, a series of bugle calls echoed throughout the barracks. Troops were running from everywhere and hastily assembling on the large parade ground. From a distance, the increasingly louder sound of a regular drumbeat could be heard. Councillors, generals, and their wives gathered on the steps of the officers' quarters.

Luke found Alvaro and asked, "What is happening?"

"I cannot believe it. The queen is coming. Apparently, Delgado, when he arrived yesterday, forewarned Da Silva," answered an angry Alvaro.

"Is it not risky for her to be so close to the border? The Spaniards could carry out the very plan we are about to hatch. Seize a key figure from the enemy camp! And there is no one more central to Portuguese aspirations than Queen Luisa," commented a now equally alarmed Luke.

"Plain stupidity! What is wrong with my sister-in-law? She should have prevented such an ill-considered move," uttered an increasingly furious Alvaro.

Within half an hour an ornate royal coach, escorted by a full company of household cavalry came through the gate of Magellan. Luke was impressed with their turnout and, above all, their horses—a stronger yet lighter variety of Arabian steeds than those known in England. The officer in charge dismounted and spoke to Da Silva, who advised everybody to disperse as the queen was moving directly into seclusion.

As the welcoming party moved away, a heavily veiled female figure alighted from the coach and, surrounded by several soldiers, disappeared into a section of the officers' quarters that was now clearly out of bounds to those not of the queen's party.

Luke caught up with Madalena before she reached her quarters. "Forgive me for my behavior toward Teresa Pinto. It was designed to elicit information, not to progress a seduction. What do you make of this surprise visit?"

"If you believe even half of what Teresa told you this morning, I am not surprised by it. If the queen suspects that a plot is developing among her ladies-in-waiting, it would be wise to have them all in one place."

"Surely, it would have been easier and safer to have ordered them all back to Lisbon," suggested Luke.

"No. In a strange way, she is safer here and most able to deal with her enemies than in Lisbon. She has her ultra-loyal household cavalry to protect her, whereas many of her enemies are deprived of the resources they could bring against her in the capital," explained Madalena.

They had just about reached Madalena's rooms when they were almost knocked down by Alfredo Matos and two other men running toward the rooms of Paola da Costa, the Marquess of Estrela.

"What's your hurry?" shouted a ruffled Madalena.

"I am sorry, baroness, but there has been an unexpected death. I and the two army surgeons based at Magellan must examine the body."

"Who is dead?" asked a mollified Madalena.

"Joana da Costa, marchioness of Estrela!"

A shocked Madalena entered her room.

Luke followed the surgeons. Alvaro emerged from Joana's room as they approached and was pleased to see Luke. "I was about to send for you. Joana's death is a mystery, and given your reputation as a sleuth, I want you to join the surgeons and myself in its investigation."

Luke had only spoken to Joana briefly on the occasion she comforted Madalena when Diego's disappearance was first revealed. The marchioness was fully and lavishly clothed, ready to receive her cousin the queen. She was small and olive skinned with short black hair. She lay slumped on her back across the bed. Matos explained that she had been strangled from behind.

"Where's her husband, Paolo?" asked Luke.

"He found the body. I suggested he move to my brother's room while the examination is conducted," replied Alvaro.

"When exactly was she killed?" probed Luke.

"About the time we were all gathering to receive the queen. Joana was missing from the group. She never made it outside into the parade ground, yet she was clearly dressed for the occasion. Her absence caused Paolo to return here immediately after we were all dismissed. He wanted his wife to explain her most undiplomatic absence."

"What could be the motive for this murder? Joana wasn't a courtier! Should you be conducting this investigation, Alvaro? Are you acting as an intelligence officer or a family member? Is the murder personal or political?" asked Luke.

"I was never close to my cousin. I do not know enough of Joana's background to help me determine any motives. The only political fact of note is that she was Spanish born. Maybe one of the ultranationalists who distrusts everything Spanish is making a statement—perhaps a warning to the queen regent."

"If so, it is perfectly timed," declared Luke.

"That is the worry. Joana today, the queen tomorrow," was the blunt reply.

Luke left Alvaro and retraced his steps to Madalena's room. Aileen welcomed him but was quickly supplanted by Madalena. Luke went straight to the point. "Tell me all you can about Joana."

"Surely, Alvaro da Costa filled you in on his cousin by marriage."

"Only that she was Spanish born."

"That is odd. He did not mention her impeccable family connections?"

"No."

"The Marchioness of Estrela was Joana de Guzman, a cousin of Queen Luisa and, like her, a granddaughter of the Duke of Medina-Sidonia, who led the armada against you English in 1588."

"Don't you think it strange that the woman is murdered just before her powerful cousin arrives?" asked Luke.

"What are you implying?" asked Madalena.

"That someone did not want Joana to speak to her cousin the queen."

Madalena drew a deep breath. "Whom do you suspect?"

"Alvaro tried to direct my thinking toward ultra-Portuguese nationalists who are suspicious of all Spanish-born nobles."

"It's possible and, if so, a clear warning to the queen herself."

"Exactly the conclusion of Alvaro da Costa. On the other hand, if I believe even a little of what Teresa Pinto said, I would suspect the Da Costa clan. Perhaps Joana discovered that her husband and his relatives were plotting to overthrow her cousin the queen. Maybe she had proof of this and was about to reveal it to Luisa."

"Question Carlos de Cipriano and Alfredo Matos on the domestic life of Castle Estrela. Were Joana and Paolo close? I will act as your interpreter," suggested Madalena.

"An excellent idea! But I prefer to start with Ana de Cipriano. Tell me about her."

"I can't. I had never heard of her, let alone met her, before I arrived at Castle Estrela."

Ana was surprised to receive a visit from the Baroness Albuquerque and the English general. She was a short plump woman with a round and cheerful face. Her once black hair showed streaks of gray. She had been crying, and several damp handkerchiefs were littered across the room.

"Joana and I were friends for decades. We have been a comfort to each other through many a crisis."

"Was there anything bothering the marchioness in recent weeks?" asked Luke.

"Yes, and it was something very important."

"Such as?"

"I don't know exactly, but she said the future of Portugal depended on what she did."

"And what did she do?"

"She wrote a letter."

"To whom?"

"I don't know."

"What happened to the letter?"

"It was given to the castle's chaplain, Francisco Diaz, who was to deliver it personally to the designated recipient. It must have been important because it was the only time since I have known her that she lied. She lied about the priest's absence, claiming she did not know where he had gone or why."

"This annoyed whom?"

"Her husband and mine. The chaplain absented himself just when he was needed to preside over the Feast of Our Lady of Estrela and to welcome the council of war."

"Why didn't Joana explain the situation to Paolo?"

"When I asked her that question, she did not answer."

Luke suddenly changed the direction of his interrogation. "Was Joana close to her cousin the queen?"

Ana was struck dumb. She seemed to fall into a trance. Luke looked at Madalena for assistance.

Madalena took Ana's hand and gently stroked it and remarked, "The English general is determined to find Joana's killer. Anything you can tell him that might uncover the murderer will be helpful—even if you have to reveal long-held secrets."

Ana smiled and snapped out of her strange condition. "I am very sorry. The general's question went straight to the heart of a matter that had remained a secret between Joana and me from the day we first met."

"Which was?"

"To the outside world, Joana was a country noblewoman with no interest in politics, to the extent that she never bothered to visit or communicate with her cousin the queen. In reality, it was the opposite. They communicated regularly, and the queen clearly sought Joana's advice on a number of matters."

"Is it possible that the letter that the chaplain carried was to the queen?"

Ana was again partly traumatized and murmured, "Do you think the letter has something to do with her death?"

"Yes, and if it was to the queen, it might, as Joana said, influence the future of Portugal."

Luke and Madalena returned to the latter's room. Concerned by what they had just heard, they recovered their equilibrium in each other's arms.

It was nightfall before Luke found his way back to his room. He was dressing for supper when there was a knock on the door. It was Father Antonio, who addressed him in Dutch.

"Luke, come with me immediately. Put on this cassock and pull the hood over as much of your face as you can. You must not be recognized!"

Antonio led him through the corridors into the officer's section and, beyond that, into a darkened chapel. Kneeling at the altar rail was a cassocked and hooded figure. Antonio approached, bowed, and knelt beside the figure, beckoning Luke to do the same on the figure's other side.

Antonio whispered, "To the outside world, we look like three monks at prayer. Your Majesty, this is the English general Tremayne to whom you wished to speak."

"General, my cousin informed me that she had discovered a plot by those close to me to remove me as regent or even to murder me. She felt it was being hatched on the frontier and that I should come immediately, and by the time she also arrived here, she could give me more details. It is clear that the plotters became aware that their plans had been discovered and killed Joana before she could tell me more."

"How can I help?" asked Luke.

"I want you to return to Castle Estrela while the marquess and his servants are here and search Joana's possessions. I want you to retrieve any letters of mine that she failed to destroy and hopefully find some evidence of the plot to which she has alerted me. As the Da Costa family is possibly involved, this mission must be concealed from Alvaro. Father Antonio will act as your interpreter, although I would prefer he stayed with me here."

"No problem, Your Majesty. My government was concerned that any interpreter may put his own spin on what I was told. My equerry, Capt. Peter Frost, speaks fluent Portuguese. He and I can sneak away from Magellan and hardly be missed."

"Take my faithful servant Ramiro de Lima and a few of his men with you for protection. God be with you. Take this letter of authorization with the royal seal. This indicates that whatever you do, you do in my name."

The queen rose and left the chapel. Ten minutes later, Antonio and Luke were at high table, enjoying the evening meal.

16

AFTER SUPPER, LUKE AND Peter made their way to Ramiro's room. The Portuguese warlord was surprised when Peter addressed him in his native tongue. He was further surprised when told of the queen's special mission and amazed at his selection in it.

Luke probed, "Ramiro, you have been a neighbor and tenant of Estrela for decades. Tell me anything about Joana that might possibly explain her murder."

"I can't. Of all the people whom I know, she was the least likely to have an enemy and certainly no one ready to murder her."

"She was popular with her tenants and workers?"

"Extremely so."

"Were her Spanish origins held against her?"

"Only by her chamberlain, Carlos de Cipriano."

"What was his grievance?"

"Apart from a general hatred of the Spaniard, I know of nothing specific. Even that hatred may have been concocted as he is closely related to the Spanish governor of Castle Passos. This animosity was more than counterbalanced by Cipriano's wife, who was Joana's long-standing and loyal friend. Joana's Spanish origins actually made her popular among many of her tenants who had relatives in Spanish-occupied territory. She often used her Spanish connections to improve their situation."

"She maintained contact with the Spanish authorities?"

"Yes, and she often reprimanded me, claiming that my raids into Spain undid the good work she felt she had done in the borderlands to protect Portuguese peasants from Spanish oppression."

"Did you know she maintained a close relationship with the queen?"

"No, she never gave any indication of any interest in politics other than where it affected her tenants and workers."

"Did Paolo have any strong views on the current state of Portuguese politics that may have contributed to his wife's murder?"

"No. Unlike his cousins, he never expressed strong support for or against the queen regent. He was a local lord determined to maintain his estates and powers. He resented any interference from Lisbon as he would from Madrid."

"Could he be ready to renounce his allegiance to the Portuguese Braganzas and return Estrela to Spanish control?"

"Never! The one political belief that Paolo held was to keep all government officials, Portuguese or Spanish, as far away from Estrela as possible. He was not happy when he was asked to host the council of war."

"We leave at dawn. Nobody is to know where we are going. I will hint that we are embarking on another secret expedition into Spain and may be gone for a week or more. No one outside of this room, except the queen and Father Antonio, know our real destination," said Luke.

Peter asked, "Ramiro, you gave no indication that the queen even knew you. Why did she expressly select you or all her Portuguese subjects for this enterprise?"

"In the early days of our revolutionary wars, when Luisa accompanied her husband, King John, on campaigns, on one occasion, she was cut off from her bodyguard and was in danger of being taken by the Spaniards. I managed to defend her until we were both rescued. That was almost twenty years ago. I am surprised that she even remembered me."

"Maybe Joana mentioned you on occasions," suggested Luke.

As they approached Castle Estrela, Luke was struck by the change in its appearance. The lower fields were empty of tents and people. A few sheep grazed on each. The castle gave the appearance of being deserted. Its main gate was closed, and a single guard manned the wall.

Ramiro announced himself. "You know me—Ramiro de Lima. I come not in my own right but as a special emissary of the queen to bring you sad news."

After some time, the gate was opened, and Ramiro's party was confronted by a soberly dressed middle-aged man, Vitor Abrega, who claimed that in the absence of Cipriano and Matos, he was the acting chamberlain and castellan.

He was shown the queen's letter of authorization and asked, "What is so important that the queen herself sends you here?"

Peter answered, "Gather everybody in the courtyard immediately, and the reasons for our visit will be revealed!"

Abrega went inside the castle, and they could hear the sound of several gongs alerting the indoor staff. From the parapet of one of the towers, a cornet blast clearly summoned the outdoor inhabitants to gather in the courtyard. Luke was surprised that so few people maintained the castle in the absence of the marquess and most of his troops.

Ramiro, still on horseback, raised his hand to gain silence from the gathered staff. "I have been sent here with my English comrades by the queen to inform you that your mistress, the marchioness Joana, is dead."

The gathering erupted into a cacophony of cries of disbelief, anguish, and wailing. Ramiro hushed the distraught congregation. "You may wonder why the queen has sent two foreigners with me. Unfortunately, your mistress was murdered, and most of the Portuguese close to her must be considered suspects. In addition to informing you of this tragic news, we are required by the queen to investigate the marchioness's last few days here and to search her quarters for any evidence that will help us understand her murder. Any of you who can assist us with relevant information, please come forward over the next few days."

The queen's three investigators, adhering to protocol, first summoned the acting chamberlain and lawyer, Vitor Abrega. Luke led the proceedings, with Peter translating his questions and the answers he received.

"Abrega, in the weeks before your master and mistress departed for Magellan, was there any major disagreement between them?"

The chamberlain remained silent.

Ramiro interjected, "Answer the question!"

Abrega responded, "I am a servant of Estrela. A loyal servant must keep confidences and not betray his master or mistress. I cannot answer that question."

Ramiro struck the table with his fist. "And we are servants of the queen. Read again this letter from her, bearing the royal seal. If you refuse to answer us, you are refusing an order of the queen. Time in a royal prison will not pleasant."

Luke could see that the unfortunate Abrega was torn between loyalty to his employers and the fear of royal punishment. He moderated his questioning. "Whatever you tell us will not go outside of this room, except to the queen. Your reticence in refusing to discuss events in the weeks before the marquess and his wife left for the barracks suggests that there was something you felt should not be revealed. What is it?"

"The marquess and marchioness led very separate lives. The marquess spent most of his time with his horses—and hunting. The marchioness was inseparable from Ana de Cipriano, and they spent most of the day together without the benefit of servants. If you want fuller answers to these questions, ask Ana. She was the confidante of the marchioness."

Luke persisted. "What happened that made you reluctant to comment?"

"In all the time I have worked here, I have not heard or even heard of any argument between the marquess and his wife, but during the recent visit of the council of war, the marchioness was furious with her husband. I was sent out of the room by Cipriano, but even through closed doors, it was obvious that the marchioness was extremely angry."

"What made her so?" asked Luke

"It had something to do with the master's behavior toward Teresa, Countess Pinto."

Ramiro whistled and muttered, "The sly old dog. I didn't know old Paolo had it in him, although as a young man, he had quite a reputation. Estrela is full of his illegitimate offspring."

The acting chamberlain was quick to counter Ramiro's innuendo. "The relationship between my master and the countess was not romantic. From the comments I heard from Cipriano afterward, it was political. The marquess had made the mistake of agreeing to some views of the countess that the marchioness found unacceptable. It had something to do with what happened at court involving ladies-in-waiting."

"Do you know what those views were?"

"No. Even if Cipriano had told me, I would not believe him. He never liked my mistress and was always feeding unfavorable information concerning her to the marquess."

"Did the marquess accept any of these negative views from his chamberlain?"

"Probably not. The marquess had a soft spot for Ana de Cipriano, and her favorable views of his wife probably far outweighed the negative influence of her husband."

"Are there any of the marchioness's maid servants here, or did they all go with her to Magellan?"

"I will send the twins to you."

"The twins?"

"Nobody can tell them apart. They are very young and a bit empty-headed. My mistress took pity on them, and in return, they proved obsessively loyal. They will be especially distraught over her death. Be gentle with them," requested a concerned Vitor.

The twins arrived. Luke did not bother with names or trying to separate them. They answered as one, completing each other's sentences. Luke gently explained, "The queen has asked us to find your mistress's killer. Can you help us?"

"Everybody loved our mistress—except the bad baron."

"The bad baron?"

"Carlos de Cipriano," they said in unison.

"Before she went to Magellan, was your mistress especially cross?"

"Especially cross? Very cross!"

"What made her cross?"

"The ladies from the court."

"Was it the ladies from the court or your master?"

"Not our master. He is very kind. He calmed her down when she got angry."

"Which ladies of the court?" asked Peter.

"There were two of them—Teresa, Baroness Pinto, and Madalena, Baroness Albuquerque."

"What did these ladies do to annoy your mistress?"

"The baroness Teresa spent a lot of time with the bad baron, bad-mouthing our mistress."

"She spent time with Cipriano, not with your master, the marquess?"

"Why would she spend time with the master?" they asked naively.

Peter asked, "Were the bad baron and the countess Teresa kissing?"

The twins looked appalled, if not disgusted, at the suggestion. "No, but that is why the baroness Madalena upset our mistress."

"Madalena was kissing the bad baron?" asked Peter.

"No, not the bad baron."

The girls suddenly stopped and looked embarrassed, and then both whispered in Peter's ear, and then fled the room.

Peter laughed. "Apparently, the marchioness was upset that Madalena was having an affair with you, Luke."

Ramiro commented, "I can understand that. Joana was very friendly with the Albuquerque family, and to see Madalena flirting with you, Luke, would have annoyed her as a betrayal of her friends and also as a breach of good manners that undermined her position as a good hostess."

"Be that as it may, my relationship with Madalena has little to do with the main aim of this investigation," replied Luke. "Bring Abrega back!"

Luke asked him a simple question. "The twins kept referring to Cipriano as the bad baron. Was that a common description of him among the staff?"

"Yes, Carlos is not popular among the workers at the castle. It was an issue that heightened the tension between him and the marchioness. She was loved by the staff, and the chamberlain felt that she undermined him in his relationship with the employees for whom he was formally responsible."

Ramiro asked, "If the tension between Cipriano and the marchioness was well known among the staff, why did the marquess retain him?"

"Ask the marquess!" replied Abrega abruptly.

Peter intervened. "We are about to search the areas of the castle frequented by the marchioness. Accompany us so that you can report back to the marquess as to what we did."

"What do you hope to find?" Abrega asked.

Luke gave the trite non-answer. "We won't know until we find it."

17

“GET THE TWINS BACK! They would know where their mistress put her papers and valuables,” suggested Abrega as he departed. They did.

Luke asked, “Where did your mistress put her letters after she had read them?”

“Into the fire,” they replied in unison.

Luke persisted. “All her letters?”

“Yes. If they did not require a reply, she gave them to us just before supper every night to burn in the grate. We had to tend the fire until the letters had burnt into a powdery ash.”

“Why did she burn them?” asked Peter.

“She said strangers might read them and cause trouble for a lot of innocent people.”

“She kept no letters beyond the day she received them?” repeated a skeptical Ramiro.

“Only those that she needed to reply to.”

“Where did she put those?” continued Ramiro.

“Into the box with her embroidery wools.”

The girls led the soldiers into an adjoining room, and on a small table in the corner was an ornate box of different woods, richly inlaid with gold, silver, and precious gems that depicted a coat of arms. It was locked.

“Will I force the lock?” asked Peter.

"No," advised Ramiro. "Out of respect for Joana, we should take it with us. Maybe Ana Cipriano knows where the key is. Failing that, we must give it to the queen unopened."

An intensive search of the rooms frequented by Joana revealed little of interest to the soldiers. Luke sought out Abrega and asked if any of his staff had come forward offering information.

He replied, "No, but a little incentive might bring a host of volunteers. They would love to report bad things about their superiors, especially about Cipriano. A small silver coin would be stimulus enough."

"Unfortunately, we have no money," replied Luke.

"And I have no access to the coffers of the marquess," added Abrega, a little too quickly.

Ramiro intervened. "I am only a few hours' ride from my own residence. I need to see if everything is running well there. I will collect a little silver from my own resources. I am sure you Englishmen can influence the queen to recompense me. I will be back in the morning."

Luke asked Abrega to inform everybody in the castle that if they came forward to talk to the soldiers, they would receive a silver coin, and if their information was considered especially valuable, a second coin would be forthcoming.

Once alone with Peter, Luke commented, "This is an unexpected opportunity to pursue our basic mission. We can question most of the employees of the castle about anything they heard or saw out of the usual during the visit of the war council and the Feast of Our Lady of Estrela. Our high nobility would never notice the behavior of servants, but those servants would surely notice every move of their superiors."

"What do you make of Joana burning her letters on the same day as she received them?"

"The queen will be pleased. Joana certainly made sure that her constant communication with Luisa remained a secret. But why would she burn other letters as well?"

"Perhaps she was a Spanish spy, and she burnt any letters that might incriminate herself."

"Or maybe she was a conduit for Queen Luisa to deal secretly with the Spaniards," muttered Luke.

"There must be more to all this than appears on the surface. Why would the queen leave Lisbon to have an urgent meeting with Joana at Magellan? Could rumors of a plot really be sufficient?" mused Peter.

"And who discovered Joana's real secret and killed her?" added Luke.

As soon as Ramiro returned the next morning with a bag of silver coins, the line of castle employees joining the queue to speak to the soldiers was never less than five all throughout the morning. Luke soon developed a template of questions that attempted to elicit which of the guests were seen in places that were unexpected and with persons who were surprising.

The first informant of the morning had Luke's immediate attention. A scrawny young stable boy was still seething weeks later over his treatment by the Spanish envoy Barbosa and his troop of cavalry. The boy was thrown out of the area he worked in, and the horses under his care had to be jammed into stalls with other horses.

"What have you to tell me, boy?" asked Peter.

"When my horses were moved to free up stalls for the Spaniards and their horses, I was relocated in a stall adjacent to the last of those occupied by the Spaniards. One night I was trying to sleep when I overheard raised voices. It was a major argument, and it was conducted in Spanish."

"Good lad. We always suspected the Spaniards must have had a base within the castle," commented Luke.

"There is more, sir. I poked my head out of the stall, and to my dismay, I recognized my master, the marquess, arguing with the man who led the Spanish troop, the man we all call the Chameleon."

"Did you hear what they were saying?"

"I heard every word but understood none of it. They continued speaking Spanish."

"Was it generally known that the marquess spoke Spanish?" asked Luke.

"Yes, most of the borderlands' superior classes speak both Spanish and Portuguese," replied the boy.

The next informant was a slovenly plump girl, whom Luke, without any evidence, immediately assumed had slept with most of her fellow workers.

Ramiro also didn't hesitate to destroy her credibility from the start. "Which of your superiors do you wish to tell us lies about?" he asked.

"Lord Ramiro, I have slept with many of your men and could tell your friends here a few things about yourself. Now give me a silver coin! Then you consider whether what I have to say deserves another."

Luke was pleasantly surprised at the girl's confidence. She was not to be intimidated.

Peter probed, "What do you have to tell us?"

"Maybe all the nobles from Lisbon prefer men to women, but one of our visitors spent nearly every night he was here for at least a couple of hours with our hated chamberlain, Cipriano."

"Who was it?"

"It was a Da Costa, not our marquess nor the man who was often with you English—the other one."

"Rodrigo da Costa?" suggested Luke.

"Yes."

"Has your chamberlain Cipriano a reputation for sleeping with men and boys?" asked Ramiro.

"Cipriano would sleep with anything that moved—man, woman, or animal. He has even slept with me," she purred.

"You don't like him?" asked Peter.

"No, I hate him. Everything will get worse for us now with the death of our mistress. The marchioness protected us all from Cipriano's rages and abuse."

Luke nodded as he handed the girl her second silver coin.

"That was a surprise," remarked Peter.

"But can you believe a word she says?" cautioned Ramiro.

"We need to take what she says about Cipriano with a grain of salt, but the fact that Rodrigo visited him every night warrants probing," replied Luke.

Next to come before the soldiers were the giggling twins.

"Why are you two back again?" asked Ramiro.

"Everybody is getting paid for information, and we know more than most. Can we have a silver coin?"

Peter was sympathetic. "You certainly earned a coin each. Can you tell us anything about the important guests who came to the castle a week or so ago?"

Luke asked, "Did any of those visitors spend a lot of time with your mistress?"

The girls giggled. "Yes, one man came most nights."

"Your mistress entertained this man most nights?"

"Only for an hour or so before supper."

"Were they very close?" asked Ramiro obliquely.

The girls giggled again. "They were not lovers, silly. Our mistress frowned on that sort of behavior. The man spent most of the time crying. She was trying to comfort him."

"Who was this man?"

"The councillor who was later hit on the head and kidnapped."

"Diego de Albuquerque?"

"Yes."

The next informant was a class above the earlier witnesses. She explained that she was one of the late marchioness's leading ladies-in-waiting and had been left behind to manage her mistress's affairs while Joana was at Magellan. During the visit of the council of war, she had been selected to assist the minister's wife, the marchioness Beatrix.

"I have never been to Lisbon and was shocked by the behavior of some of women associated with the court when they were here. I was a novice nun for several years, but before I took my final vows, I had to leave because of my family's poverty. I needed to work to support my aging parents. Therefore, I do not know what is accepted in worldly society. Maybe what I have to say is not important. And I don't want any money."

"What can you tell us that might be important?" asked Ramiro.

"The lady Beatrix, the wife of the minister, entertained a man who was not her husband on several occasions."

"Entertained? What did that entail?" asked Peter.

"What we saw before we were sent from the apartment—or returned too soon—were two semi-naked bodies engaged in a lot of cuddling and fondling."

"Who was the man?" asked Luke.

"General Caro."

Ramiro burst into laughter. "My god, that must have been a sight. Beatrix is a large voluptuous woman whose whole body is a sequence of ample curves—and Caro is a very small man."

"One last question," said Peter. "Was your master the marquess faithful to his wife?"

"It is not expected of the Portuguese aristocracy to be faithful to their wives, but the marquess is the exception. It was always a surprise to polite society that he never sought an annulment of his marriage when Joana failed to produce children."

"Do you know who will become the marquess on Paolo's death?"

"Yes, the man who was here at that time, his cousin Rodrigo da Costa."

"Please take three coins to help with your parents. Your information has been invaluable," concluded Luke. He then turned to Ramiro. "Does Rodrigo have any children to succeed him?"

"No. He had two sons by his first wife, but both were killed in colonial conflicts, the eldest in Ceylon, and the youngest disappeared in Brazil. His body was never found. His second wife, Micaela, has had a number of miscarriages."

"So the ultimate possessor of the marquisate of Estrela is our comrade Alvaro da Costa?" concluded Luke.

"Unless Micaela produces an heir, you are correct," replied Ramiro.

The next half dozen informants contributed nothing of significance. The final informant was a servant who was responsible for ensuring that the countless fires within the castle were lit before the important guests were awake. In such a role, he wandered the castle in the early hours of the morning just before dawn.

"Did the influx of so many dignitaries present you with any unusual scenes in the early hours?" asked Ramiro.

"None of the visitors, except for one, rose until four or five hours after I lit the fires."

"Who was the exception?" queried Peter.

"That cousin of the master who was always with you English."

"Did you see him entering or leaving anybody's rooms?" probed Ramiro.

"No, I saw him wandering the corridors throughout the castle and well away from his own room."

"Did you speak to him?" continued Ramiro.

"No, but we acknowledged each other's presence as we passed with a nod or wave of the hand."

Over supper, the three soldiers discussed their very informative day.

"As far as explaining Joana's murder, we need to know exactly why she burnt her letters and whether there are any in the box we will take to the queen. Why was Paolo talking to the Chameleon? Why was Rodrigo spending time with Cipriano? Could they both be homosexuals? Why was a weeping Diego comforted more than once by Joana? Does Alvaro's ultimate succession to the marquisate have any relevance, and why was he wandering the castle while everyone else slept?" summarized Luke.

"Yes, only Caro's meetings with the minister's wife seem potentially unrelated to our investigation," added Peter.

"Do we leave first thing in the morning and return to Magellan and report this to the queen?" asked Ramiro.

"No. Today has been successful. Let's offer a little more remuneration and make ourselves available for another day. There has been little or no information on a number of the key participants whom we need to probe," concluded Luke.

18

T HE NEWS OF INCREASED remuneration and the continued opportunity to throw mud at their superiors brought forth a new stream of willing informants. First in line was a large burly man in his mid-forties who said he was an outdoor servant who had been responsible for ensuring that the tents on the lower field were stable and withstood the vagaries of the weather. It had been his practice to inspect the tents after the entertainment had finished, which was usually around midnight.

"And what did you see that might interest us?" asked Peter.

"Activity continued in three of the tents throughout the night—those devoted to gambling. There was a tent for card players, another for dice, and a third for the wealthier visitors, in which both games were played."

Ramiro commented, "Undoubtedly, most of the visitors and leading members of the castle spent some time in one or another of the tents. I spent a night or two myself playing cards."

"My lord, you limited yourself to the tents where the stakes were low. One man spent every night playing for high stakes and lost a fortune. Two men played most nights and always won."

"The loser?"

"That pompous General Pinto."

"And the winners?"

"Your comrade Colonel da Costa and my immediate superior, Alfredo Matos."

"Did they play for cash?" asked Luke.

"Initially, yes, but as Pinto's losses increased, he had to write bills of credit to the winners."

"So it is reasonable to assume that at this moment, Pinto owes Matos and Da Costa a lot of money?"

"Yes."

The next informant was one of the chamberlain's men, responsible for moving through the castle to maintain security after everybody had retired.

"I have not come forward for the money but because what I witnessed one night could have been the work of the devil. I reported what I saw to both the chamberlain baron Cipriano and to the visiting priest, Father Antonio, but nothing seems to have been done."

"What did you see?"

"I was walking past the chapel when I heard a raised voice speaking in a tongue I have never heard and murmurs of disquiet from a dozen or so nuns who were present. When I entered, I saw a woman partly clad, kneeling in front of the altar, pleasuring herself. She seemed to be in a sort of trance. One of the nuns said that the woman had entered this state of religious euphoria after touching the relic of the person that Our Lady of Estrela had saved centuries ago. The nun was greatly disturbed, as were others, because they doubted that this experience came from God. Most saw it as the work of the devil and asked me to put an end to it."

"What did you do?"

"I cleared the chapel of the nuns, and knowing that these trances lasted for only a short period, I observed the victim until it was obvious that she was coming back to reality. When this happened, the woman adjusted her clothing and, I assume, returned to her apartment."

"Did you recognize the woman?" asked Peter.

"Not at the time, but later, one of the nuns told me that it was Camilla, the viscountess De Mota."

"The tongue she was using when under the trance—was it Spanish?" Ramiro asked.

"No."

"Are any of the nuns still within the castle?"

"Yes. A small number of them who have a special dedication to Our Lady of Estrela spend an additional month in the chapel after the feast observing a range of rituals associated with Our Lady. Since you all left, the nuns are now housed in the northern wing of the castle. I will ask the mother superior to speak to you."

The mother superior was a small elderly woman with a sense of humor. "Our friend Gil has been telling tales out of school," she commented.

"Reverend Mother, could you describe to us what exactly happened during the night in question?"

"During most nights of the feast, we held a service in which religious relics and icons were paraded, and people were invited to deepen their closeness to God by touching or meditating upon the sacred objects. This is a deeply moving spiritual experience. That night, Viscountess de Mota was so overwhelmed that she began to speak in tongues and then engaged in self-abuse that immediately alarmed me."

"Why so? Is not such behavior a common form of religious ecstasy? And Camilla was brought up within the highly emotional Spanish church," Peter commented.

"Quite so, young man, but present in the castle at that time was the evilest of inquisitors, Father Zarco, whom I believed was here simply to declare the worship of Our Lady of Estrela heretical or, even worse, diabolical. This would have given him all the ammunition he needed to destroy us. I brought the service to an end and relied on Gil to ensure that the viscountess came out of the trance without damage to herself."

"Did any other important guests attend any of your services?"

"The mistress of the castle, Marchioness Joana, and her companion Ana de Cipriano were there but only during our midmorning services, never at night."

"Did no one sneak into your late-night rituals to hide their attraction to your devotions?" asked Ramiro.

"I suppose all these questions are necessary?" asked the astute nun.

"Yes. We do not know what any apparent innocent piece of information might enable us to uncover the marchioness's murderer," explained Luke.

"There were three surprise visitors—General Caro, the Irish woman Madalena Albuquerque, and her maid."

"Did you report the disturbing case of Lady Camilla to the priests?"

"The castle's chaplain was absent on business for the marchioness Joana, and the council's chaplain, Father Antonio, quickly dismissed what he called superstitious talk about the devil."

"You have been visiting the castle over the years to participate in your special devotion to Our Lady of Estrela. Did you hear or see anything different on this visit that might relate to the murder of Joana?" Ramiro asked.

"I spoke to the marchioness Joana on a number of occasions during this visit. She did seem to be distracted and asked me for a favor. She made a large donation to our order for us to pray several times a day for the safety of the queen."

Just as the mother superior left, Abrega jumped the waiting queue. "Gentlemen, there is something I must report about my immediate superior, the deputy chamberlain Alfredo Matos."

"Is it fair to assume that if Matos is proved to have acted in any way against the interests of the marquess, you might be promoted to his position?" Ramiro stated.

"Yes, and you can disregard what I say as an ambitious underling trying to climb the ladder as quickly as possible."

"What do you want to report?" asked Luke.

"I saw Matos on two occasions in conversation with that troop that we later found to be Spanish. He was supervising the provision of meals and supplies for them."

"He could explain that away easily as an officer of the castle providing visitors with the hospitality that would be expected," stated Ramiro.

"True, but the timing of those encounters is significant. The first time I saw him in deep conversation with Colonel Barbosa was just before General Caro was tricked into waiting for General Tremayne at the Bridge of the Three Angels, and the second time was immediately before Baron Albuquerque was kidnapped."

"Are you suggesting that Matos gave the Spaniard his orders?" asked a cross Ramiro.

"He may have a simple explanation," added Peter.

"Is Matos a gambler?" Luke suddenly asked.

"Yes, and it will eventually lead to his death. Many of his opponents claim he is a card cheat. One day someone won't wait for proof and challenge him to a duel."

"Does he lose much? Could he be so far in debt that the Spaniards have promised to bail him out if he does their bidding?" probed Peter.

"He claims he is falsely accused of cheating simply because he wins most of the time," explained Abrega.

"On the other hand, could his series of successes have meant that many important people owe him money? Did the marquess, the marchioness, or the chamberlain play against him?"

"The marchioness, never, the others on rare occasions when there were important visitors."

"Is Matos using gambling debts as a weapon against his superiors?"

"The wealth of the marquess is enormous. He would not be a debtor. Cipriano is another matter."

"Have you any comments on any of the visitors during their time here that may be relevant to our inquiry?"

"I was asked to assist the minister of war during his stay. There was nothing unusual in his behavior. Apart from spending a lot of time alone with his fellow councillors Da Costa and Albuquerque, he did receive visits from most of the wives. To my knowledge, Teresa Pinto, Camilla de Mota, Madalena Albuquerque, and Joana da Costa visited him—without their husbands. The visits were never long enough to involve an affair, and his secretary was present at all times."

Ramiro commented, "Why did that civilian cabal meet so regularly without the military? This is very disturbing."

"And the women were probably only trying to advance the careers of their husbands," muttered Peter.

"I wouldn't be too sure," Luke disagreed. "Da Silva could help advance Pinto and Mota but could do little to help Albuquerque and would appear irrelevant to the career of the Marquess of Estrela. An explanation from those ladies will be very illuminating."

"Anyone else you wish to comment on?" asked Peter.

"Only that De Mota was up to his old tricks."

"What old tricks? asked Luke.

"I can answer that," said Ramiro, surprising his comrades. "De Mota likes children. When I was in the royal army, it was a standing joke that Mota's regiments had three times the drummer boys deemed necessary. Was he engaged in such activity while here?"

"Yes. He disappeared whenever possible to the lower fields and paid willing parents to spend time alone with their children."

"Surely, not many parents would agree," commented an appalled Luke.

"Some certainly refused. Did you not see the bruised face and black eye that De Mota displayed just before you all moved to Magellan?" explained Abrega.

"Are De Mota's vices limited to children?" asked Peter.

"He is also fond of young male clergy," added Abrega.

"Are you making this up because Mota is pro-Spanish and a very ineffective general?" asked Luke.

Ramiro answered, "What has been said about Mota's sexual vices has been common knowledge within the army for years, but I cannot see how in any way it can be related to Joana's murder."

"The only person we have not heard a bad word about is Ana Cipriano. Have there ever been negative rumors about her?" asked Luke.

"Few people know her personally. She spent most of the time isolated with Joana. Her only entries into the real world won her applause. She always sided with Joana against her husband in matters involving the treatment of servants."

Luke thanked Vitor Abrega for his information.

Once he had left, Peter expressed what Luke had been thinking. "Perhaps those two virtuous women, Joana and Ana, had a very close relationship, close enough to be a possible factor in the murder of Joana."

"No, I have known Joana for years. Close friends with Ana, yes, but nothing more," proclaimed a shocked Ramiro.

"We have exhausted our sources of information here. Let's return to Magellan in the morning and report to the queen," concluded Luke.

19

THE THREE SOLDIERS WERE led by Father Antonio into the queen's private quarters. Ramiro reported on their investigation and handed Joana's casket to the queen. Peter offered to force it open if she so desired.

The queen replied, "There is no need. My grandfather gave each of his five granddaughters an identical casket—with the same key. I have mine with me, and it will open the box." She left the room and returned a few minutes later. "What do we expect to find in this box?" she asked.

"Perhaps the few letters that she did not burn," Ramiro replied.

"Hopefully some information about the matters that she wanted to urgently discuss with you," added Luke.

The queen opened the box. There was universal disappointment. It was completely empty. She asked, "You did not find Joana's key?"

"No, Your Majesty," replied Ramiro.

"Perhaps her murderer did and discovered incriminating material, which he destroyed before killing Joana," mused the queen.

"Some of the information we gained from the visit to Castle Estrela might, with further probing, lead both to the murderer of Joana and the traitor or nest of traitors within your administration. Do you want us to continue with both our initial mission and solving your cousin's murder?" asked Luke.

"Yes. Joana's murder may make your intrusive questioning of my courtiers and generals less suspicious. I informed them during your absence that I had appointed the two English officers and Lord Ramiro to investigate the murder. I explained that I had chosen three people far removed from the court and administration of the state as, unfortunately, all of them had to be treated as suspects."

"Any objection to our appointment?" asked Peter.

"Not to my face, but Father Antonio heard some rumblings of discontent."

Antonio explained, "None of the courtiers complained. Nor did the generals. Caro, in fact, thought it was an inspired choice. He seemed to be well informed of General Tremayne's previous reputation in solving murders for English military intelligence, and the queen's senior lady-in-waiting, the countess Micaela, cited evidence from her own family in France to support Caro's assessment. The only objection—and quite nastily expressed—came from the chamberlain, Baron Cipriano."

"What do you mean nastily expressed?" asked Ramiro.

"He turned it against Her Majesty, saying it was typical of Spanish-born noblewomen to recklessly open Portugal's state secrets to foreign agents. Caro responded aggressively and said that while those gathered around the table did nothing, the navy of these two foreign agents was, at that very moment, ensuring that the sugar fleet from Brazil would reach Lisbon safely, thereby guaranteeing the country's and most of their own individual wealth for another year."

"Cipriano! He was certainly the most disliked person at Castle Estrela, and he never hid his dislike of Joana," added Luke.

The queen rose to leave and announced, "Gentlemen, question Cipriano and the Marquess of Estrela in the next two days before they leave. I will go to Castle Estrela with Paolo and his officials, including Cipriano, for Joana's funeral. She made it clear to me years ago that she wished to be buried in the chapel of the castle where she had spent most of her life. I have given safe passage for some of our Spanish relatives to attend. Caro managed to negotiate a suspension of the current hostilities with Spain for fourteen days. The council of war and all the generals and their wives will stay here at Magellan. Joana wanted her funeral to be an internal Castle Estrela affair. I will attend not as queen but as her cousin. It will be conducted by her loyal and faithful chaplain, who, for decades, delivered our secret correspondence to each other. He should have returned to the castle by the time we get there. If not, Father Antonio will have to step in."

The next morning, the trio questioned Paolo, Marquess of Estrela. Peter explained that they had just returned from his castle, having been sent there by the queen to find any evidence that might explain his wife's murder. They now wished to question him on some aspects of the information they had gathered on that visit. Luke, who was gaining confidence with his Portuguese, asked directly, "Was there anything bothering Joana in the weeks before you moved here?"

"She was not happy with the council meeting at the castle. All her life, she avoided the court and government officials."

"There were no specific occurrences that she discussed with you that may have upset her?"

"Joana and I did not discuss many issues. She ran the day-to-day affairs of the castle with little reference to me. Most of her discussion on this would have been with Cipriano, and all her private conversation would have been with his wife, Ana."

'We were told that she and Cipriano detested each other."

"Joana detested nobody! That is why I find her murder so unbelievable. Nobody disliked her."

"Except Cipriano," added Ramiro.

"Given the long-standing tension between your wife and your chamberlain, why did you not dismiss him?"

"I intended to years ago, but Joana persuaded me not to."

"She wanted you to retain a man who constantly undermined her not only with the servants but with you. Why?" asked Luke.

"Her closest friend for decades was his wife, Ana. If Cipriano left, Ana would have to go. To keep Ana, Joana was willing to put up with Carlos."

"Did you know that Joana, for decades, maintained a regular correspondence with the queen?"

"No, it was a secret she kept well."

"If she kept that a secret, is it possible there were other secrets that may have led to her murder, which she concealed from you?" probed Peter.

"I would never have thought so, but now I cannot be so sure."

Ramiro suddenly changed the subject. "Paolo, are you a traitor negotiating, even when the council of war was at your castle, with the Spaniards?"

Paolo's face reddened. Luke expected an outright denial. He was surprised with the answer.

"I am no traitor, but I have had regular dealings with the Spaniards, and I faced an awkward situation during the council's visit."

The three investigators waited for the marquess to expound.

"I am a frontier magnate who keeps the lines of communication open with my counterparts across the border. We regularly correspond using the clergy to transfer letters across the frontier. Recently, I received a proposal from a Spanish official suggesting that with the death of King John and the accession of the retarded Afonso, I consider transferring my allegiance back to the Spanish Habsburgs. I was amazed that a troop of elite Spanish cavalry had infiltrated my castle during a visit of the Portuguese war council. The leader of that troop, Colonel Barbosa, required an immediate answer, which I gave him late one night in the stables. It was a total rejection. I am Portuguese."

"Were you offered any sweeteners to accept the offer?"

"Yes. I was to be made a duke, with Estrela and its lands elevated to a duchy."

"Did Joana know about this offer and your response to it?"

"Yes."

Luke asked, "If the Spaniards made another attempt to persuade you, how would they go about it?"

"There is a Portuguese priest just across the border who has links with the Spanish inquisition—a Father Nicodemo. He often carries both my messages and those of Barbosa."

"We know Father Nicodemo. We will certainly probe his role further," said Ramiro.

"The queen has granted safe conduct to Joana's Spanish relatives to attend the funeral. Might that be another occasion where offers for your betrayal might be renewed?"

"Yes. In fact, one guest will be the powerful grandee of Spain—Joana's cousin and the queen's brother, the Duke of Medina-Sidonia."

Peter muttered to Luke, "That would be a very effective abduction."

Ramiro overheard and protested, "The queen would never agree. The duke is her brother, and it would breach all the rules of diplomacy. It would be counterproductive." He turned to Paolo, "At least, my lord, in time, you can remarry and sire a son to inherit your title and lands."

Paolo gave a weak smile and replied, "If only! I can never sire a child. It was my wild youth and the remedies adopted to cure my problems that created this unfortunate condition."

Ramiro was stunned. "I am sorry, my lord. Local gossip was that after Joana and you failed to produce an heir, you did not seek an obvious annulment because she had such powerful relatives in Spain that the Spanish church would ensure that the pope would not grant it—"

Luke interrupted. "My lord, you might consider a not-uncommon practice among the English aristocracy. Never willing to admit impotence, many a high-ranking lord had their wife impregnated by a third party and claimed the ensuing child as his. Succession ensured."

"It would be delightful to thwart Rodrigo, although he is not as avaricious as that French whore, his wife, Micaela. Her lover has just arrived in camp. If she becomes pregnant, I would certainly have doubts about that paternity."

"You dislike Micaela?" queried Peter.

"She is too powerful and acts in her own interests and not those of the queen. She is the only person whom I heard Joana ever say a bad word about."

"Can you remember the exact focus of Joana's displeasure?" asked Luke.

"No, I came in on a conversation between Joana and Ana. Ana may be able to tell you more."

"You will have years to modify the succession in ways more to your liking," commented Ramiro.

"No. That will not be the case. Micaela will be Marchioness of Estrela sooner than she thinks. Joana and I made a solemn pledge to each other that when one of us died, the other would also leave this troubled world."

Ramiro was aghast. "My lord, you surely do not contemplate suicide. It is a mortal sin that Joana would certainly abhor."

"Don't stress, Ramiro. I will be leaving this world by joining an order of monks. As soon I can get my affairs in order, I will renounce my titles and estates, and Rodrigo and Micaela will become the new lord and lady of Estrela."

Ramiro began the questioning of Carlos de Cipriano. "Baron, we would like to ask a few questions arising out of our visit to Castle Estrela on behalf of the queen. Did you ever see or have access to Joana's casket, which bore the arms of the Guzman family and where she kept her letters and private papers?"

"Even though I have been chamberlain for over a decade, I was never admitted to the antechamber in which the marchioness kept her private documents. No servant ever entered that room. Only my wife had access."

"Most of the information that we gathered from the servants consisted of the usual complaints and lies by the lower orders against their superiors. But one issue that intrigued us were reports that Rodrigo da Costa visited you on several nights during his stay at the castle. Were you trying to get on side with the man who would one day be the marquess?" asked Peter.

"Yes, I am no fool. Paolo is not a well man, and the death of Joana may contribute further to his ill health. I was preparing for the worst."

"Surely, that preparation did not require visits every night," Luke emphasized.

"I am not an idiot, General. I did not immediately require Rodrigo to give me an undertaking that I would remain chamberlain. Rodrigo has a reputation as a chess player. I also play. The time we spent together was taken up by a series of chess games, during which I gradually tried to influence him in my favor."

"You want to continue as chamberlain under a new marquess. How do you think you would relate to the new marchioness, Micaela?"

"I have had years of experience in not relating to the late marchioness. Joana and I hardly tolerated each other. But Micaela is a scheming, untrustworthy female who cannot wait to assume the mantle of a marchioness. She is desperately trying to get pregnant to stop her brother-in-law, your ally Colonel da Costa, succeeding her husband to the title."

20

LUKE SUGGESTED THEY QUESTION Micaela da Costa before she left with the queen for Castle Estrela. Ramiro objected. "No! We have nothing to question her about except deeply personal issues regarding her desire to be a marchioness and her marriage fidelity—based on gossip from two men who are far removed from court. I need a lot more information before I would question the queen's closest confidante and a powerful figure in the Da Costa clan."

Peter agreed. "There is no obvious link between Micaela and the murder of Joana, which is our current focus. But let's question Ana Cipriano before she returns to Estrela."

Luke opened the questioning. "Baroness, we are interested in the small casket in which Joana kept her valuable papers and embroidery wools. When did you last see it?"

"She called it 'Grandfather's box.' It contained only letters of current interest. She did not keep any papers for a long period. The last time I saw it was on the day we came here."

"Was it full of papers?"

"No. Just before we left, she opened the casket and handed most of the papers to the twins to immediately burn in the grate. Two letters, she retained, which I assume she brought with her here. There was nothing left in the casket."

"Did she lock the empty box?"

"No, she could not find the key, but as it was empty, she was not concerned."

"That is indeed a mystery," said Ramiro.

"Why?"

"Because when we found the box, it was locked," he replied.

"No mystery. I imagine one of the servants found the key after we left and locked the box."

"We were told that servants other than the twins were banned from that room. You were the only person other than Joana to have access," added Peter.

"True, while the marchioness was in residence, but according to my husband, servants just love to enter forbidden places when the master and mistress are away."

"Did Joana ever express her views on the succession following Paolo's death?"

"She hoped that she would die first because she wanted to end her life in Castle Estrela. If Paolo died before her, she would have to return to Spain. She would not live on in the castle with Micaela da Costa as the new marchioness, even if that woman offered her a place."

"There seems to be much resentment against Micaela from both Paolo and your husband. Why is that?"

"The Da Costas were appalled that Rodrigo took as his second wife a member of the French court whose reputation had preceded her."

"I know the French family of which Micaela was part. I never heard of any such salacious rumors," lied Luke. "Can you be more specific?"

"According to Teresa Pinto—and it has been accepted at the Portuguese court for years—Micaela took a Portuguese nobleman as her lover before she married Rodrigo."

"There is no problem if this happened before her marriage," proclaimed the pragmatic Peter.

"Her enemies claim the relationship has renewed and that her lover has just arrived here, the heir to the richest duchy in Portugal—Roberto, Viscount Delgado."

"Before she came to Magellan, Joana visited the minister of war on at least one occasion. Do you know why?"

"Yes" came the surprising and pleasing answer.

The soldiers waited.

At last, Ana expounded, "During that last week at Estrela, Joana expressed a general concern about her cousin the queen. She said she had taken steps in the matter, but in case they came to nothing, she would give the minister a letter to carry to Her Majesty."

"A letter that she kept in her casket until delivered to Da Silva?" Luke asked.

"Did she deliver the letter?" added Peter.

"I assume so. She visited the minister—and there was no letter left in her casket."

The trio next questioned Alvaro.

Luke asked, "Why were you wandering around Castle Estrela in the early hours of the morning when we were stationed there?"

"I don't see how my wandering the castle when everybody slept is related to your investigation."

"Let's say it looks suspicious. You could have been meeting secretly with any number of people or simply seen on your way from a romantic liaison," suggested Peter.

"In time, I will be Marquess of Estrela. I was taking my time inspecting every part of the castle so that I could to assess whether I would be up for great expenditure in maintaining the infrastructure. Rodrigo is so mean, he will not spend anything during his tenure."

Ramiro was almost lost for words. "That's very presumptuous of you! You may not outlive your cousin Paolo nor your brother Rodrigo. Far more likely is that either man could produce an heir who will scuttle your chances. Paolo is now in a position to remarry, and your sister-in-law Micaela is not too old to produce a child."

Alvaro did not comment but seemed to treat the possibility of his relatives producing children as remote. Luke wondered if he knew more about this situation than he revealed.

Peter continued, "You are a successful gambler. We heard that you drained General Pinto of his dwindling fortune during your mutual time at Estrela."

"Yes. A few nights playing against Pinto would enrich all his opponents. The man is both foolhardy and a fool. He is the last general in Portugal I would entrust to command our armies."

Luke changed the subject. "Did you know that your cousin Paolo is in constant communication with the Spaniards across the border?"

"The border nobles on each side of the frontier communicate with each other, but little of it involves national security. My agents know most of what is going on."

"Then how do you explain—"

Ramiro's question was interrupted by Luke. "I don't think we need detain the colonel any longer," he said.

After Alvaro left, Luke explained, "Let's not alert Alvaro to the fact that his cousin was entertaining a suggestion to change sides and deliver his person and estates to the Spaniards and that the Spaniards had a troop within his castle waiting on an answer. It suggests the military intelligence gleaned by Alvaro is full of holes."

"Can we trust him? Should we interview his superior? Who does he report to?" asked Peter.

"Alvaro, as head of military intelligence, reports directly to—and only to—the queen," explained Ramiro.

The next aristocrat interviewed was Rodrigo.

Luke was aggressive. "Joana's death must have been one of the last things you wanted to happen."

"Of course. Her death is a tragedy."

"Especially for you and Micaela."

"Why us?"

"Paolo is now in a position to remarry and in a position to sire a son to inherit his title and estate."

"If so, I will be delighted. I have no desire to inherit a large border estate and the difficulties it entails."

"Is Micaela of like mind?"

"My wife is a very able woman with ambition. I don't think she will wait quietly until my cousin dies to become a marchioness. Recent rumors at court suggest that the queen will reward her for her devoted service to the Portuguese crown by granting me a new and superior title. The queen has discussed it with Micaela, but for the time being, it is to be kept secret. What happens to the Estrela title therefore may be irrelevant to what satisfies Micaela and me."

"Yet recently, you discussed the situation at Estrela in some depth with Paolo's chamberlain, Baron Cipriano."

"Only as part of social chatter while we played chess."

"If you were lord of Estrela, would you keep Cipriano as your chamberlain?"

"I don't see how any of this relates to your inquiries."

"Cipriano is a possible suspect in the murder of Joana. His dislike of her was well known. However, how her death would benefit him is problematic. Your succession, on the other hand, would confront him with a possible life-changing event. Did you tell him he would be sacked, or did you encourage him to expect a positive result?"

"What I told him made him very happy. In the light of what I have just mentioned, I informed him that if I became the Marquess of Estrela, it was highly unlikely that Micaela and I would live there. We would both remain at the royal court. In those circumstances, the chamberlain would become the effective master of Estrela."

"From what you say, there was no evidence in recent weeks of the queen withdrawing her favors from Micaela?"

"Precisely the opposite."

"There has been a concerted campaign to blacken the name of your wife. Are you aware of it, and what is its motivation?" asked Luke.

"Micaela is the conduit to the queen. Those denied access bear grudges. Others would like to replace her in such a position. And there are others who want to bring down all the Da Costas. Many courtiers play their part in this constant undermining. The most virulent are the Pintos, especially the countess Teresa."

Luke decided to upset Rodrigo with the hope of an enlightening outburst. "Is your wife pregnant?" he asked.

"No!"

"So does that mean that should you succeed to the marquisate of Estrela and receive an even higher honor from the queen, your younger brother, in time, would eventually inherit all your titles and estates?"

"Yes, but considering the dangerous life he leads, I will probably outlive him. That is why I have been agitating that Alvaro marry and produce as many sons as he can. If he does not, Estrela will revert to the crown on his death."

"Are you returning to Estrela for the funeral?"

"Yes, only relatives and Paolo's chamberlain have been released from their duties here to attend."

"While you were at Estrela the last time, why did you and your fellow councillors have a series of meetings without we military?" probed Ramiro.

Rodrigo replied calmly without any hint that such a question might cause embarrassment. "There were a lot of administrative matters requiring our consideration that did not involve the army. A box of papers arrived from Lisbon every second day needing action—most of it to do with our naval activities against the Dutch."

Alfredo Matos expressed surprise that the soldiers wished to question him.

"As deputy to a man who openly disliked Joana, I would have thought you were a possible suspect in her murder," said Luke provocatively.

"I may be Cipriano's deputy, but that does not mean I agree with what he thinks or does. Nor do I necessarily follow his instructions."

"Whose instructions were you following at Estrela when you had at least two private conversations with the Spanish would-be assassins who were harbored in the castle and who openly attempted the destruction of General Caro?" asked Ramiro.

"Not Cipriano! I was acting directly for the marquess."

"Your timing of these meetings has aroused suspicion—just before the attempt on Caro and then just prior to the abduction of Albuquerque."

"On both occasions, the master had heard that the Spanish troop was about to leave, and he wanted me to suggest to them that they not return because they had his final answer—and it would not change."

"Why did they return after both occasions?"

"I am not sure, but their leader, Col. Marcos Barbosa, indicated that they might assist the inquisitor Zarco—if his enterprise would benefit Spain."

"Surely, there was enough treacherous talk for the marquess to expel them immediately."

"That is why he encouraged Lord Ramiro and his troops to stay at Estrela."

"We also hear that you led a charmed life," noted Peter.

"In what way?"

"You are incredibly lucky at cards. And you have avoided being killed by opponents convinced that you cheat."

"Losers always complain. There are many idiots playing cards who can be beaten by common sense, whatever cards you get. For example, there are many born losers like General Pinto. I made more money out of Pinto in a week than the marquess paid me in six months."

21

"LET US QUESTION THE noblewomen concerned before we confront the minister," suggested Luke.

Camilla de Mota could not conceal her disdain—a Spanish noblewoman being questioned by a Portuguese rogue and two heretical Englishmen of dubious status.

Peter was immediately aware of her obvious sensitivities. "My lady, is there anything that you could tell us that might help us find the murderer of the Marchioness Joana?"

His gentle approach was shattered by her dismissive and haughty response.

"How would I know anything about such a horrible event?"

Peter tried again. "We have to put together different facts and see if there is any connection. For example, you and the murder victim did exactly the same thing on the same day."

"And what could that have possibly been?"

"You both visited the minister, Pero da Silva, without your husbands or any servants. We know why Joana did so. Why did you?"

"I am a daughter of the Spanish grandee family of Cerda. I went to the minister to emphasize the advantages of such a connection, should my husband be elevated to his rightful place as commander-in-chief of all Portuguese forces. I pointed out strongly that both sides would achieve more by negotiation, in which I personally could play a part, than by petty skirmishes along the frontier."

"A view with which I strongly agree," announced Luke surprisingly. He pushed deeper, "My lady, I understand you are especially blessed of God—that in perusing the sacred relics, the Holy Mother herself came to you."

"Sacrilege! How does a heretic know such things unless he is controlled by the devil?" was the unexpected and disappointing reply.

Luke persisted. "During these periods of ecstasy, did Our Lady tell you anything that might stop the evil that is enveloping Castle Estrela?"

"Not that I recall. You do not always remember what happens during such beautiful periods," said Camilla, falling into a long silence.

There was no point in continuing the interview with such an antagonistic subject.

Teresa Pinto took the opposite approach to Camilla de Mota. She set out to charm her interrogators. Her habit of pulling her long dark locks across her face was immediately displayed as she purred, "How can I help?"

Luke, attracted to the woman, asked in faltering Portuguese, "My lady, why during your stay at Castle Estrela did you visit the war minister without your husband?"

"I would have much preferred to have visited you, my English general. I was seeking to help my husband become commander-in-chief—but to no avail."

"Da Silva did not accept your arguments?" asked Luke.

"Don't be stupid, Englishman! Far worse. He did not accept me. I am Teresa, one of the most beautiful women in Portugal. I cannot understand it. His own wife is an elephant of a woman with nose and ears almost as big as that creature."

Luke had to smile. Her description of Beatrix Silva, while ludicrously exaggerated, contained recognizable essentials. Teresa continued to concentrate on Luke. "Have your comrades leave, and I will tell you everything you want to know. I will make you so happy that you will never leave Portugal," she pouted.

Luke played along. "Countess, I will revisit you later, but for the moment, the three of us must pursue our inquiries. Are you aware of your husband's gambling addiction?"

"Yes, but I prefer him chasing a fortune at cards than the wives of our friends. My family is especially wealthy, so Baltasar's indiscretions enable me to exert influence on our relationship by persuading my brother to pay off my husband's gambling debts. He did lose a lot of money at Estrela and has had to pay the winners initially with bills of credit. I hope your English navy escorts our sugar fleet safely to Lisbon. Otherwise, I will have to plead with my brother once again to cover Balty's debts."

Madalena Albuquerque was the most relaxed of the three aristocratic women interviewed. "What have you gentlemen been saying to Teresa Pinto? She left here on a high. Told me I would enjoy this experience!"

Peter took up the questioning. "Just before Joana left Estrela to come here, she visited the minister of war without her husband or servants. You did likewise. Why?"

Luke intervened. "Most wives visited Da Silva to advance their husband's career. This could hardly be the case with yourself and Diego."

"No, it wasn't. Diego is seeking an annulment of our marriage. Pero da Silva is on the same committee as Diego, advising the queen on matters of religion. I thought he might know how far Diego's case had progressed."

"Did you get a satisfactory answer?"

"Yes. The minister was blunt. He said our case had become a pawn in the battle for the control of the Portuguese church. The archbishop of Lisbon and the provincial of the Jesuits advised that it should go to Rome with a positive recommendation. The provincial of the Dominicans and the Inquisition wanted it rejected unless approved by the Spanish church. In the end, it was agreed that it be referred to the cardinal archbishop of Toledo for final recommendation."

"On an entirely different matter, what has happened here during our four days' absence?" asked Ramiro.

"Hostilities have been suspended because of Joana's imminent funeral. The queen and her councillors have met each day on matters of state, and Micaela da Costa has been frequenting the evening banquet. To everybody's surprise, the only person to have seen much of the queen alone has been Viscount Delgado. For an aristocrat who was believed to be the head of a group of pro-Afonso, anti-Luisa nobles, that is surprising."

"Indeed!" agreed the soldiers in unison.

The minister of war welcomed the trio into the large room that had become his office while at Magellan.

"Minister, you were one of the last people to speak to Joana alone a few days before she left Estrela to come here. Why did she want to see you?"

"She or her servants had picked up some information that she thought should be transmitted to the queen. She said she had sent some details to Lisbon, but should anything happen to her or her messenger, I was to deliver a letter that she had written to Her Majesty."

"And have you?"

"No. In the end, she never gave me a letter. She said she would bring it to me before we left Estrela. She never did."

"You also had visits from the wives of Pinto, De Mota, and Albuquerque. What did they want?"

"I doubt whether any of their requests can help you in your investigations. Pinto and de Mota wanted me to promote their husbands, and Albuquerque sought advice on the state of her husband's annulment petition."

"As the most senior person here next to the queen, have you been informed of any fact or rumor that might help us to determine Joana's murderer?"

"No. Until the queen told us at a council meeting that Joana had corresponded with her for decades, I have not considered her in any way pertinent to the political life of Portugal. Her only claim to fame was that she was a member of the great Spanish house of Guzman. Her death must have resulted from whatever she discovered. If only she had given me that letter!"

"Why is Viscount Delgado here? He is not a supporter of the government, and you do not need his troops."

"The very question I put to the queen."

"With what response?"

"It was in the interests of Portugal—and I was not to raise the issue again."

The soldiers were about to leave the minister's office when there was a loud knock on the door, and without waiting for a reply, an officer burst into the room. Luke recognized him as the commander of the queen's personal bodyguard.

"What is it, Captain?" asked Da Silva.

"There has been another murder" was the reply.

The four men followed the captain out into the barrack square, and below one of the upper windows, a body lay on the ground, covered with a blanket. Alvaro was already there and had taken charge of the investigation. When the blanket was taken away, there was no mistaking the identity of the victim, although she was lying facedown. The magnificent tresses identified the body as that of Teresa Pinto.

Within minutes, the queen herself was in the courtyard. She ordered that the investigation be conducted by Ramiro, Luke, and Peter, overtly removing Alvaro from the scene. She immediately canceled her trip to Estrela and the proposed transfer of Joana's funeral to the castle. Nobody would leave Magellan. Both noblewomen would have their funerals there. Their bodies could later be taken by their respective spouses for internment on their own estates. The Spanish visitors for Joana's funeral would come to Magellan instead of Estrela.

Luke and Matos inspected the body. Teresa had been strangled and thrown from the window onto the hard barrack square. She must have been returning from her interview with the soldiers when she was set upon. A heavy abrasion on the back of her head may have been the incapacitating blow before she was strangled. Luke, Peter, Ramiro, and Alfredo considered the situation.

Luke advanced his usual theory. "Assume that the same person murdered both women. In this way, we can deduce who might have had reasons to remove both women."

Ramiro was blunt. "Teresa hated the Da Costas, wanted to be senior lady-in-waiting, and wanted her husband as commander-in-chief. She cherished a hope that her family, and not Luisa's, would reign in Portugal. While her husband was intensely loyal to the queen, Teresa's family were strongly anti-Spanish and wanted a Portuguese nobleman such as Delgado as regent instead of the Spanish-born Luisa."

"What you are implying is that the interests who would be happy to see Teresa dead are the queen and the Da Costas," summarized Luke.

"I don't think your theory will work in this situation, Luke. What might account for both murders is to consider Teresa's killing as revenge for the murder of Joana. Joana's friends, who may be the Da Costas and the queen, think she was murdered by a Teresa-favored clique, so they murdered her. None of this theorizing helps. Treat them as two separate murders that have no links—unless we can establish them. Teresa was a beautiful woman who did not hesitate to use her charms on many a married man to gain what she wanted. Her death might have resulted from some jealous wife who felt her husband was too close to Teresa," said a thoughtful Alfredo.

"Or a jealous husband such as Baltasar Pinto who was fed up with his wife's affairs," suggested Peter.

"No, I would rule out Pinto as a suspect. We know he is heavily in debt. His one way out is if his wife's family pick up the debt. He is not going to kill the goose that lays the golden egg, especially at this time. I still prefer to work on the assumption that we have one murderer. Maybe Teresa discovered the same crisis that was about to confront the queen as had Joana," persisted Luke.

"In that case, our immediate task is to find out, hour by hour, how Teresa spent her time since she had arrived at Magellan," concluded Ramiro.

The next morning, the three investigators paid their respects to General Pinto, who seemed completely unnerved by the death of his wife.

Ramiro asked gently, "How did Teresa spend her last few days here?"

"She was very happy. The queen wanted her back in attendance as a lady-in- waiting to help prepare for the funeral of Joana and the reception of the Spanish delegation."

"She spent most of the last two days within the queen's quarters?" said Luke, seeking confirmation.

"Yes, except for when you interviewed her yesterday—just before her death."

"Did she tell you anything that had troubled her since her return to the queen's service?"

"Only her age-old gripe that I heard every day in Lisbon, that Micaela da Costa continued to bully the queen, but she did say yesterday that the queen did not appear as compliant as she used to be, so much so that Micaela had to ask her brother-in-law Alvaro to support her on a number of issues she had raised with the queen."

"She believed that Micaela and Alvaro combined to bully the queen?" reiterated Luke.

"Over what issues?" added Peter.

"The presence of Roberto Delgado in the queen's quarters was annoying them both."

22

A S THEY LEFT PINTO'S room, Luke suggested that Ramiro visit the queen and obtain details of everybody who was within her compound since Teresa resumed her role as a lady-in-waiting. Ramiro returned with the information within half an hour. "Apart from the queen and her personal bodyguard, the only persons to enter the royal compound in that period were Micaela, Alvaro, Teresa, Father Antonio, Pero da Silva, a Spanish envoy, and Roberto Delgado."

"It is reasonable to assume that something that Teresa heard or saw within the royal compound provoked her murder," concluded Luke.

"The queen has given us authority to interview on her behalf all but one of those I just named," added Ramiro.

"Who is exempted from our probe?" joked Peter.

"Viscount Roberto Delgado. And the queen thinks it will aid our investigation if we conduct it from a room within her compound. Pero da Silva is currently with her, and she will ask him to see us before he leaves the area," reported Ramiro.

The royal compound took up the two upper levels of what had been the original commandant's residence. The room allotted to the trio overlooked the barrack square. Pero arrived and immediately expressed his concern that two leading noblewomen had been murdered within a week of each other in the very premises in which the queen was located, and which currently housed the bulk of the Portuguese army's high command.

"This is not good for morale. Is one person responsible for both deaths?" he asked.

"Tremayne thinks so, but Lord Ramiro and I have a more open mind," replied Peter.

"Was Teresa Pinto privy to any state secrets over the last few days that may have provoked her murder?" Luke asked.

"No, the queen has always been cautious about speaking about state matters with her ladies-in-waiting. Micaela da Costa is the only one of them in whom she confides. Teresa was always anxious to replace Micaela in the queen's affections and hierarchy, but she was viewed as potentially unreliable—a view I expressed personally to Her Majesty not so long ago. Micaela, cattily, always emphasized that Teresa's generosity toward men would prove an Achilles heel that could provide entry to the queen's inner circle for enemies of the state."

"Was anybody within Magellan currently benefitting from Teresa's generosity?" continued Luke.

Da Silva smiled. "The gossip around the barracks is that you, General Tremayne, were her current interest."

"Nobody else? Who did she speak to over the last few days?" continued a slightly embarrassed Luke.

"She argued with Alvaro, was closeted with the queen alone for some time, was seen flirting with Delgado, and received a message from Paolo," added Da Silva.

"Delgado is your opponent. Why has the queen invited him here—and into her private compound? Is she about to replace you, Rodrigo da Costa, and Diego de Albuquerque with a new set of councillors representing the pro-Afonso views of Delgado?" probed Luke.

"Is the queen about to stage a coup against herself?" emphasized Peter.

"It is the queen's prerogative as regent to appoint whom she likes to her council, but she only confided to me a few minutes ago that she has no intention of replacing me or Albuquerque. Joana's death has raised a few doubts in her mind about Rodrigo da Costa, but she is awaiting your report before she acts."

"Why did Teresa spend so long with the queen?" asked Ramiro.

"Teresa was made responsible for executing the queen's decisions regarding the funeral of Joana. It was beneath Micaela's view of her own importance to be bothered with such trifles."

"Why would Teresa spend time with Delgado?" probed Peter.

"An obvious one! Teresa came from one of the most powerful and ancient Portuguese families related to the old Portuguese monarchy, as does Delgado. If the Delgado group were anxious to replace the Spanish-born regent with someone who would appeal to the Portuguese nationalists, Teresa's family would be their first choice."

"It does not make sense. What is the queen up to?" asked the frustrated Ramiro.

"Would an extreme supporter of the queen kill Teresa to thwart a pro-Afonso coup?" asked Luke, largely to himself.

Next to front the investigators was Micaela. Luke asked a routine question regarding Teresa's return to the queen's service.

She replied, "Teresa was given leave by the queen to accompany her husband to Estrela. It seemed ridiculous that when she was here in Magellan and I was struggling to cope with the added problems of the marchioness Joana's funeral and the visit of a Spanish grandee that she not return to duty immediately. When Teresa resumed her role with the queen, she was immediately made responsible for those extraordinary events, while I concentrated on the day-to-day issues of the queen's household on tour."

"Was Teresa happy to be back in the queen's service?" asked Peter.

"Delighted! She always hoped to replace me as the senior lady-in-waiting and was out to impress the queen with her efficiency and loyalty—despite her family supporting the pro-Afonso nobles."

"And the leader of such a group, Roberto Delgado, is invited here and into the queen's compound. How do you explain that?"

"Ask the queen. She absolutely refuses to discuss Delgado's presence with anybody."

"You must have some thoughts on the matter," probed Ramiro.

"The queen is trying to broaden her appeal to the more nationalistic Portuguese factions."

"In that case, the murder of Teresa would be a major blow to her plan. It might suggest that Teresa was murdered by current supporters of the queen who do not wish to lose their influence," commented Luke undiplomatically.

Micaela seemed caught off guard and reacted, "Teresa was so unimportant that murder was a remedy that need never be considered. I have kept her insidious influence at bay for years. Except in her own eyes, Teresa Pinto was a nobody. Nothing has changed over the last few weeks."

"What has changed is the arrival of Delgado," asserted Peter, contradicting the overconfident Micaela.

Luke took up the questioning. "Countess, we have been informed that Delgado was once your lover and that you manipulated the queen to have his militia units mobilized so that he would be sent here. Forgive my bluntness—is he still your lover? Did you persuade the queen to order his unit here?"

Micaela blushed, and her bright blue eyes deepened as she responded aggressively. "No, no—to both questions."

"But you were acquainted with Delgado at the French court?" continued Luke.

"Yes, we were good friends."

"Since Delgado arrived here, have you had any private conversations with him?" Luke asked.

Micaela hesitated. "No."

"If you were such great friends in Paris, why do you not talk to him when he is located in the same compound here?" asked a suspicious Ramiro.

"One scenario is that you renewed your deep friendship and were seen or overheard by Teresa, which necessitated her removal," suggested Peter bluntly.

"Outrageous! The queen did not intend that I should be insulted and accused of murder. I will report your misconduct immediately."

She stalked out of the room.

Alvaro was the next to arrive. "You have certainly upset the countess Micaela. She is demanding an immediate audience with the queen to protest against your behavior."

"Yes, we accused her of murder. She and Teresa have been enemies for years, and now with the advent of her former—or is he her present—lover, the victim may have seen them alone in a compromising position."

"A bit far-fetched! Micaela is a petite woman who would not have the strength to strangle anybody. On the other hand, Delgado could have," admitted Alvaro.

"We assume that it was something that Teresa heard or saw in the last two days since she resumed duty with the queen that led to her murder. As only a few of you have been within this compound, we must conclude that one or more of you contributed to her death."

"There is something amiss in your assumption. The queen and Micaela could not physically have killed Teresa. That leaves only Pero da Silva, the minister of war, Antonio Mendes, a priest who was formally employed by Teresa's family and had known her since childhood, Delgado, and myself—and a fleeting visit from Cipriano."

Luke was taken aback by the last statement. Cipriano visit had not been noted earlier.

Ramiro replied to Alvaro's comment, "Precisely! That is what upset Micaela. Mendes was a friend of Teresa, Delgado of similar political views, and Cipriano irrelevant. Only Pero and yourself would benefit from her death."

"Not necessarily. Teresa's overt opposition to the Da Costas and a Spanish-born regent and her open advancement of her own family's claim to the Portuguese throne might have been too radical for even the ultranationalists such as Delgado. She may have been an embarrassment to his cause," Alvaro countered.

"Have you had any discussion with him?" asked Ramiro.

"Only about the deployment of his militia in the presence of Da Silva."

"There was another person admitted to the compound, the Spanish envoy helping arrange the visit of the Duke of Medina-Sidonia. Could he have murdered Teresa on the orders of some Spanish interest?" continued Ramiro.

"That would be a very convenient answer, but it was impossible. The envoy was escorted by two of the queen's household guard every minute he was in the compound and indeed in the barracks in general."

The last of the queen's inner circle to be questioned was Father Antonio. He was still visibly distraught.

"She was a lovely child, beautiful beyond belief. As a mature woman, she tried to use her beauty for personal and political gain. Yet she was never quite the femme fatale. There was always something of the child about her. She seemed a strange mixture of the predatory vamp and naive innocent."

"Was it her generous attitude to a large number of men who contributed to her death?" asked Luke.

"Yes. Her death most likely resulted from some personal issues rather than anything political. Her constant flirtations could easily have been misinterpreted by males whom she sought to charm. Her death does not seem to have been planned. Someone on the spur of the moment took advantage of a small window of opportunity to kill her."

"Did she speak to you about anything since her return to the queen's service?" asked Ramiro.

"Yes. She seemed to be obsessed by the presence of Roberto Delgado, who, on the one hand, led that faction of the nobles with ultranationalistic views with which her family agreed and, on the other, was the rumored lover of her hated superior, Countess Micaela da Costa."

"Did you ever see Teresa with Delgado?" probed Peter.

"No."

"What do you make of Delgado's presence?"

"The Da Costas and Da Silva are trying to turn it into a major issue. The queen is simply trying to expand her base of support. To involve Delgado and his militia in this current campaign would assist in this plan. The queen is beginning to distrust some of those around her and therefore needs to bring others into her inner circle."

"Was there any particular male whom Teresa had been involved with in recent weeks?" asked Peter.

"I cannot reveal the secrets of the confession, but from other sources, I would say Teresa has had no serious lovers for some time but was using her charms on Da Silva and you, General Tremayne, to gain advantages for her husband."

"Or her own gratification," muttered a cynical Ramiro.

"If you think her murder has something to do with the misuse of her charms and Da Silva and Tremayne are the most recent recipients—and we obviously reject them as suspects—who killed her?" continued Peter.

"It could go back months. I don't know whom she was close to before I became royal chaplain."

"Was there nothing over the last few days involving Teresa that you thought unusual?" asked Peter.

"No, except a slight altercation with Alvaro, which surprised me because their paths did not cross. There seemed to be no reason for them to argue."

"Interesting," muttered Luke.

23

THE FUNERAL SERVICE FOR Joana, Marchioness of Estrela, and successive granddaughter, niece, and cousin of the grandee of Spain, the Duke of Medina-Sidonia, was conducted by the archbishops of Lisbon and Évora and the Spanish primate, the cardinal archbishop of Toledo. It was immediately followed by that of Countess Teresa, from which the Spanish primate and guests withdrew, accepting the anti-Spanish sensitivities of Teresa's family. At the conclusion of that service, Baltasar, Count Pinto, was given permission to take the body of his wife from Magellan to her ancestral home in northwestern Portugal.

During a week of mourning and the continued suspension of hostilities with Spain, Luke decided that he and Peter would once more reconnoiter across the border. It would enable them to better assess the deployment of the Spanish troops against whom they would soon be arrayed. As they left Magellan, Luke asked that they converse in Portuguese as he was determined to improve his grasp of the language. He was now able to conduct an interview and engage in basic social chitchat.

As they trotted slowly in the direction of Corba, the village and parish in which Father Nicodemo was priest, Luke was surprised not to see or hear Spanish troops. Peter concluded that the Spaniards must have used the cease-fire to withdraw most of the troops that had been facing the Portuguese.

"But where have they gone?" mused Luke.

On reaching Corba, they were warmly welcomed by the Nicodemo.

"Why are two Englishmen wandering about the Spanish borderlands?" he jokingly inquired.

"While both sides endure a week or two cease-fire, focused around the funeral of Queen Luisa's cousin and fellow Guzman, Joana da Costa, I wanted to establish the exact deployment of enemy troops before hostilities resume," Luke explained.

"The Spaniards have not been idle during the cease-fire. Troops have been withdrawn either into Castle Passos or moved much farther north," related Nicodemo.

"That explains why we saw no Spanish troops on our way here," affirmed Peter.

"Are they simply moving to a new border, which they will defend at all costs, but are willing to surrender the land between the current frontier and the vicinity of Castle Passos?" queried Luke.

"Probably, they are willing to surrender land that was Portuguese and which is inhabited by Portuguese speakers such as this area if we do likewise for Spanish speakers within Portugal."

"Can we just move in and reclaim this village and its surrounding lands?" asked a skeptical Luke.

"Yes, very soon and with the support of the Spanish government."

"You have been negotiating such a transfer for some time?" commented Luke.

Nicodemo smiled.

"How does Jorge Zoritas react to this possibility?" asked Peter.

"That is a surprising and worrying fact about which I was about to inform Colonel da Costa. Zoritas told me some time ago that he would soon be rid of us. He was returning to Estremadura to recruit landowners to control expected captured Portuguese territory, and for his services, he would receive a larger and richer grant for himself somewhere to the northwest."

"Which suggests that the Spaniards are confident of a relatively easy land grab somewhere along the frontier—but not here," summarized Peter.

"No more intelligence to Alvaro da Costa! He is under investigation," said Luke with such vehemence that Nicodemo reacted angrily.

"Gentlemen, I do not take my orders from the English. How do I know that Alvaro is no longer trusted, or that you have authority to act in this way?"

Luke searched in his saddlebag for the letter of authority he had received from the queen.

Nicodemo perused it and nodded. "What has created doubt concerning Alvaro?" he asked.

"Before she died, Joana da Costa indicated to the queen that she might be betrayed by those close to her. Unfortunately, she was murdered before she could provide names. That is also why the queen, who felt she could trust nobody around her, asked a couple of foreigners to conduct the investigation into Joana's murder and into the conspiracy against her," explained Peter.

"The matter has intensified with a second murder—that of Teresa, Countess Pinto," added Luke.

"It must be a relief that Jorge Zoritas is away," said Peter, changing the subject.

"Quite the opposite. While Jorge's away, his delinquent son, Mendo, is terrorizing the neighborhood. On my last visit to Castle Passos, I complained to the authorities, and they now send a patrol through the area on a regular basis, but Mendo is cunning and devious."

It was as if the mention of the name had conjured up this diabolical personality. A villager burst into the room, claiming that three men led by Mendo had abducted not only his obsession, Marabella Gomes, but her two younger sisters, Marisa and Martina, who were but children.

"He must be taught a lesson," muttered Nicodemo.

He asked the villager to inform the girls' two male cousins and ask them to report back at the manse, heavily armed, immediately.

"We will help, but two English soldiers, two villagers, and an unarmed priest may not be enough," said Luke.

"Forget the unarmed priest! Before I joined the church, I was a soldier in our army in Brazil. Mendo is a coward and can now only convince two or three other degenerates to join him in his escapades. The rest of the Zoritas clan and their servants are terrified of Jorge, who has confined Mendo to the family home in his absence. They will not assist this wayward wretch. He will not dare take the girls back to his house because the steward whom Jorge left in charge would very quickly put an end to any immoral activity."

"So where would he go?" asked Luke.

"My parishioners tell me that he uses a shepherd's hut on the side of the mountain to drink and fornicate with his cronies. My guess is that he is heading there."

Two strapping young peasants arrived, armed, to Luke's surprise, with swords.

Nicodemo noted Luke's reaction and explained, "Over the years, I have kept my hand in as a swordsman by teaching some of the village lads the finer points of swordplay. These boys are my best pupils." The priest then strapped a sword around his cassock and led the small troop of four others out of the village, heading for the mountain shack.

As they trotted along, Nicodemo observed, "The last time Mendo saw you two, you were allegedly part of the Inquisition. I will continue that fantasy. We may be able to terrify Mendo by the threat of an inquisitorial prison as he clearly has ignored the order not to molest the women of the village, especially Marabella."

Luke expressed some disquiet. "If Mendo and his cronies are intent on raping these girls, we may not be in time to stop them. They would have at least half and hour's lead over us. Animals driven by lust are not patient."

Nicodemo and the two village lads smiled.

The priest answered, "You may have noticed we are climbing this narrow and potentially dangerous track. Mendo, especially if he has been drinking, would never attempt it, even if he knew of its existence—which I doubt. He will be taking the more leisurely gradual track that winds slowly up the mountainside. We will reach his destination before him. In about ten minutes, we can compare our relative progress."

The group eventually reached a point on the track that gave them an unimpeded view of the major route up the mountain. In the distance and well below them were four horsemen, all swigging from leather carafes.

Luke was surprised. "If I had abducted a woman, I would have placed her on my horse in front of me. Why has Mendo tied the women together and roped them behind one horse?"

"He spent some of his youth in the Americas, and that is how the Spaniards there treated the native women and slaves. I doubt if he considers Portuguese peasant women as much more than animals. But this makes our task easier. Instead of waiting in the hut to meet him, we shall, as soon as this track joins the main pathway, head down hill and confront them. Luke, you and I will play the Inquisition card, while Peter and the lads will move directly to free the girls."

"Let's add a bit of terror to this. There is a long gentle slope from the intersection of the tracks to where we will confront Mendo. A cavalry charge downhill straight at him should more than alarm him," said Luke.

"I doubt if he will even see us. He can hardly stay on his horse. He appears hopelessly drunk," added Peter.

"Make as much noise as you can—and stay in line. The two village lads will be on either flank and continue through the charge and free the girls. You and I, Luke, will stop in front of Mendo and deliver our diatribe," affirmed Nicodemo.

Mendo saw a row of five horsemen galloping downhill at a furious pace—directly toward him. Given his level of intoxication, he saw but did not comprehend—but two of his followers did. They turned and rode, as if possessed, down the slope, away from any imminent conflict. The man who led the roped women froze to the spot with fear.

The village lads swept past Mendo, cut the rope, placed the two younger girls on their horses, and, waving at Nicodemo, rode slowly back toward the village. Marabella strode past Mendo and his lone frozen supporter and stood beside Nicodemo as he berated the degenerate Spaniard.

"Mendo Zoritas, the gentlemen with me last saw you when they were with the Inquisition in my village. The man on my left removed you from your horse with a flying tackle. At the time, you were ordered, under threat of spending time in an Inquisition prison, that you were never to molest any of the women of Corba. You have clearly disobeyed that order."

Mendo tried to dismount but, in the process, fell to the ground. As he lay semi-helpless on the ground, Luke drew his sword and placed its point at Mendo's throat.

"Father, I would not waste the time of the Holy Inquisition on this scum. Escort Marabella back to the village and leave it to Peter and myself to tie up the loose ends. We will return to Corba later in the day."

"I am a priest. I do not want the blood of anybody, even Spanish filth, on my hands," said a suddenly pious Nicodemo.

"Mendo and his friend will not be murdered by us, but two very drunk horsemen on a narrow mountain track might find it hard to avoid an accident," replied Luke with a smile.

The priest lifted Marabella onto his saddle, remounted himself, and reluctantly rode off.

Peter asked, "Do you intend to execute these two in cold blood?"

"No, but they are both scared and drunk. Under the threat of death, they might yield information that could be useful for our mission."

Peter tied both the hands and feet of the two Spaniards together, and Luke's improving Portuguese was readily understood by the victims as he asked, "Your father will soon be leaving this area to take up richer estates to the north. Where exactly is he going?" Luke pricked Mendo's throat with the point of his sword, which drew some blood. "My sword could easily slip farther," he whispered in the ear of his prisoner. "Tell me now."

Peter began to pile rocks that lay about the slope on the body of Mendo's companion, who had been forced to lie on his back. If completed, this cairn-building exercise would have crushed the Spaniard to death. As the pressure increased, he pleaded with Mendo to tell their interrogators everything. Mendo began to blubber but gave no coherent answer. With a very dexterous movement, Luke removed the sword from Mendo's throat and sliced off part of his ear. Blood streamed profusely from the excision.

"Can you hear my question better now?" he asked.

"Yes!" Mendo screamed. "But I do not know where we are going. All I know is that we will occupy part of Portugal that is to be handed over to us willingly. It will not be the result of an invasion. That is why Father is in Estremadura recruiting farmers and shepherds rather than soldiers."

Luke tossed the man a large handkerchief to stop the bleeding from the ear, which was now missing the lower part of the lobe. "I will not waste the time of the Inquisition by taking you to its prison," Luke announced.

"Kill us quickly then," pleaded Mendo's companion.

Luke primed his pistol, and the two Spaniards prayed.

24

T O THEIR SURPRISE, PETER freed both Spaniards, and Luke gave them a specific order. "Remount your horses and disappear down that steep track to our right before I change my mind."

"You will shoot us in the back," moaned the companion.

The two Spaniards galloped away at breakneck speed and began the descent of the treacherous path—too quickly. On the first bend, there was a loud scream.

By the time Luke and Peter reached the scene, Mendo's companion was pointing down the precipice, and Mendo's unmanned horse was quietly nibbling some grass.

"What happened?" asked Luke.

"As Mendo rode around this sharp bend, his saddle strap must have broken, and he was catapulted over the cliff. His horse pulled up on the very edge," explained the terrified companion.

"Oh dear, he must have been in such a hurry to escape us that he did not check his saddle straps," remarked Luke innocently and smiled at Peter.

Luke, Peter, and Mendo's surviving accomplice made their way back to Corba.

Nicodemo immediately noticed the obvious absence and, before he upbraided the Englishmen, asked gently, "Where is Master Zoritas?"

Mendo's friend gave the priest a surprising and reassuring answer. "The young master was so drunk that he did not check his saddle straps, and at the first sharp bend, the saddle moved and catapulted him over the cliff."

Luke smiled to himself.

"Did you find the body? He will need a Christian burial," asked the priest.

"No, we could not descend from the path to the valley floor. It will be easier to search for the body in the morning as the light has already begun to fade," answered Luke.

Later that evening, as Luke and Peter enjoyed a meal with Nicodemo, he asked, "Did your questioning of Mendo reveal anything of significance?"

"Yes. He is convinced that Spain is about to gain a large tract of Portugal by gift rather than conquest."

"That would require negotiation at the highest level," remarked Nicodemo.

"From the Portuguese side, the very highest level of government is the queen regent, who is currently on the border," mused Peter.

"And the third highest-ranking member of the Spanish government, the cardinal archbishop of Toledo, primate of all Spain and chancellor of Castile, is currently with her," said Nicodemo with obvious delight.

This attitude intrigued Luke. "But surely, the primate is in Portugal simply to take part in the requiem mass for Joana da Costa."

"Rubbish! Why would a seventy-year-old who hardly leaves Madrid journey to the frontier to share a mass with Portuguese bishops for a distant relative of the Guzmans, whose family is out of favor with the Spanish government? No, he is Spain's high-powered negotiator for whatever transfer of land is proposed."

"Surely, the queen is not betraying Portugal and surrendering territory to Spain," said Luke.

"More likely, she is exchanging Portuguese-speaking parts of Spain such as here with Spanish-speaking parts of Portugal," Nicodemo responded.

He continued, "What do you intend to do tomorrow?"

"After we search for Mendo's body, I will visit Castle Passos to see what we can discover, but we will need your help to achieve that."

At first light the next morning, Nicodemo, Luke, Peter, and a dozen villagers set out along the valley to search for Mendo's body. They searched all day without success.

"He must have survived and wandered off," declared Luke.

"Impossible! The fall was too great, and the landing would most likely have been onto sharp rocks," observed Peter.

"They say that the devil looks after his own" was Nicodemo's unhelpful advice.

"There must be a simple explanation," said Peter.

"Perhaps there is. His body may have been caught somewhere on the precipice. I will get two of the village boys who are expert climbers to make their way up the sheer face of the cliff first thing tomorrow."

On the way back to the village, Nicodemo said, "Given the current cease-fire, I have greater access to Castle Passos than normal. I will make a visit tomorrow, accompanied by two lay brothers of the Franciscan order. I have a couple of spare cassocks that should provide sufficient disguise."

The following morning, two young climbers left Corba to scale the precipice over which Mendo had been flung. Luke and Peter slept in as Nicodemo had parochial business to complete before he was free to leave for Passos. They spent some time deciding how they could conceal their weapons while wearing the cassocks. They adopted the simplest approach— simply wear the cassock over their other clothes and weapons. Nicodemo, on returning to his house, was surprised at his two portly companions who did not walk as freely as they might.

Eventually, the three were ready to leave. They had just reached the crossroads that marked the boundary of the village when Marabella came running down the slope, shouting for them to stop. She was distressed and weeping, explaining that one of the climbers sent to find Mendo's body had fallen, and his injuries were too severe for the locals to rectify.

"What do you in such cases of severe injury?" asked Peter of Nicodemo.

"We take the patient to the monastery of St. Juan, the nearest religious house that has several monks who are experts in medicine. In fact, the abbot there is an old friend. We will wait for the wagon carrying the injured lad and escort it to San Juan, which is only a few miles beyond Passos."

After a short wait, the wagon arrived. Its driver and the villagers who had assisted in the recovery of the injured man were anxious to return to their own work and were delighted when Peter offered to drive the wagon. Luke and Nicodemo rode beside it. The injured lad was in great pain, and despite his heroic efforts to control himself, he screamed from time to time. Constant doses of brandy eased the situation a little.

The monastery amazed Luke. It was a massive structure that had walls twenty-five feet high and undoubtedly many feet thick. It looked a more efficient defensive structure than many a castle.

Nicodemo explained, "During the reconquest of this region from the Moslems, this monastery was an early Christian outpost that was built to withstand the then constant counterattacks that Islam launched against it. Many of the early monks were warriors as well as religious, fully imbued with the crusading spirit. Nowadays, the monastery belongs to the Cistercian Order, who emphasize scholarship, medicine—and very profitable sheep farming."

As they approached the main entrance of the monastery, Nicodemo became apprehensive.

"What's wrong?" asked Luke.

"I have never known the main gate to be closed during daylight hours. This is most unusual."

Nicodemo dismounted and approached the entrance. After considerable conversation with the gatekeeper, the gate was finally opened, and Nicodemo returned to Luke and Peter, accompanied by three monks. "We are not permitted to advance any farther. The brothers will take over the wagon and our patient."

Peter climbed down from the wagon and unhitched his steed. The three monks pulled and pushed the wagon into the monastery. The other monks followed it on foot, and the gate closed with a resounding clang. "What is going on? This is not normal monastic hospitality," observed Luke.

"It certainly is not," agreed Nicodemo.

"Did the monks offer any explanation?"

"Yes. It has been closed because it is about to become the location where some very important people are to meet and stay if necessary. My friend, the abbot whom I asked to speak to, apparently opposed the closing of the monastery just because it was to house important guests and has, as a result of his objection, been temporarily confined to his cell."

"On whose orders?" Luke asked.

"That is a most worrying aspect—the primate of all Spain, the cardinal archbishop of Toledo."

"That is indeed worrying. I would assume that the cardinal is to stay here after he returns from Magellan on his way back to Toledo and Madrid.

But why here and not Castle Passos as one would expect?" asked a bemused Peter

"What has the monastery got that the castle has not?" added Luke.

A serious Nicodemo almost whispered, "Secrecy. As you know, even enemy agents can pick up a lot of information in the castle. That is why you are going there. It would be difficult to conceal the identity of any visitors in the castle. What happens behind the monastery walls and who is there is another matter. Ecclesiastical discipline alone would curtail much of the gossip, and the small monastic cells could keep dozens of people unaware of each other's presence and identity."

At least the gates of Castle Passos were open and the guard gave Nicodemo a cheery welcome. The hostlers approached the horsemen and took their steeds to the stable. Nicodemo and his two plump religious brothers entered the prison, where the commander of the guards joked, "If I had had my way, there would have been nothing for you to do. For weeks, I have moved any ill or wounded prisoners of war into the monastery of San Juan for treatment or the last rites. The able-bodied men were distributed among the local farmers as part of the workforce and, as of yesterday, will remain on those farms until further notice."

"If you have been so successful in emptying your prison, why are there still people here?"

"As of yesterday, I was ordered not to send any more prisoners to the monastery until further notice."

"Do you know why?"

"Rumors. Someone of importance is in the area, and his activities need to be kept secret. But everybody knows that the cardinal archbishop of Toledo and the duke of Medina-Sidonia have passed through here on their way to a funeral in Portugal."

"How many men have you left for me to visit?"

"Three men whose superficial wounds have become infected and who really need the help of the monks. Five men who were picked up by a patrol deep within Spain who could be spies for you Portuguese—and a couple of madmen."

Nicodemo whispered to Luke and Peter, "Come with me. Keep your faces covered but see if you can recognize any of the group just picked up by a Spanish patrol. How many illegal forays is Portugal conducting during this cease-fire?"

Nicodemo heard a few confessions, conducted the last rites for one distraught character whose wounds did not appear fatal, and conducted an abbreviated mass that was interrupted by one of the madmen claiming direct revelation from God. They recognized none of the prisoners.

Two hours later, Nicodemo, Luke, and Peter enjoyed a meal in the refectory. Peter remarked on how few troops were visible in the castle. Suddenly, a series of blasts on a cornet were heard. Ten minutes later, the guard commander entered the refectory.

"Sorry, Father. I have some bad news for you. The gates have just been closed and the troops within the castle placed on full alert. All Portuguese speakers are to be temporarily detained here until further notice."

"Does that mean we are your prisoners?"

"No, you will be given beds in the dormitory with the troops and not in the cells with the prisoners."

Given the alert and the obvious redeployment of troops, there were very few soldiers in the large room. "Something important is about to happen, given what is occurring here and at the monastery," remarked Peter.

"It can only be one thing—the king of Spain is meeting with the queen of Portugal," suggested Luke.

"It is all fitting into place. Perhaps the queen is handing over a Portuguese province to Spain in return for the recognition of Portuguese independence in the rest of the country," concluded Nicodemo. "That would conform to long-held Portuguese strategy."

"The queen is besieged on all sides, but I cannot see her returning an inch of Portugal to the Spaniards. She and her husband fought too hard to put Portugal where it is," said Luke.

"I hope you are right, Luke. Otherwise, our whole mission in Portugal is a farce. It is not a question of a queen besieged but of Englishmen deceived," declared a doubting Peter.

25

AS SOON AS THEY were permitted to leave Castle Passos, Nicodemo returned directly to Corba, while Luke and Peter headed by a circuitous route back to Magellan. As they entered the barracks, a soldier informed them that the queen wished to see them immediately.

Ushered into the queen's private apartment, Luke and Peter were surprised to find that only the queen and Madalena Albuquerque were present.

"I have asked the baroness to act as a lady-in-waiting in place of the murdered Countess Teresa. Her fluency in English is an added advantage in this conversation. I have been wanting to speak to you for several days. Where have you been?" she asked.

"Deep within Spanish territory, seeking information that might help with both our overt and secret missions," answered Luke.

"With what success?"

Luke decided to hold nothing back. "When does Your Majesty intend to meet the king of Spain?"

If Luke had been looking for an indication of guilt or embarrassment, it was not forthcoming. "General, you have indeed been very successful. Nobody here other than Father Antonio and Viscount Delgado know of such a possible development. My brother, the Duke of Medina-Sidonia, and Baltasar Sandoval, who is chancellor of Castile and the cardinal archbishop of Toledo, suggested that if I wished to meet with the Spanish king, arrangements could be made immediately. That offer was made over a week ago. I asked the cardinal what could be achieved by such a meeting.

He suggested that a more permanent cease-fire could be arranged and some tinkering with the border. In turn, he asked me what Portugal would want. My answer was simple and short—that Spain recognize Portuguese independence. This did not please him. How did you know of such a highly secret meeting?"

"Guesswork based on the closure of both Castle Passos and the monastery of San Juan. Clearly, a very important visitor was expected in the area. We also heard rumors of the transfer of Portuguese land to the Spaniards. As only Your Majesty would have the authority to do that, I put two and two together."

"Those rumors about land transfers are news to me. I would never cede an inch of independent Portugal back to the Habsburgs, and I am determined to have all Portuguese-speaking areas still under Spanish rule returned to Portugal as soon as possible. The cardinal, in fact, as a morsel to get me to agree to a meeting, did suggest that Spanish-occupied land between here and the original border near Castle Passos could be returned to us. He even claimed that the current Spanish landlord, a Jorge Zoritas, was about to be withdrawn and moved somewhere else."

Luke choose not reveal any more regarding the land transfers and asked, "When will you meet Felipe IV?"

"I won't, but I did agree to send a small delegation to meet with senior Spanish officials at the monastery of San Juan in three days. You will be surprised to know that the Spaniards asked for you, General Tremayne, to be part of that group."

"That's not good. I thought my mission was a secret. How could the Spaniards know I am here?"

"The traitor in our midst. That is why I am sending only three men and one woman in my place—Pero da Silva, the senior minister in my government, Roberto Delgado, and, if you accept, yourself."

"Why Delgado?" asked Peter.

"I cannot trust those around me. If only one member of my government is involved, it will be easy to trace any leaks back to Da Silva. Delgado represents the opposition nobles, who consider I am too close to Spain. It is vital that I win them over. Delgado will ensure Portuguese interests are not infringed by any agreements that Da Silva could be tempted to sign."

"And my presence?"

"You are not plotting against me, and I would very much appreciate any information concerning what Spain wants of you—and how they came to know about you."

"And who is the woman who will come with us?"

"Madalena Albuquerque as interpreter for you, Luke, and an observer for me. That is not quite the full story. She is an essential part of a charade by which I intend to conceal my location over the next week."

After the meeting with the queen concluded, Luke spoke alone with Madalena. "Anything of importance take place while Peter and I were away?"

"The queen announced that Paolo da Costa was renouncing his title and estates to become a monk and that she had accepted his request, making Rodrigo da Costa the new Marquess of Estrela and my superior here as a lady-in-waiting, Micaela, the new marchioness. It's gone to her head a little. Her overt ambition has been known for some time, but now she has suggested to the queen that she and Rodrigo could represent the monarchy at any function Her Majesty is unable to attend. Luisa was furious. Micaela herself will be enraged when she hears I have been selected to go to Spain with you."

"Why did the queen overlook her and select you?"

"Micaela is already committed to leave tomorrow with Paolo, Rodrigo, and Alvaro to take Joana's body back to Estrela and for Paolo to formally hand over his title and estates."

Early the next morning, soldiers manning the walls of Magellan were surprised to see the queen's coach with two women aboard, surrounded by a troop of household cavalry, followed by two wagons containing possessions and supplies, three gentlemen on horseback, and another troop of the queen's cavalry. They were not surprised to see the cavalcade turn right at the gates and head west toward the Tagus and, ultimately, Lisbon. The queen, they assumed, was returning to her capital.

Luke, who, with Pero da Silva and Roberto Delgado, comprised the three gentlemen, was immediately aware that they were traveling in the wrong direction. He asked Da Silva for an explanation.

"Direct orders from the queen, who wants to use our mission to falsely suggest to those at Magellan that she has returned to the capital. That is why Baroness Albuquerque and her maid are using the royal coach and have dressed to look like queen and lady-in-waiting. The commander of our escort will continue some miles west, south, and then back east to cross the border and take us to the monastery of San Juan. Part of the Spanish delegation, our recent funeral guests, leave after us this morning, and this diversion will enable them to reach the monastery before us."

"Why is the queen playing such a game?" asked Luke.

"She thinks that her pretend absence from Magellan may encourage the traitor or traitors to act. She will remain secluded in her apartment with only Father Antonio and the commander of her personal guard aware that she is still there."

Luke discovered that Roberto's English was as basic as his Portuguese, but they managed to chat amicably as they rode. Luke explained that the queen had asked him to investigate the two murders and that given Teresa's views about Micaela and himself, Roberto had to be considered a suspect in her murder.

"The court gossip that we were lovers in Paris is decades old. At the time, we were both young and single. Since we both returned to Portugal years ago, we have rarely seen each other. Micaela married and became a courtier and eventually senior lady-in-waiting to Luisa de Guzman. I became an opposition leader, seeking to remove Luisa as regent because of her Spanish birth and having a Portuguese-born nobleman replacing her until Afonso is old enough to rule in his own right."

"That is what I have been told, so why are you here?"

"I was summoned by the queen."

"Did she say why? Rumor implies that Micaela persuaded her so that she and you could renew your love affair."

"If Micaela used her influence in such a way, it was based on fantasy. There is no love affair between us, although she has not remained faithful to her husband."

"Did the queen not explain why you had been sent for?" asked a suspicious Pero.

"Only that the generals needed the assistance of the provincial militia drawn from my family estates over which I am the commander-in-chief."

"The generals did not need your extra troops. And if you are simply an additional military leader needed in the current border skirmishes, why are you secluded in an apartment attached to the queen's enclave and not living in the general barracks with the rest of us?" probed Luke.

"Ask the queen. I honestly do not know."

Da Silva muttered, "Roberto, for her own ends, which I cannot fathom, I fear the queen is playing us off against each other."

"Is it the queen or the devious Da Costa clan?" uttered Luke undiplomatically.

Delgado thought it wise not to reply to either comment.

Luke changed the direction of his questions. "What are the rumors of Micaela's more recent liaisons?"

"I am not a courtier, but over the years, two names have filtered down into the provinces—her brother-in-law, Alvaro, and the murdered woman's husband, Baltasar Pinto."

"Alvaro, as a younger brother placed in close proximity to his sister-in-law, is not a surprising subject of such gossip, but Pinto surprises me," said Luke.

"Aware that Teresa was coveting her job, she seduced Pinto to win him to her side, and in return, she ensured he retained his military command despite complaints against him," Pero suggested.

"That is an angle to Teresa's murder of which I was not aware. I did not know that her hatred of the Costas might be that personal—her husband had been seduced by her rival and superior."

The meeting at the monastery of San Juan without the presence of either monarch was a waste of time. Portugal's basic demand, recognition of her independence, was not even discussed by the Spanish representatives. They concentrated on the need for a permanent cease-fire along the Portuguese frontier, probably, Luke thought, because the demand for Spanish troops in the Netherlands, Italy, and Catalonia left few for the Portuguese campaign.

His own role was to act as courier—to carry a message to Oliver Cromwell that Spain desired peace with England, and should such an outcome occur, they would transfer some territory in the Netherlands to English sovereignty. When Luke asked if Spain would, here and now, guarantee that Dunkirk or Ostend would be that territory, he was told that was a discussion that would take place when peace was achieved.

Madalena's services were not required as the Spaniards had a number of people present who spoke English. No women were present at any of the discussions.

Their return journey to Magellan followed the same route along which they had reached San Juan. It led through a series of gorges, many of which had towering rock formations overhanging the narrow track.

The Portuguese cavalcade was progressing through one such formation when Luke heard a rumbling, and Delgado suddenly shouted out for the coachman to accelerate and for those behind him to stop in their tracks. Bouncing down toward the bottom of the gorge were dozens of large boulders. They were about to become victims of an unexpected avalanche.

Several massive rocks hit the coach. It tipped and was crushed further by two gigantic monoliths almost as large as the coach itself.

As soon as the avalanche stopped, Luke, Roberto, Pero, and a score of soldiers began moving the rocks from the coach to rescue or, at least, assess the state of its occupants. The coachman was dead, hit while in his driving seat by one of the flying missiles. He had accelerated sufficiently on hearing Delgado's cry to save his team of six horses but not himself.

Eventually, the interior of the coach was uncovered. The bodies of Madalena and her maid Aileen were carried to a grassy verge. Aileen was dead—so badly ripped apart that even the battle-hardened Luke was sickened. Her face was smashed in, and some of her limbs detached from the torso. A cannonade could hardly have rendered such shocking injuries.

Luke held the blade of his dagger to Madalena's mouth. She was still alive—just.

A soldier sent to where the rocks had been dislodged shouted down to his comrades, "This is no accident. The avalanche was man made. The rockfall was engineered by an unknown enemy."

26

THE COMMANDER OF THE escort emptied some of the goods out of a wagon and placed Madalena's body carefully into the space obtained. He ordered the driver to travel as fast as he safely could and get the baroness to Magellan. The wagon, with an escort of troopers, was quickly out of sight.

Luke, upset by the injuries to his friend Madalena, could only disparage his comrades. "Whatever happened to that concept of honor? We would all be safe because the Spaniards and Portuguese prized honor above victory. We had safe conduct, and look what happened!"

"It could even have been worse than what we see. The coach that was targeted was emblazoned with the insignia of the Braganzas. Whoever organized this attack thought they were assassinating the queen of Portugal," said Pero.

"And that frees the representatives of the Spanish government. They knew that the queen was not in the coach, and their high sense of honor, despite your comments, Luke, would prevent them breaking the cease-fire and the safe conduct that we have received," added Roberto.

"Then who is behind this?" asked Luke.

"Someone who is fairly ignorant of what has been happening and who thought that by killing the Portuguese queen, he might receive a reward from the Spaniard," continued Roberto.

"A gang of criminals?" suggested Luke.

"Criminals want material rewards. There are so many troops here that a gang would not have risked an assault on the coach. This is more likely the work of a very disaffected person who has a personal vendetta and, having seen the royal coach on the way to the monastery, took the opportunity to attack it on the way back," explained Pero.

"Let's search the area from which the rocks fell. There may be a clue as to the perpetrators of this vile assault," said Roberto.

Luke, Roberto, and Pero, accompanied by six troopers, made their way to the top of the gorge. It was clear that many of the boulders had been removed from their original resting place and relocated on the edge of the gorge, where they were ready to be more easily pushed over the edge. Some boulders had been placed slightly down the slope so that when those behind were pushed, they knocked together, creating an effective avalanche.

As they searched along the ridge, a man staggered out from behind some bushes. He was bleeding profusely.

Roberto asked, "What happened to you?"

The man replied simply, "I was shot."

"Why were you shot?" Roberto continued.

"Because when Mendo refused to pay us, I suggested we all leave."

Luke intervened. "Mendo Zoritas?"

"Yes."

"How did you come be involved with that madman?" Luke asked.

"We work for his father. Mendo returned to the family home early yesterday and said he had been beaten up by marauding Portuguese, and he appealed to our Spanish honor to assist him in an act of revenge."

"Did he have a specific act in mind?"

"Yes. He said that on his way home, he had seen a coach with the coat of arms of the Portuguese queen heading for the monastery of San Juan. He assumed that it would return by the quickest route and would have to pass through this series of gorges. If we could smash that coach and kill the occupant, it would be ample revenge."

"So you agreed to assist him?" asked Pero.

"The young Mendo is a hothead and probably a little mad. I suggested that he contact the Spanish authorities to approve this course of action. He said there was not enough time, and to persuade us to join him, he offered to pay us two pieces of silver each. We had almost finished preparing a man-made avalanche when one of our number who had to go earlier to the Zoritas manor returned and told us that Mendo had no money and that his father's steward had ordered us to desist in assisting him and return home. I was informing the men of this when he shot me and threatened the same to anyone else who argued against him."

"Surely, combined, you could have dealt with him," said a cynical Luke.

"The men who had Mendo's pistol trained on them were scared, although several managed to disappear."

"Where is Mendo now?" continued Luke.

"He has either gone home or, more likely, to Castle Passos to brag that he has killed the queen of Portugal—and seeks a massive reward."

"If he has gone to Castle Passos, he will never leave. If he tells the authorities what he has done, he will be immediately incarcerated for breaking the cease-fire and causing the Spanish authorities serious embarrassment. If he boasts of killing the queen, he will be charged with murder," explained Pero.

"As will you, my man," added Roberto.

"Did the coach passengers die?"

"Yes, one is dead and another barely alive," answered Luke.

"Was the queen the one who died?"

Pero da Silva declared, "That, we will not tell you. We will go to Castle Passos and formally complain about the breach of the cease-fire and an attempt to kill our queen. You will get medical help there, and if Mendo has been fool enough to go there boasting, we will ensure he never leaves."

As the Portuguese cavalcade approached Castle Passos, the sound of cornets and drums could be heard, putting the Spanish base on alert. Pero and Roberto decided to flaunt their status and openly adopt the posture of disgruntled victims.

On approaching the main gate, which was closed, Pero announced himself as a marquess and Portuguese minister of war and Roberto as heir to the largest duchy in Portugal. They wished to register their complaint concerning an unprovoked attack during a cease-fire and a clear breach of their safe-conduct pass. The gate was opened just wide enough for a tall Spanish nobleman to emerge.

"They are serious claims, gentlemen. I am Federico Sanchez, governor of Castle Passos and general commanding all Spanish troops within this province. Welcome!"

The gates were fully opened, and the Portuguese convoy entered the castle grounds. The general led Luke, Roberto, and Pero to his quarters, where they partook of a range of delicacies and drank light local red wine.

Pero detailed what had happened. General Sanchez was surprisingly blunt.

"Mendo Zoritas has been a disgrace to his Estremaduran heritage. His father is not much better. Thank god that family will soon be out of my jurisdiction. They will, in a short time, move farther north."

Luke was about to question Sanchez further but picked up on the disapproving glance from Pero, who was determined to keep the confrontation nonpolitical.

"What do you wish me to do?" Sanchez asked.

"As one of our number is dead and a second close to it, I would like Mendo tracked down and summarily executed," suggested Roberto.

"There will be many settlers to the west of here who will be delighted if Mendo Zoritas is removed from the scene. I have serious doubts regarding the man's sanity," confessed Sanchez.

As if to prove the veracity of Sanchez's last remark, an orderly entered the room and announced, "There is a Mendo Zoritas who wishes to speak to you, urgently bringing great news to the glory of Spain."

Sanchez suggested the visitors withdraw to the adjoining antechamber, where they would be able to hear every word. A highly elated if not agitated Mendo burst into the room and, before Sanchez could speak, declaimed, "I have just killed the queen of Portugal. What is the reward?"

Sanchez feigned ignorance and then disbelief. "You have murdered a Spanish-born monarch during a period of a cease-fire, precisely when she was traveling in my area under a safe-conduct pass signed by the cardinal archbishop of Toledo and myself. Your actions killed at least one Portuguese courtier but fortunately not the queen. You stand confessed by your own mouth of murder in circumstances that are reprehensible and unforgivable."

Mendo was shocked, "They are an enemy that have risen against our catholic monarch Felipe IV. I demand a reward!"

"I will not waste the time of the judges. You will have an immediate reward. You will be taken into the castle courtyard at once—and shot."

Sanchez summoned a couple of soldiers who grabbed Mendo and dragged him screaming from the room. The three visitors rejoined Sanchez. Roberto asked, "Will he be shot?"

"Before you leave this room, he will be dead."

Luke admired the attitude and actions of this Spanish general. He had said little because of his lack of Spanish and was surprised when Sanchez turned toward him and, in perfect, English said, "Luke Tremayne, friend and envoy of the Lord Protector of England, you do not recognize me?" He turned to the Portuguese nobles and explained, "Ten years ago, Tremayne and I were on the same side. We were both in Ireland, concerned with a missing treasure of silver that our king had sent to the Irish rebels to help prevent an English conquest of their island. I was sent to deal with a high-ranking cleric who had misappropriated the king's silver, and Tremayne was there to find it before us and redirect it to Cromwell's campaign of conquest."

Luke commented, "I would not recognize you. Ten years is a long time, and if I remember correctly, all our meetings were in the dark."

Roberto, who was interested in the events outlined, asked, "And what happened to the silver?"

Sanchez replied, "We managed to execute the treacherous cleric, but Tremayne found the silver. I know you will not tell me, but I wonder what devilish scheme the protector has up his sleeve in sending you to our borders. We know your cover story of assessing how many English troops are needed on the frontiers to sustain Portuguese resistance, but you do not need a highly experienced and high-ranking intelligence officer to do that."

"Nothing sinister, I assure you. I have been promoted out of intelligence into diplomacy and just happened to put into Lisbon after a period in North Africa."

Everybody else in the room smiled a knowing smile. The silence was broken by the sound of several musket shots, fired in unison, echoing up from the castle courtyard. Mendo Zoritas would cause no further trouble. As Sanchez had raised political issues, Luke returned to his unasked question earlier in the meeting. "Where are you sending Mendo's father?"

Sanchez cleverly sidestepped the real import of the question. "I have sent him deeper into Estremadura to recruit settlers."

"For recaptured Portuguese territory?" commented an alarmed Roberto.

"Not at all, viscount. Too much of Spain just north of here is poorly utilized. More intensive farming is possible and denser settlement necessary to achieve it. Richer soils and plenty of water will attract the poor pastoralists of this province."

"Denser population will also provide a military advantage, making it more difficult to dislodge a Spanish presence," muttered Pero.

Sanchez changed the subject. "I will be informed officially eventually, but I gather your meeting with the cardinal archbishop achieved nothing."

"Your side wanted a bit of tinkering at the borders until they are strong enough to invade in force, and we wanted nothing less than the recognition of our independence. Yes, it achieved nothing except the possible death of one of our noblewomen, the baroness Albuquerque," replied Pero.

"Unfortunate! But why was she in the queen's coach in the first place?" asked Sanchez.

"Our queen had her reasons," remarked Pero.

"Well, at least that meeting cleared the air from my point of view," confessed Federico. "The cardinal archbishop will return to Toledo and Madrid, and we locals can implement policies that are necessary—without central interference. You are welcome to stay the night."

Pero thanked Sanchez but intimated that they were anxious to reach Magellan as soon as possible to discover the condition of the baroness. Luke informed Sanchez that one of the men who had stood up to Mendo and assisted them was receiving medical treatment in the castle and hoped that the governor could see his way clear to allow the man to return to his home unpunished.

"An agent must always protect his informants," joked Sanchez as he shook Luke's hand.

As the Portuguese convoy made its way toward Magellan in growing darkness, Roberto commented, "You got on very well with that Spanish general."

"Yes, he is man after my own heart. His immediate execution of Mendo is exactly what I would have done. In his early days, he must have carried out many an execution on behalf of the Spanish state. It is always an advantage to know the opponent you face. Knowing our immediate enemy is Sanchez will certainly alter my approach to our next engagement."

27

PERO REPORTED IMMEDIATELY TO the queen, while Roberto and Luke headed for Madalena's apartment for an update on her condition. A guard at the door indicated that her husband Diego had banned any visitors. They had just turned away when the door opened, and Alfredo Matos emerged.

The army surgeon looked exhausted but was pleased to see Luke, who immediately asked, "How is she?"

"Not good but still alive. Let's get a drink, and I will bring you up to date."

The three men headed for the refectory, where an ample range of local wine was always available.

Matos asked, "What exactly happened to the baroness? I was only told that her carriage had overturned."

"It was smashed by a man-made avalanche of large boulders," replied Luke.

"That explains her injuries. They are identical to that of soldiers on the battlefield hit by cannonballs. Her bones have been crushed in many places. One leg is definitely broken in several places. Her arms and ribs have been badly damaged. She is still unconscious, which enabled us to effect some remedial manipulation without inflicting excruciating pain on her. At the best, she will walk with a limp and may lose the use of one arm. My big fear is that as her head is badly bruised, when she comes out of her current comatose state, her mind may be seriously affected. She may be reduced to the level of an idiot and may not be able to speak."

"If that be the case, it would be better if she were dead," said Luke with tears running down his face.

"How is Diego reacting to this?" asked Roberto.

"Coldly. I know he is seeking an annulment, but he displayed no emotion when his wife's body was brought to the apartment. He made no attempt to hold her hand or offer other acts of affection either before or after we had finished treating her."

"Was the queen informed?"

"Not immediately. No one knew the queen was still here. We all thought she had returned to Lisbon. Father Antonio was told of Madalena's condition, and he informed the hidden queen, who immediately came to Madalena's apartment. She was acutely aware that it could have been her in that overturned coach. She now carries considerable guilt over the matter."

As the men drank, Peter entered the refectory. Alfredo said he must give the queen an update on Madalena's condition, and Roberto, who lived within the queen's apartment, left with him, leaving the two English officers alone.

"The news of your adventure is all over the barracks. Did someone try to assassinate the queen? Why was the baroness Madalena in her coach?" asked Peter.

Luke explained in detail what had occurred. Peter was delighted that Mendo Zoritas had finally been dealt with. Luke made several favorable remarks concerning the local Spanish commander whom he explained he had met ten years earlier in Ireland.

"Sanchez is a very able man. Whatever Spain is planning regarding the annexation of Portuguese land, I am sure the driving force and organizer of such an enterprise is the local command and not distant Madrid. What has happened here in my absence?" he asked.

"The high table has been almost deserted. The queen—with the baroness Madalena, we thought—had returned to Lisbon. The four Costas and two Ciprianos had gone to Estrella to bury Joana and finalize the transfer of power to Rodrigo. Pinto had taken the body of his wife home. Da Silva, Delgado, and yourself had disappeared on a secret mission. The only people appearing for supper were Beatrix da Silva, Diego de Albuquerque, Alfredo Matos, Generals Caro and De Mota, De Mota's wife, Camilla, and Father Antonio."

"What about our partner Ramiro de Lima?"

"He disappeared about the same time as you did. He has not yet reappeared."

"Despite the absence of so many people, did you uncover anything that will help us solve the murders and locate the traitor?"

"Caro doesn't seem to have time to be a traitor. He spent most of the time Pero da Silva was away with the minister's wife."

"Anything else?"

"Yes, Camilla de Mota has disappeared into Spain—without her husband. When Father Antonio chided her, before she left, she replied haughtily that if it was good enough for that Spanish traitor, the Duke of Medina-Sidonia, to visit his sister the queen of Portugal, it was reasonable for her to visit her relative, the Spanish commander-in-chief, the Duke of Medinaceli."

"That is interesting. He was obviously present at our meeting at the monastery of San Juan, although he was never introduced. I am gathering the impression that the government of Spain in Madrid is seeking peace in all parts of the empire, including the Portuguese frontier, whereas local commanders such as Sanchez want to continue a more aggressive policy."

"What's been happening militarily? Hostilities resume in a few days."

"Caro believes that there is no point in occupying land that the Spaniards withdraw from and which they will soon reenter when Portuguese troops withdraw. He is arguing for an all-out assault on a major Spanish town, which, when taken, can be defended. Diego, not anxious to make any decisions in the absence of so many, preferred to concentrate on a possible abduction as a symbolic act that would not lose many lives. The council awaited the return of the minister, yourself, and Roberto, whose infantry militia Caro had targeted for the offensive. You meet first thing in the morning."

The meeting began with Pero in the chair with Luke, Peter, Diego, Roberto, Matos, Caro, and Mota present. Ramiro's absence was still not explained. Caro outlined his plan for the coming renewal of hostilities.

Suddenly, the door was flung open, and two heavily armed soldiers entered the room, followed by Queen Luisa. She signaled for them to stay seated and announced, "This meeting is ended! General Caro, there will be no further offensives in this local area. You are to organize my army in such a way that this garrison will be adequately manned to resist any possible attack, but all other troops, including the two militia regiments, are to be ready to be deployed anywhere else in my kingdom. Da Silva, Delgado, and Tremayne, follow me!"

The queen turned and strode out of the room, followed by the named officers. On entering the queen's apartment, they found seated at the queen's desk a very elderly cleric, who looked decidedly unwell.

She explained, "This gentleman was, for two decades, chaplain to my cousin the late Joana da Costa, Marchioness of Estrela. He carried throughout that period letters between us, maintaining absolute secrecy. He left Estrela just before the start of the Feast of Our Lady with a letter for me but was turned back by the floods. He returned to Estrela just before the family moved here. Joana replaced the letter he had with an updated epistle. She told Father Francisco she hoped to discuss its contents with me here, but should anything happen to her, the information contained within it must get to me. As you know, she had previously alerted me to the fact that I might be in danger from those close to me, and given her situation, it cast doubt on the loyalty of the Da Costa clan—but whom? Paola, Rodrigo, Micaela, or Alvaro? A member of the royal council, my senior lady-in-waiting, or my head of intelligence? And was this potential Da Costa conspiracy in any way related to the leak of critical information to our enemy?"

"And does the latest letter tell us more than we already know?" asked Luke in almost perfect Portuguese.

"Not as to the exact source of the danger, but it certainly explains Joana's death. Let me read the relevant passages.

> One of my servants who speaks Spanish overheard two of the Spanish officers who came to see Paolo comment that while Paolo was intractable, his successor would be much more easily persuaded. When the other officer remarked that Paolo was reasonably young and may not die for decades, the first officer replied that he had just discovered an interesting and very useful piece of information that might speed up the process of succession. This was our

agreement that if I died first, Paolo would renounce his title and estates and enter a monastery.

"Tremayne, you thought that Joana was murdered because she overheard the details of a plan. Now it appears that she may have been murdered as the first stage in that plan," declared the astute queen.

Delgado spoke. "I am new to this situation. What exactly was the offer that Paolo refused?"

The queen replied, "That the marquess renounce his loyalty to the house of Braganza and pledge obedience and fealty to the Habsburgs, returning a vast segment of current Portugal back into Spanish hands."

"And what was to be the reward?" continued Delgado.

"The marquess would be made a duke and given a place on the Spanish council of state," the queen replied.

Delgado muttered, "Micaela would certainly covet being a duchess."

"How are we to approach this?" asked Pero. "Rodrigo, Alvaro, and Micaela may be completely innocent. Is there a shred of evidence in any way suggesting any of them have even been approached with such an offer, let alone have accepted it?"

"Your Majesty, in terms of your own safety, all three should be stood down from their current positions and either placed under house arrest or very closely monitored," advised Luke.

"If you do that, it will alert a potential traitor that something is afoot. It may make it more difficult to discover further information," said Delgado.

"Why not extend the current temporary suspension from their duties to give them time to grieve for Joana and to effect the transfer of lands and titles? That should not arouse their suspicions and give us time to investigate further," suggested Luke.

"I sent Ramiro de Lima and his men to Estrela ahead of the Costa's return, ostensibly to protect the family as many of the household servants were here as part of the local militia but, in reality, to spy out the situation."

Pero commented, "Any such declaration by the Da Costas of a change of allegiance is not uncommon in recent years. Her Majesty and her husband, John, renounced Habsburg sovereignty over most of Portugal. At the same time, her brother, the Duke of Medina-Sidonia, who was recently here, did the same for the southern province of Andalusia but failed. There are others in Catalonia at the moment who want to transfer their allegiance to the Bourbons of France. Many of the border aristocracy on both sides of the current frontier are periodically tempted. We should not treat it as a rare event but as a commonplace possibility in border areas."

Suddenly, the elderly priest gurgled and slumped forward.

Luke moved forward and inspected the inert body and, after some time, announced, "He is dead."

A tear ran down the face of the queen. She was about to dismiss the gathering when, following a loud knock, two soldiers followed by Ramiro burst in.

"Forgive this intrusion, Your Majesty. I have ridden nonstop from Estrela. The new marquess, Rodrigo da Costa, is dead."

"How?" asked Luke.

"Same way as Joana and Teresa—strangled."

"Who inherits the lands and title now?" asked Delgado.

"Alvaro," answered Luke.

"So Micaela was marchioness for a few days at the most. The loss of the title will mean more to her than the loss of her husband," commented Delgado.

Luke had picked up on Roberto's references to Micaela. What did they signify? Had Delgado's attitude to his ex-lover turned into antagonism or was it a ploy to conceal the opposite feelings.

The body of the elderly priest was taken from the room under the supervision of Father Antonio. The concerned queen asked Ramiro to expound on his dramatic news.

"The Costas buried Joana in the family crypt within the chapel, and Paolo took Rodrigo on a tour of the castle. Paolo then told the family that he was departing immediately for the monastery of his choice and that Rodrigo and Micaela were, from that moment, the undisputed owners of the titles and estates of Estrela. He took over an hour to say farewell to his staff, and then, unaccompanied, he rode out of the castle for the last time.

"Micaela asked me to have supper with them that night. When I arrived for supper, the great hall was empty except for one small table at the far end, at which Micaela, Alvaro, Carlos, and Ana Cipriano were already seated. There was a vacancy at the head of the table for Rodrigo and, on the side next to Ana Cipriano, for myself. After waiting for some time, I volunteered to find Rodrigo.

"I did. He was sitting in the large favorite chair of the former marquess. He had placed it so that he could view much of the immediate estate through a large double window. He had his back to the door and was obviously enjoying some fine red wine. The killer must have crept up behind him and strangled him. The goblet fell from his hand and spilled wine over his clothes and the floor. There was no sign of a struggle."

28

"**W**HAT DID YOU DO on discovering the body?" asked the queen.

"There was no priest or doctor at Estrela, so I had the room closed off and mounted guards, forbidding Cipriano's staff from dressing and preparing the body for burial. I left Alvaro and Micaela comforting each other, sent a man after Paolo in case, given the circumstances, he wished to return, and then rode through the night here."

"I will return immediately with you to Estrela," said the queen.

"Is that wise, Your Majesty? There is a killer at Estrela. Return to Lisbon and leave the Estrela situation to Ramiro," counselled Pero.

"And a coach would not make it by any direct route from here to Estrela," added Ramiro.

"Her Majesty no longer has a coach at Magellan. It was destroyed by an old friend of yours, Mendo Zoritas, and in the process, the baroness Albuquerque was seriously injured," explained Luke.

"I will ride to Estrela with a troop of my personal guard, Viscount Delgado, the two English officers, the surgeon Matos, and Father Antonio. Pero, you and Diego will return to Lisbon and assemble a full meeting of my council to act as the government in my absence."

"Rodrigo was a member of your council, but is your visit to Estrela really necessary?" asked a worried Roberto, agreeing with Pero.

"Three people close to me—my cousin Joana, a lady-in-waiting, Countess Teresa, and now a member of my council, Marquess Rodrigo da Costa—have been murdered. Accepting the advice of our English friend

Tremayne that these murders are the work of the same person who, by this latest report, is active at Estrela, I want to supervise a thorough investigation, culminating hopefully in uncovering the monster behind these acts. Micaela da Costa has been my faithful servant and closest confidante for many years, and I wish to be near her at this time of loss. In recent weeks, because of certain suspicions, we have not been as close as usual. Also, if certain rumors are to be believed, the Spaniards may attempt to seize the Estrela estates at any time. Finally, I can claim I am inspecting property that—if the new marquess, Alvaro da Costa, does not produce a male heir—reverts to the crown on his death. My immediate visit to Estrela is essential for all these reasons."

"I seek leave for Diego that he be permitted to stay here until his wife is fit enough to travel," requested Pero.

"No. Leave is denied. There are many more qualified physicians and surgeons in Lisbon. Madalena must be taken there immediately as there has been no improvement in her condition," answered the queen somewhat abruptly.

The queen, on her arrival, immediately took control of Castle Estrela. She indicated that Ramiro would be responsible for the security of all those in the castle. The castle was deemed a crime scene, and she ordered Ramiro and Luke to investigate Rodrigo's death. Alfredo Matos had returned primarily in his role as a surgeon to examine Rodrigo's body and Fr. Antonio Mendes to conduct the funeral service.

Alvaro's first sentence immediately aroused Luke's suspicions. "Your Majesty, while the presence of your bodyguard and Lord Ramiro's troops are welcomed in the immediate circumstances, the return of the local militia, which contains many of the castle's servants, would be appreciated as soon as possible."

"Do not worry, Alvaro. You are a long way from the border, and in the event of trouble, our troops from Magellan and Lisbon could be here very quickly to protect you," the queen replied with obvious relish.

Luke whispered to Ramiro, "You cannot hand over your estates to Spain if you do not have troops on the ground to deal with recalcitrant tenants who won't go along with you. Do you think the queen is issuing him with a subtle warning?"

She continued, "Alvaro, in the circumstances, you are to remain suspended as my head of intelligence until further notice. Pero da Silva will act in that role until matters settle down. In any case, as the new master of Estrela, you may not wish to return to Lisbon and your former employment. If you have any relevant recent information, pass it on to Lord Ramiro. Are you keeping Cipriano and Matos in their current positions in the short term?"

"For the moment. I will discuss their futures in due course," Alvaro replied.

Cipriano, despite the absence of so many servants and tenants, had the household accommodating the visitors and running effectively within twenty-four hours of their arrival. His wife, Ana, acted as the queen's only lady-in-waiting.

Ramiro and Luke decided to question Cipriano to determine where everybody was in the hours leading up to Rodrigo's murder.

"The household were all together to bid Paolo farewell at about three in the afternoon and then again at supper around eight. Where were you during the five-hour gap?" asked Luke.

"I was everywhere in the castle and its surrounds, checking that we were operating once again as well as we could with the absence of so many staff. Ramiro and I ran into each other many times during that period. There would be one staff member or another who could vouch for my presence during all that time," replied a confident Cipriano.

"When you have time, give us a list detailing your activity at specific times. We would like to eliminate you from our inquiry as soon as possible," continued Luke.

"During this period, did you see Rodrigo, Micaela, Alvaro, or your wife?" asked Ramiro.

"Immediately after Paolo's departure, Rodrigo and Micaela moved to the respective areas of the castle that had been exclusively Paolo's and Joana's. I never saw Rodrigo alive again and did not see Micaela until we came together for supper—but my wife may be able to tell you more concerning the new marchioness. Alvaro is a different matter. He lingered at the stables and had a long discussion with the grooms. He was still there when I passed by on two or three later occasions—"

Ramiro interrupted. "My men remarked on that as well."

Cipriano continued, "Then I saw him later in the corridor near Micaela's apartment and just before supper back at the stables. There is another piece of information concerning Rodrigo. About an hour and a half before supper, he sent one of servants into the castle's cellar for a very expensive bottle of red wine. The servant, used to Paolo's abstemious ways, came to me to see if it was acceptable to take such a wine to the new master. I told him that Rodrigo was the new master, and he should hasten to bring the marquess his wine. Rodrigo was still alive an hour and a half before supper."

Luke thanked Cipriano and asked him to send them the servant who had taken the wine to Rodrigo.

Ramiro stopped Cipriano leaving. "Chamberlain, before you go, where did you all spend the night following the discovery of Rodrigo's body after I left for Magellan?"

"With little to do in the situation, Ana and I retired almost immediately to our bedchamber."

"What about Micaela and Alvaro? When I left, they were consoling each other," asked Ramiro.

"Because I retired when you left, I have no knowledge of what the former marchioness and new marquess did."

"No direct evidence, but the servants would have been agog with those two spending the night together immediately following the death of their husband and brother," asked Luke, guessing what may have occurred.

Cipriano appeared uneasy and admitted, "I did hear rumors to that effect."

"What was their mood the following morning?" Luke probed.

"They both appeared distraught, which I attributed to the death of Rodrigo, not the result of any nocturnal activity or discussion."

"Could they have been arguing throughout the night?" asked Ramiro.

"There is no way I can answer that question. I will send you the servant who brought Rodrigo his wine."

The elderly servant was delighted to see Ramiro, who later explained to Luke that the man had, decades earlier, been his father's servant.

Luke asked, "Were you specifically summoned to Rodrigo's room regarding the request for the bottle of expensive wine?"

"Yes."

"When you entered the room, was Rodrigo seated behind his desk or on the chair placed near the window?"

"He was behind the desk, and he asked me to move the chair to the window, which I did."

"Did he give any indication as to why he wanted that bottle before supper?"

The servant's answer astounded Luke and Ramiro. "Yes, he wanted to share a celebratory drink with his brother before supper. Given that, when I returned with the bottle, I also placed two silver goblets on the desk."

"Two silver goblets?" repeated Luke.

"Yes."

"There was only one goblet on the floor when I found the body," said Ramiro.

Luke probed further. "Did you see Colonel da Costa as you left the marquess?"

"No."

After the servant left, Ramiro commented, "It is not looking too good for Alvaro."

"I never picked up any antagonism between the brothers that would lead to fratricide," said Luke.

"Let's question Alvaro immediately," said Ramiro.

"Send one of your men to find him. While we wait, let's question the women," proposed Luke.

As a matter of courtesy, the two officers sought permission to attend Micaela in her apartment.

Luke began the questioning. "Between bidding farewell to Paolo and meeting for supper, a period of five hours, what did you do?"

"For an hour or so, I was so overwhelmed with the honor of becoming the Marchioness of Estrela and rising several ranks within the Portuguese nobility, I just sat in my apartment, meditating on my good fortune."

"Surely, this did not last for five hours," said Ramiro.

"No. I soon realized that as mistress of such a vast estate and large castle, I was totally ignorant of my duties. I asked Ana de Cipriano, who had been the confidante of the previous marchioness, to give me the advice I needed. We talked for more than two hours until we both changed for supper."

"During this period, were you interrupted?" pressed Ramiro.

Micaela hesitated—a brief second that Luke did not miss.

"No," she eventually replied. "Why do you ask?"

Luke lied. "We have been told that your brother-in-law, Alvaro, visited you."

"Whoever told you that lied, but I can understand the mistake. When Ana arrived, she said she had seen Alvaro in the corridor, but he never visited me."

"Have you spoken to Alvaro since the death of your husband?" said Ramiro.

"Yes, at length this morning."

"More like the whole night, according to our sources. Alvaro spent the night with you," declaimed Luke.

"That may have been true, but we spent the whole time talking."

"Concerning what?" asked Luke.

"Much of it very personal, largely lamenting my loss and his self-perceived inadequacies for the position."

"Nothing more specific?"

"He, a bachelor, did make the magnanimous offer that I could stay here indefinitely as the dowager marchioness."

"Will you accept?"

"I have to discuss the situation with the queen and weigh the advantages and disadvantages of being a lady-in-waiting at the center of power or a rural dowager marchioness. Alvaro's offer could not last forever. The queen has made it clear that he must marry and beget a male child, or the estate will be lost to the family."

"How is Alvaro taking his sudden and unexpected advancement?" asked Luke.

"He is a little lost—and overwhelmed."

"How has he taken the death of his brother?"

"Badly. They were very close."

"Now that is not true. We have had several reports from different sources that the brothers have been estranged since Alvaro's alleged affair with yourself, which may still be continuing," Ramiro announced bluntly.

Micaela bristled, "In recent times, rumors have spread that I was having an affair with Roberto Delgado, Alvaro da Costa, and even the queen herself. It stems from anti-French feeling provoked by my closeness to Her Majesty."

Luke was far from convinced. Micaela's evidence was a mixture of half-truths, outright lies, and obvious concealments. Luke could not help feeling that the answer to Rodrigo's murder might lie in the desire of Alvaro for his sister-in-law—and in her possible complicity in the plot.

29

T HE SOLDIER SENT TO bring Alvaro to his interview with Ramiro and Luke returned alone.

"Where's Colonel da Costa?" asked Ramiro.

"Gone" was the unhelpful reply.

Ramiro glared at his man, who was ultimately provoked into expounding on his answer.

"I don't know where, but he was seen leaving the castle and heading up the mountain on the track that leads to the border."

"When was this?" queried Luke.

"Just now. I saw him myself."

"He is heading into Spain to finalize his treacherous deal," Luke concluded.

"We must follow him. It may be our only chance to catch him red-handed," suggested Ramiro.

"How many men should we take with us?" asked Luke.

"None. He would quickly realize that he was being followed by a troop of dragoons. I am pretty good at tracking animals—and humans. Just you and me."

It was dark as they left the castle alone. Only Peter knew of their plan with orders to inform the queen—but only if she asked. There was little need for Ramiro's tracking skills during the night hours. There was only one track over the mountain so that their quarry could not diverge from his assumed path. Nevertheless, as the sun rose and they emerged from the mountain forest, they were relieved to see a lone horseman moving along the valley floor.

As the horseman passed a major crossroad and continued south, Luke commented, "That is a surprise. He could have turned east into Spain, but he is continuing toward Magellan."

"That is a disappointment. There can be a host of legitimate reasons as to why he is returning to the barracks," added Ramiro dolefully.

The two men reached Magellan around noon and immediately reported to its commanding officer, General Caro.

Caro was relaxed. "What have I done to deserve this, a visit from three people of whom I thought I had seen the last?"

Ramiro pretended ignorance. "Three people? There are only two of us."

Caro gave the officers a knowing look. "Ramiro, I have known you for years. You are either part of whatever Colonel da Costa is up to or following him to find out what his secret is."

"And what did Alvaro tell you he was up to?" asked Luke.

"Why should the commander-in-chief of the Portuguese army reveal confidential information regarding the country's head of intelligence to a foreign officer and a local bandit?" asked Caro only half-jokingly.

"Because Alvaro is no longer the intelligence chief, and we have direct authorization from the queen herself to act in any way we see fit to secure the borders of the country, unearth one or more traitors, and solve three murders," Luke responded.

"Is Alvaro part of your team, or is he a suspect?" probed the astute Caro.

"He was once central to our team—but he is now a suspect," said Ramiro with surprising honesty.

Luke was more cautious. "We must follow up on every lead. Does it not seem suspicious to you that the end result of two suspicious deaths is that Alvaro succeeds to the marquisate of Estrela and then immediately heads into Spain, with whom Portugal has just resumed hostilities? Who benefits from the death of Joana and Rodrigo? It is clearly Alvaro."

"No, that's a very prejudiced conclusion. These deaths could conversely be part of a vendetta against the Da Costas. The family's Jewish ancestry is constantly held against them—and not only by deranged inquisitors. My family has suffered similar discrimination and antagonism. The power that the Da Costa family wields provokes inexplicable hatred. Alvaro may be the next victim rather than your prime suspect," argued Caro with clear conviction.

"You raise an interesting point. At one stage, I thought that Joana had been murdered by supporters of Teresa Pinto, who, in turn, had been murdered in a vengeance killing by the Da Costas. She hated the Da Costas and is now dead—murdered. Did the Da Costas have her removed?" asked Luke provocatively.

"That seems to be your problem, gentlemen. I only have to protect the country militarily" was Caro's lighthearted reply.

"Why did Alvaro come here? Who did he speak to?" asked Ramiro.

"Only me, and he asked only one question—my latest information regarding the disposition of Spanish troops across the frontier, especially the location of the Spanish general Federico Sanchez."

"And your answer?"

"My reports have dried up. The latest was days old and placed Sanchez still at Castle Passos."

"How did he respond?"

"He was disappointed but indicated he knew of another possible source of relevant information. He left the castle about fifteen minutes before you arrived."

"And we know where he is headed," replied Ramiro. "One of his best agents is just across the border in Corba and has regular access to Castle Passos."

As Luke and Ramiro trotted out of Magellan and took the shortest route they knew to Corba, Luke commented, "This looks increasingly like a major conspiracy against the Portuguese state. We know Nicodemo is a double agent. Maybe his real loyalty is to Spain and he is a major participant in Alvaro's treachery."

"Even worse, Nicodemo may be the mastermind behind this enterprise to transfer large areas of Portugal to Spain rather than Barbosa. Nicodemo could come and go across the border even more easily than Colonel Barbosa and carry out negotiations without arousing suspicion," added Ramiro.

"I have a lot of time for Father Nicodemo. I hope you are wrong," muttered Luke.

It was late in the afternoon when they reached the outskirts of the village.

"What do we do?" asked Luke. "Alvaro is probably with Nicodemo. It is too late for them to go anywhere today. We need to remain concealed."

"We can visit Marabella Gomes and shelter in her house," suggested Ramiro.

"No. She is too close to Nicodemo. If he is part of, if not leader of, the Spanish conspiracy, we do not want him to know we are here. We will sleep in the forest. Let's hope it does not rain."

The next morning, they quickly realized that they could not remain concealed and, at the same time, keep an eye on Nicodemo's house and any movements out of the village. Luke remembered that a little way up the mountain track from which Mendo had fallen was a clearing from which one had a good view of the village yet remained completely concealed from the villagers.

Not long after they arrived at the clearing, they saw movement in the village. A parishioner brought two horses to the hitching rail outside of Nicodemo's house, and within minutes, the priest and Alvaro appeared, mounted the horses, and headed out of the village in the general direction of Castle Passos.

Luke and Ramiro descended the mountain and went immediately to the home of Marabella Gomes.

She was pleased to see them, lamenting, "You have missed Father Nicodemo and Colonel da Costa. They have just left. They said nothing about expecting you."

"It is a pity we have missed them. We had hoped to talk to them before they departed for Castle Passos."

Marabella looked bemused. "There must have been a change of plan. I cook for the priest and was with them most of the early evening. There was no talk of going to Castle Passos. They were going to Toledo to finalize the transfer of some lands between Spain and Portugal. When he was at the monastery of San Juan, Father Nicodemo had several conversations with the cardinal archbishop. I assumed that Colonel da Costa is representing the queen of Portugal in these land negotiations."

"Yes," lied Luke. "The colonel is a very important man. He is now the Marquess of Estrela and owns most of the land just across the border and well into the mountains."

"If you hurry, you will catch them just beyond the first crossroad," replied Marabella.

It was Ramiro's turn to lie. "No, my dear, we have come only to ensure that the colonel and Father Nicodemo have begun their trek into deepest Spain. We shall not follow them on this very important and secret trip."

"I don't know how secret it is. For weeks, the whole village has been convinced it will be the major beneficiary of this mission."

"In what way?"

"Father Nicodemo said it was dangerous to speculate until everything was in place."

"So Nicodemo thought that whatever he and the colonel are up to, it would benefit the village?"

"Yes, Nicodemo was very pleased with whatever he is about to achieve."

Luke and Ramiro decided to return directly to Castle Estrela. They were not equipped for a long journey into Spain and had decided that following Nicodemo and Alvaro would not add greatly to their basic incriminating information—a now wealthy Portuguese border aristocrat was negotiating with the Spanish chancellor, the cardinal archbishop of Toledo, regarding the transfer of land.

Ramiro and Luke's return to Portugal was halted immediately after they left Marabella's house. The village was swarming with Spanish troops, and advancing toward Luke and Ramiro, having just left the house of Father Nicodemo, was the Spanish commander. This was no routine Spanish patrol. Luke estimated that it was a full company of cavalry, and it was led by the commander-in-chief himself, General Sanchez.

"Well, well, well," commented the Spaniard. "We came to arrest a devious priest, and we find a Portuguese officer and an English general. You are now formally my prisoners as the cease-fire ended yesterday morning. What are you doing here?"

Ramiro, adept at playing a role, started laughing. "Incredible! We are here for the same reason—to arrest that treacherous priest Nicodemo Oliveira. We have long known he was a double agent, but until recently, he convinced our government his ultimate loyalty lay with them. We now have information to the contrary, and because he was privy to some of our secrets, we were asked to escort him back across the frontier to be dealt with."

"But he was gone when we arrived," lied Luke.

"And you have not been able to find where he went?" asked Sanchez, not expecting a reply.

"Yes, we have, and it confirms our assessment of the priest's Spanish loyalty. He is going to meet with the cardinal archbishop of Toledo, King Felipe's right-hand man," answered Ramiro.

Sanchez seemed taken aback by this information.

Luke continued his lying. "He has gone to thank the Spanish authorities for removing the Zoritas as landlords of his parish."

Sanchez seemed even more unhappy with such a comment. "The priest is confused. The eventual removal of the Zoritas is part of my local policy. The central administration is probably completely ignorant of it. All Nicodemo had to do was to thank me on his next visit to Castle Passos. What made you suspicious of him?"

Again, Luke lied. "We discovered that his true loyalty was not to Portugal nor to the Spanish state but to the Spanish Inquisition. It is lucky you did not find him. Any mistreatment of a favorite agent of the Inquisition would have been the end of your career."

"Maybe, but for the time being, my career will be enhanced by my capture of an English general of high renown. I am freeing you, Ramiro, to return to your queen and inform her that for the ransom of fifty thousand ducats and the return of ten loads of stolen arms and ammunition, General Tremayne will be released."

"No, Federico, that will destroy your career. You were not present at the meeting at the monastery of San Juan, but Tremayne was specifically instructed by the cardinal archbishop as a matter of urgency to deliver a personal message from Felipe IV to Oliver Cromwell," said Ramiro.

Luke was about to ask why the local commander-in-chief was not at that meeting but thought it might not help his cause.

Sanchez was inwardly seething. He had been excluded from that meeting.

He was never informed of Nicodemo's status with the Inquisition nor of his government's use of Luke, and now a local irritating priest was heading for a meeting with one of Spain's most powerful men. He asked Ramiro, "Do you know how long ago the priest left this village?"

Luke suddenly saw an opportunity of stopping Alvaro and Nicodemo. "Apparently less than half an hour ago. Your cavalry should catch them in no time."

Sanchez's reply worried Luke. "Was he alone?"

Luke surprised himself when he answered, "No."

"Do you know who he was with?"

It was Ramiro's turn to lie. "No. It was probably a villager accompanying the priest for protection. The road to Toledo is not free of brigands."

Sanchez was silent for some time but finally announced, "Gentlemen, leave Spanish territory immediately! I will pursue the double-dealing priest. I might even escort him personally to the cardinal archbishop."

30

A S THEY MADE THEIR way to the border, Ramiro asked, "What do you make of all that?"

"One thing is certain—the central government and its local military commander are not working in harmony. I did find it strange that Sanchez was not at the San Juan monastery meeting, and he did seem quite ignorant of Nicodemo's formal role with the Spanish Inquisition," commented Luke.

"Another thing troubles me," continued Luke, "is it more than a coincidence that a treacherous Portuguese nobleman intent on transferring his loyalty to Spain should come to the same village at the same time as the local Spanish military commander? Why did Sanchez ask if Nicodemo was alone?"

"Luke, your view of events stems from your as-yet-unproven premise that Alvaro is a traitor. He may even be on this trip as the senior intelligence officer still acting for Queen Luisa."

"But the queen has removed him from that position," countered Luke.

"Has she? You are a foreigner, and I am a frontier nobleman not highly regarded by the courtiers. Is the queen more likely to confide in the Da Costas and Albuquerques—or in us?"

A now depressed Luke trotted slowly toward the border. After half an hour, he exclaimed, "Damnation! My horse has gone lame. I will have to walk."

"You cannot reach Estrela on foot. We will head for Magellan for new horses. If we are walking, it is shorter to cut through the forest than to keep to the main track," advised Ramiro.

After walking for some time and as the heat of the day increased, the men decided to rest in a clearing and allow their horses to drink at an adjacent stream.

Luke slumped down at the base of a large tree. He suddenly jumped back in alarm. "A snake!"

"Was it black with white markings?"

"No, it was olive."

"Don't panic. Most Portuguese snakes are venomous, but only one is fatal to humans—the black-and-white viper."

"I am particularly wary of snakes. I lost a friend to a viper in the Maghreb and nearly died myself of a snake bite, both incidents only a few months ago," Luke explained, sweating profusely.

"Anything to eat in your saddlebag?" asked a hungry Ramiro, deliberately changing the subject of their discussion.

"No, I expected to gather supplies at Corba, but Nicodemo's departure and the arrival of Sanchez and his men put it out of my mind. Water from the stream and a few berries and nuts will have to suffice until we reach Magellan. I am going to catch up on some of the sleep we missed last night while the temperature peaks."

Luke and Ramiro were both soon asleep, breaking the quiet of the forest with their almost rhythmic snoring.

Sometime later, Luke awoke slowly to a hideous smell and the sensation of a hairy object rubbing his neck—and a nauseating hot breath blowing into his face. The hideous monster of his initial waking thoughts slowly transformed into a large goat who was trying to sample Luke's lace collar. He pushed it away and was surprised to find the clearing overtaken by a small flock of wild goats. Ramiro's continued snoring kept the inquisitive and obviously hungry animals away from his face, although the straps of his leggings were obviously a tasty treat.

The goats suddenly disappeared. Luke eventually heard what the animals had heard much earlier—the sound of gunfire. He ran to his horse, which was grazing at the edge of the stream, retrieved his musket, and proceeded to prime it. He awoke Ramiro and alerted him to potential danger. The sound of the shooting came closer, as did the noise of animals crashing through the forest. Into the clearing came three large wild pigs. One of them lowered its head and, without missing a step, headed straight for Ramiro.

Luke took no chances and fired at the animal as it neared Ramiro, who had drawn his sword just in time to defend himself. The wounded animal veered away at the last minute and disappeared with its companions. Unfortunately, they had spooked the horses, which fled at a gallop. Ramiro was upset.

"We must retrieve our horses quickly. This forest is home to the lynx, and wolves occasionally descend from the north. A pack of wolves would enjoy a meal of horsemeat."

"You claimed to be the great tracker. Now is the test," said Luke, trying to lighten the conversation. "Are wolves really a problem?"

"There are more in the far north and in the Estrela mountains. I keep dozens of Estrela dogs who bond with the flocks and, in numbers, are a match for any pack of wolves."

"Do the wolves attack humans?" asked the ignorant Luke.

"Unless absolutely starving, a single wolf will not attack a human, but with a pack, the single human is in great danger, although they much prefer deer, which, luckily for us, are plentiful in this forest."

After following the horses' tracks for half an hour, Ramiro proudly announced, "They are close. They have stopped their frenzied gallop and appear to be ambling slowly along as they eat the young grasses."

Ten minutes later, they came upon the two horses, who were sharing a particularly grassy area of the forest floor with several deer, who seemed oblivious to the human presence. As they headed back to the clearing where they had slept, the noise of musket fire intensified and appeared much closer.

"Have hostilities broken out despite Caro's orders to withdraw his men and only defend Magellan?" Luke wondered.

"No. Given the intermittent firing, this is a hunting party. The woods are overstocked with deer, wild goats, pigs, rabbits, and hares—all good eating."

"Then we can relax," announced Luke.

"No! With a hunting party heading in our direction, there is always the danger that we will be hit by a random musket ball that misses its intended target. We must make them aware that we are here."

"How do we do that?"

"In the gaps of silence from them, we will fire our weapons, and it would be wise to shout out or even sing."

"How successful will that approach be?"

"It depends on whether this is a hunting party of individual villagers out to find a meal or a properly organized expedition to increase the provisions of Castle Passos or Magellan."

"So this could be an armed party of Spaniards. Calling out in Portuguese might be self-defeating. Spanish junior officers are not as likely to be as generous as General Sanchez," lamented Luke.

These worst fears were not realized. Following a burst of gunfire by Ramiro and Luke, the forest went silent. Suddenly, a voice in Portuguese demanded that they show themselves to avoid being shot accidently. The sergeant leading the party immediately recognized Ramiro and explained that Caro had sent them out to replenish the larder at Magellan before their mass exodus. They had almost completed their hunt and would now return to the barracks with the wagon that followed them, piled high with deer and rabbits. The amused sergeant, made aware of the lame horse, offered Luke a ride in the wagon beside the carcass of a giant stag.

The arrival of the hunting party with Ramiro and Luke also amused Caro. As it was getting late, he suggested they stay the night and leave for Estrela with fresh horses first thing in the morning.

"What happened to Colonel da Costa? Were you not to join him on some secret mission?"

"He has headed farther into Spanish territory, and with the renewal of hostilities, we did not think it appropriate that we should follow him," said Ramiro.

"A good decision. I have just ignored the queen's orders not to cross the frontier by sending a company of well-armed cavalry deep into Spain to rescue that idiot De Mota. We would not want him captured by the Spaniards."

"What is De Mota doing in Spain when hostilities have been renewed? Is he not your deputy now that Pinto is out of the picture?" asked Luke.

"He is trying to find his treacherous wife!"

"What do you mean by *treacherous*?"

"Camilla de Mota was born Camilla de la Cerda within the high Spanish nobility. Her first cousin is Antonio de la Cerda, Duke of Medinaceli, who is captain general of the sea and, in that capacity, has overall control of all Spanish forces engaged against Portugal."

"Her birth is hardly evidence of treachery. The queen herself has an almost identical background," said Luke.

"It was the arrival of the queen's brother, the Duke of Medina-Sidonia, that infuriated Camilla and revealed her intense Spanish loyalties. In Spanish eyes, Medina-Sidonia is a traitor to Spain, having led a revolt of Andalusian nobles against King Felipe at the same time that his sister and her husband led the Portuguese insurrection. The king has forgiven Medina-Sidonia, but most of the nobles have not. Consequently, Camilla decided to avoid a confrontation with Sidonia when he came here for the funeral of his cousin. She decided to visit her cousin whom she thought might be at the monastery of San Juan."

"That meeting was some time ago. We were there. I can't recall whether Medinaceli was or was not," commented Luke.

"Apparently, he was not, or Camilla missed him. De Mota became agitated when she did not return and asked permission to enter Spain to escort her home, but he did not know where she was. When Colonel da Costa passed through here the other day, I asked him as the former intelligence officer if he knew whether the De la Cerda family had any property near our borders. He said that they had a hunting lodge in the forest just south of where you were earlier today. De Mota, with a few men, left to find his wife. He has not returned, nor has the cavalry company I sent to find him."

Later that evening, when Luke and Ramiro were alone in the room they shared, Luke underwent an epiphany. A shocked Ramiro heard him confess.

"Could I be completely wrong? I have assumed from the beginning that the traitor and the murderer were one and the same—and that he was a male. Maybe there is more than one murderer and traitor, and one of the traitors is a woman, Camilla de Mota."

"That is a possibility. Unlike other officials and generals, Gaspar de Mota was known to have been dominated by his wife, and he probably told her everything he heard at the war council or in meetings with other generals," remarked Ramiro.

"What a perfect cover! Openly pro-Spanish, bitterly opposed to the queen, anxious for a reconciliation with Spain, and with a husband who has been considered soft on the Spaniard. Too obvious for idiots like us to see through," lamented Luke.

"The De Motas might be the traitors, but I cannot see them as the murderers of Joana and Rodrigo. Camilla was already in Spain when Rodrigo died," Ramiro added.

"Let's hope Matos and Cipriano have unearthed more evidence about Rodrigo's murder than we have."

31

IMMEDIATELY AFTER THEY ENTERED Castle Estrela, they were directed to the queen's quarters.

"We are in trouble," muttered Ramiro.

On entering the royal reception room, they were confronted by an irate regent.

"And where have you gentlemen been the last few days? I don't expect our English visitor to be aware of protocol in these matters, but Lord Ramiro, even though you are a country aristocrat, you are aware that when the monarch is in residence, anybody leaving such premises must seek the monarch's permission to depart."

"I am sorry, Your Majesty, but we were following up a lead in our investigation of Marquess Rodrigo's death. Our leading suspect left the castle secretly—and we had to follow him immediately."

"With any positive results?"

"No, Your Majesty, but we did discover some relevant news when we visited Magellan on our way back. Viscountess de Mota visited relatives in Spain and has not returned. Her husband went in search of her and has not returned. General Caro has a troop of horse scouring the borderlands looking for them," Luke replied.

"I was well aware that Camilla went into Spain to avoid meeting my brother, the Duke of Medina-Sidonia, at Joana's funeral. These cross-border visits by Camilla are not unusual, but the delay in returning is suspicious."

"So much so that it may answer one of the tasks you gave to me—uncover the traitor among the councillors and generals that attended your council of war. The De Mota family were very slow to come across to the rebels led by you and your husband, and Lady Camilla has never hidden her hatred of you. Gaspar de Mota, by all reports, is dominated by his wife. Probably, he discussed confidential matters with her, who then transmitted this sensitive information to her Spanish relatives," continued Luke.

"A possibility. Her open pro-Spanish position on every issue may have proved a very effective cover. She was not just an embittered member of the court but also an active agent of our Habsburg enemies. Is she also behind the murders?" asked the queen.

"I don't think so," replied Luke.

"Which means you have to approach the killings in a different way. They may have nothing to do with state security and have resulted from differing personal tensions. There may have been more than one murderer, which undermines your basic approach, Tremayne," argued the queen.

"Not completely. The evidence of your cousin that people close to you were engaged in transferring large sections of Portuguese territory keeps one or more of the Da Costa family as suspects. The murder of Rodrigo confirms that this transfer may involve Estrela lands, although Teresa's murder may not be related," admitted Ramiro, coming to Luke's defense.

After they had left the queen's apartment, Ramiro asked, "Didn't you find that strange?"

"Yes, the queen did not ask us who we were following or whether we had seen the absent Alvaro on our travels," agreed Luke.

"The queen must know where he is," declared Ramiro.

"Because she sent him on this mission," added Luke.

"Sometimes I think that we are expendable outsiders being used by the establishment for their own ends—whatever they may be," concluded a depressed Ramiro.

The next morning, Luke and Ramiro called on Alfredo Matos.

Luke asked, "Did your examination of Rodrigo reveal anything that might help in locating his murderer?"

"Yes."

"Why didn't you mention it at supper last night?"

"I was scared. The same person has murdered at least two people, and I have discovered a clue that might bring him to justice. He is almost certainly one of us, and alerting him to my find would put my own life in danger. I was so anxious that I have written you a detailed report just in case I became the next victim." Alfredo handed Luke a sealed envelope.

"What did you find?" asked Ramiro.

"Rodrigo was strangled from behind by a man with unusually large hands. There was a pressure mark where something metallic had bitten into the skin. There was a similar mark on Joana's throat."

"So what made such a mark?"

"The underside of a ring. The murderer was wearing a ring."

"Well, that's no help," said Ramiro. "Everybody except our English friends wear one or more rings."

"But how many wear a ring that comprises of so many jewels that it requires two circlets of metal melded together? Most rings are a single circlet of metal with the jewels placed on the top of the circlet. The ring worn by the murderer required two adjacent circles strong enough to hold a large piece of gold into which the jewels were embedded. A man with large hands who wears a ring with an extensive range of jewels based on a golden strip which, in turn, rested on two parallel bands for support is your murderer."

"That certainly makes our task a little easier," said Luke half-seriously.

"Not really," Ramiro remarked. "Most people with massive rings that Alfredo describes would not wear them on a day-to-day basis. They would be brought out of the jewel box only on very special occasions."

"Such as a planned strangulation. It may have given the murderer confidence or justification for his action," mused Alfredo.

"If we were in Lisbon, we could ask the six or seven gold or silversmiths if they had made a double ring for anybody of late," said Luke.

"We can't, and it would be useless. Most of the jewels you seen worn around you are family heirlooms that were made centuries ago," retorted Ramiro.

"And you can't break into everybody's jewelry box to examine the contents," said Alfredo.

Luke thought to himself that that was not completely out of the question.

Ramiro asked, "Alfredo, is there anybody you know of at Estrela or among the recent visitors who owns such a ring?"

Again, Luke was surprised by a positive response.

"Yes, there are two owners of such a ring—and their rings are very similar if not identical."

"Who are they?"

"The two individuals who could not possibly be your murderer."

"Can you be sure?"

"Decide for yourself. The owners of such a ring are the queen and Ana Cipriano."

"This inquiry is frustrating—one step forward and two steps back," announced an annoyed Luke.

"Let's talk to Ana about hers," said Ramiro.

Luke began with a long series of lies. "The Portuguese government, in appreciation of my service to them and the potential help from the lord protector, wishes to reward me with an ornate ring. I have been told that you have a very large beautiful double ring that might give me some ideas of what would be appropriate."

Ana sent one of the servants to bring her jewel box to her. It was indeed a massive ring. It was the size of a large pendant, covering much of the hand as Ana struggled to put it on her finger.

"It is too heavy for a woman to wear other than for a short period. I am surprised you needed to look at my version of the ring. The queen has one that is identical, which the silversmiths of Lisbon could have had ready access to from the queen's treasurer."

"How is it that you and the queen have identical rings?" asked Luke.

"No secret. They are known as the Guzman golden garnets. A previous duke of Medina-Sidonia had one each made for his granddaughters, which included our current queen and my late friend Joana da Costa. Joana gave hers to me several years ago in appreciation of my devoted service."

"I am most intrigued by the double ring. Are there many others in Estrela or among your recent visitors who have similar construction to their jewelry?" probed Luke.

"Up until a few days ago, I would have said no, but then I saw a beautiful ring of very large sapphires of varying hues. The overall effect was not of a massive ring, but it did have a double circlet of gold."

"And whose ring was it?"

"When Rodrigo succeeded to the marquisate, I was asked to assist the new marchioness settle into her position. Part of my initial duties was to locate and check on her jewelry case. That's where I saw the ring."

"The sometime marchioness Micaela da Costa?"

"Yes."

After the two men left Ana, Luke remarked, "That woman could not have been the murderer. Did you see how tiny her hands were? They could hardly have fitted around Rodrigo's wrist, let alone his neck. No wonder she rarely wears the ring. It is too large to stay on her finger."

"Which means it remains in a jewelry case to which our murderer could have had easy access," concluded the practical Ramiro.

"Luke, you question Micaela about her ring. I will talk to my men to see if they have come across any interesting information."

Luke was delighted to be able to talk to Micaela in English.

"And why has the English general come to visit me?" she pertly asked. "Am I still a major suspect?"

"I don't think you murdered anybody," Luke remarked. noticing her small hands.

"What do you want then?"

"To look at your jewelry."

"Any particular item?"

"Yes, a double gold circlet of large sapphires."

"A gift from a French nobleman on my departure from the Bourbon court," explained Micaela.

She left the room and returned wearing the ring. Luke took her hand and turned it over revealing the double circlet. He was immediately struck by a major difference in construction to that of the Guzman golden garnets. The double circlets here were much thinner and fused together only at three points; the garnets were built on two wide rings fused together over their entire circumference.

Alfredo could determine which one was worn by the killer, thought Luke.

Micaela asked, "What is so fascinating about the underside of the ring?"

Luke avoided the question. "It was an excuse to hold your hand." He then quickly changed the subject. "Ramiro and I have just returned from

Magellan, where we may have solved the initial secret mission you gave to me on arrival—the traitor among the generals and in the council of war."

"Have you told the queen?"

"Yes, but she needs further evidence. At the moment, it is circumstantial."

"Who is it?"

"Nobody on the council deliberately betrayed secrets to the Spaniards. One member dominated by his wife discussed state secrets with her, which she, in turn, passed on to the enemy. It was the most obvious suspect of all—the Spanish-born Spanish-loving hater of Queen Luisa, Camilla de Mota."

"What made you suspect her?"

"Nothing until a day or so ago. She entered Spain just before Joana's funeral and has not yet returned. Nor has Gaspar de Mota, who went looking for her."

Luke sensed that as a result of this news, Micaela relaxed. He decided to strike.

"Where is your brother-in-law, Alvaro?"

Micaela quickly controlled a momentary flash of anger that Luke was astute enough to detect.

"How should I know?" she replied offhandedly.

"He is your closest-living relative in Portugal. He has just succeeded to the marquisate of Estrela, and he is, by all sources, a very close friend. He suddenly leaves his new estate while the queen is in residence, and nobody wants to talk to us about it. Do you know why he left Estrela secretly and in such a hurry?"

"He used that meaningless phrase—'unfinished business.'"

32

LUKE ASKED ALFREDO IF he could tell whether Micaela's sapphire ring or Ana's golden garnet caused the marks on Rodrigo and Joana's throat. "A simple experiment will give me an answer. Bring the two rings here, and I will pretend to strangle you wearing each in turn and see which mark more closely resembles that on the victims."

Ramiro, on hearing of the experiment, felt he could not miss the entertainment. Alfredo found the rings were too loose on his small fingers, and Ramiro was asked to wear them and try to strangle Luke, deliberately putting pressure of the ring-bearing finger into the throat. Luke hoped that it would be Micaela's ring. This would further incriminate Alvaro, who would have had easy access to his sister-in-law's jewels—especially if she was his accomplice. He was disappointed.

Alfredo proclaimed, "There is no doubt the ring worn by the murderer was or was similar to that of Ana, Baroness Cipriano's golden garnets."

The conversation was interrupted by the arrival of Roberto, Viscount Delgado. "Gentlemen, my apologies. A courier has arrived from Magellan bearing bad tidings. Caro received a message from his Spanish counterpart, Sanchez, that he had in his custody Gaspar de Mota, Alvaro da Costa, and a priest, Nicodemo Oliveira. He is willing to negotiate their release with representatives of Queen Luisa. The queen has nominated myself as leader, assisted by Lord Ramiro and General Tremayne. We leave immediately for Castle Passos."

"Has the queen given you any specific instructions?" asked Luke, anxious not be kept in the dark.

"Only a surprising comment that not all of them might be worth rescuing. Some may deserve to rot in a Spanish prison. When I asked which of three might be in that category, she told me to rely on the judgment of Ramiro and Tremayne. Can you enlighten me?"

"Colonel da Costa is a suspect in our investigations into treason and murder, and Father Nicodemo is a double agent whose real loyalty is unknown. De Mota may have innocently given his wife secret information that she passed on to the enemy. If we fail to negotiate the release of any of them, I would not lose much sleep," announced Ramiro.

"A Spanish prison might save us the trouble of a firing squad or decapitation," added Luke.

Two days later, Roberto, Ramiro, and Luke were sitting opposite General Sanchez in his chambers within the tower of Castle Passos.

"And what does your queen offer for the safe return of my three prisoners?" he asked optimistically.

"Nothing. Why should she? Mota is a suspected traitor, Alvaro is implicated in several murders, and the priest is a confessed agent of the Spanish Inquisition. It is surprising that you have not been reprimanded by your superiors for arresting three of your own agents," remarked Roberto aggressively.

Luke was surprised at this direct approach.

Roberto continued to reveal his ultranationalist Portuguese position. "General, you well know that twenty years ago, we were all part of the same state, loyal to Felipe IV of Spain. Intermarriage between Portuguese- and Spanish-speaking members of the kingdom was common, as was the possession of multiple estates within each linguistic area. Since our revolution in 1640, everybody within Portugal has had to decide to join our independent state or cling to the effete Habsburg dynasty. Most people have made a clear decision one way or another. There are a few who pretend loyalty to our queen but have not really committed themselves to the Portuguese state. These people such as your three prisoners are not welcome in the new Portugal."

"In other words, General, you need to convince us that it is worth our time negotiating for any of these three," emphasized Ramiro.

"Come, gentlemen, this attempt to convince me that these three are not valuable members of the Portuguese government does not wash. Colonel da Costa is the head of military intelligence and a confidante of the queen. If, in that role, he may have had to murder people, does not necessarily affect his loyalty to the Portuguese state, as General Tremayne would attest."

"If Da Costa was a Portuguese loyalist, why is he trying to reach the cardinal archbishop of Toledo, one of Spain's leading politicians?" asked Luke.

"Thank you, General, for that piece of information. Colonel da Costa refused to reveal where he was heading when we apprehended him. A bit of torture now might elicit why he was trying to see His Eminence."

Both Portuguese nobles glared at Luke.

Sanchez seized his opportunity. "To save your comrade from torture is surely sufficient reason to negotiate his release."

Luke, anxious to redeem himself, made a suggestion. "Not at all. If you wish to torture Alvaro, we would like to be present. Like you, our queen would like to know why he wants to see the cardinal. And as I understand it, the Spaniards are much more efficient at torture than the gentler Portuguese."

Delgado summed up, "Regarding Alvaro, both sides want to know why he is going to Toledo. If he is a Spanish agent reporting to his master, your detention and possible torture of him would not enhance your career. If he is acting for Portugal, you could be a hero—but can you take the risk of making the wrong call? It might be better to release him into our custody than be too heavily involved. You can always claim that you arrested Father Nicodemo and his companion, whose identity you only discovered later."

Sanchez turned to Luke. "As a fellow long-time intelligence officer, do you believe the murders you think Da Costa committed were part of his intelligence work?"

Luke replied honestly, "At this stage, it is an open question, but I am more inclined to believe that it relates to women and property rather than the security of the state."

"What is your position on De Mota?" asked Sanchez.

Roberto reverted to his earlier theme. "We do not want him back. His family was favored under Spanish rule. He is married to the most anti-Portuguese woman among the nobility, who is closely related to your commander-in-chief, the Duke of Medinaceli. He has always been half-hearted in the pursuit of Portuguese independence and, on the battlefield, is reluctant to take Spanish lives. He belongs in Spain."

Ramiro asked, "How did he come to be your prisoner?"

"He simply turned up at the gates of the castle, asking to see me. He wanted to know if I had any news of his wife or of her illustrious relative, the duke. I had not and immediately arrested him. It is not often in time of war that the deputy commander of your opposition visits your headquarters, seeking assistance."

Delgado added, "De Mota has never been trustworthy and has already been removed from his position. You can keep him until his wife chooses to claim him. They will both be arrested immediately they reenter Portugal. The queen will confiscate their property and reassign it to a worthier subject."

Luke wondered whether the queen would actually act in this way, or had Delgado's imagination run riot?

Ramiro summed up, "Keep De Mota. We do not want him back."

"We are not progressing far," uttered the frustrated Sanchez. "Let's hope we can reach an agreement regarding the troublesome priest. His pro-Portuguese activities are well known to us."

"And the fact that he is an agent of the Spanish Inquisition to us," countered Delgado.

Luke intervened, "Nicodemo struck me as an honest man. Why not bring him here and question him? He may answer the question Alvaro refused to. Why were they going to Toledo?"

Sanchez nodded, and the Portuguese mission were offered a range of hot chicken nibbles with an admirable wine as they awaited the arrival of Nicodemo.

He entered the room and was visibly surprised to see Ramiro, Roberto, and Luke with General Sanchez, who addressed him immediately.

"Father Oliveira, your Portuguese friends are here to decide whether to take you home or to allow you to rot in my prison forever. None of us trust you. Are you loyal to Felipe of Habsburg or Luisa of Braganza?"

"That is not an appropriate question," Nicodemo replied.

"Why not?" asked Sanchez.

"Whether I give my loyalty to Habsburg or Braganza is of little importance to me. My loyalty is to Mother Church. When I entered it, there was no division between Portugal and Spain, and I trained and served essentially within what is now the Spanish Church. For decades, I have been an agent of the now Spanish Inquisition, and in that role, I have acted in ways that may seem to support the Habsburgs. On the other hand, I was born Portuguese, and my parish is one of the few Portuguese-speaking areas still within the reduced Spain. Next to the church, my loyalty is to my parishioners, and in that role, I have acted at times to support what outsiders would see as assisting the Braganzas."

"Whose cause are you furthering in seeking to talk to the cardinal in Toledo?" asked Luke.

"My parishioners."

"In what way?" asked Ramiro.

"I have had discussions with both the Spanish and Portuguese governments to transfer my little parish to Portuguese control. The Spanish authorities are happy to trade my little rural parish with a Portuguese-occupied town of Spanish speakers in the Algarve. Final discussions have taken place above my head, but while he was at the San Juan monastery, the cardinal sent a message that if I visited him in Toledo at my earliest convenience, I would have an answer to my formal petition."

"Why was Alvaro da Costa with you?"

"I don't know. I guess he was sent to protect Portuguese interests in any discussion I had with the cardinal."

"Did you know before he arrived at your house on the eve of your departure to Toledo that he was coming?" asked Luke.

"No, he seemed delighted when I told him he was lucky to catch me as I was leaving for Toledo in the morning. He offered to accompany me."

"He never actually said he was sent by the queen to assist you?" asked Ramiro.

"No."

Roberto turned to Sanchez. "General, it seems you have nothing to bargain with. With the loyalty of all three men suspect, it would be unwise for Portugal to negotiate their release. On the other hand, your action in arresting them could be seen as obstructive by both the cardinal and the

Duke of Medinaceli. If I were you, I would release all three but not into our hands. These negotiations are at an end."

Sanchez was furious. His Portuguese visitors were right, but he was not going to admit that in the presence of Father Nicodemo.

Ramiro tried to ease the tension. "The negotiations may be at an end, but our enjoyment of your food and drink should continue at least until those carafes are empty."

Father Nicodemo was not as diplomatic. "Release me now! And the cardinal need not know of this unfortunate interruption to my journey."

Sanchez winced. "You may go, but Da Costa remains."

As the Portuguese delegation rode away from Castle Passos, Ramiro questioned Roberto. "Was it wise to leave Alvaro in Spanish hands? As an intelligence officer, he could still reveal a lot of our secrets to the enemy."

Roberto was firm. "If he is a traitor, the harm has already been done. If not, Alvaro da Costa is not the sort of man to reveal anything, even under torture."

As he watched them leave from his tower window, Sanchez wondered if he had fallen into a trap. He had acted too quickly on the information he received from an unknown source in Portugal that Alvaro was heading for Spain and would probably make his first night in the village of Corba. Certainly, he would have to make his peace with the cardinal and the Duke of Medinaceli. He would send Colonel Barbosa to Toledo immediately.

33

I MMEDIATELY ON THEIR RETURN to Estrela, the three men reported to the queen. Roberto detailed their discussions with Sanchez.

The queen, silent for some time, finally responded, "Gentlemen, I agree completely with two-thirds of your decisions. We are well rid of De Mota and his imperious wife. I shall have great delight in confiscating all their lands within our borders. And it is imperative that Father Nicodemo visit the cardinal. But why did you do nothing about Alvaro da Costa?"

"Because we have accepted Tremayne's analysis of the situation, which holds Alvaro responsible for three murders," said Ramiro.

"And what exactly is your hypothesis, Tremayne?" demanded the queen.

"That Alvaro is a spoilt, jealous younger brother who lusted after his elder brother's wife. Micaela returned his affections, and together, they planned this series of murders. In removing Joana, Alvaro knew that Paolo would renounce his titles and estates to his nearest relative Rodrigo. On Rodrigo's death, Alvaro would succeed, and after an appropriate lapse of time, he would marry Micaela."

"And where does the murder of Teresa Pinto fit into this pattern?" asked the queen.

"Teresa, as a lady-in-waiting and often in your privy apartment at Magellan, probably overhead Micaela and Alvaro plotting and had to be silenced," continued Luke.

"You may as well tell Her Majesty your theory about Estrela and Spain," Ramiro commented.

"I did not think the English were renowned for their fantasy," the queen replied jokingly.

"Your cousin Joana overheard a Spanish officer revealing that, ultimately, a possessor of Estrela would hand over the whole of the Estrela lands, which cover half a province, to Spain. I believe it is Alvaro who is about deliver that prize to the enemy."

"In return for what?" she asked.

"An offer of a duchy. Alvaro da Costa, Duke of Estrela and subject to Felipe of Spain."

"I have known Micaela and Alvaro for decades. They are among my closest confidantes and, I believe, most loyal supporters," retorted an unconvinced queen.

"Your cousin Joana warned you that the traitors were those close to you," added Roberto.

The queen turned to Luke. "Your hypothesis explains many of the facts, but do you have any definite proof?"

"Not as yet, but I can see no other credible explanation for what has happened," answered Luke.

Ramiro commented, "Did you send Alvaro into Spain to assist Nicodemo achieve the transfer of his parish to Portugal? Perhaps he was to reveal which part of Portugal you were trading in its place."

"I would love to say Alvaro entered Spain on my orders to negotiate with the cardinal, but my part of this bargain was negotiated weeks ago. When my brother, the Duke of Medina-Sidonia, was at Magellan, I agreed to transfer a town of Spanish-speaking inhabitants in the Algarve but currently occupied by a Portuguese military unit back to the Hapsburgs. It would raise the duke's tarnished reputation within the Spanish court and would free up a company of soldiers we badly need elsewhere, as well as bringing Corba back into the Portuguese fold, where it belongs. Nicodemo did not require any assistance from Alvaro."

"Then why is he going to Toledo?" Ramiro probed.

The queen ignored Ramiro's question and turned to Luke. "Do you really believe that Micaela is complicit in these murders?"

"She is a very ambitious woman, and given her family's high status in France, to be a countess in Portugal is beneath her expectations. A marchioness was a little better, but to be a Spanish duchess would be bliss," Luke replied.

The queen gave Luke a strange look and commented, "I am sorry, Tremayne. You must have had a very bad experience with women. I wonder if, in your eyes, she would be content with a Portuguese duchy."

Luke thought this may have been the reward that Rodrigo had been expecting. Or was she intending to raise Alvaro to that dignity and had seen it as a way to satisfy her two ambitious courtiers by supporting their marriage?

Ramiro continued his interrogation of the queen. "Your Majesty, do you have any explanation for Alvaro's trip to Toledo?"

"No, and for him to attempt it after the renewal of hostilities and without informing me of his departure, let alone destination, does seem strange. What do you gentlemen intend to do next?" she replied.

Roberto answered forcibly, "While we track down the murderers and traitors, it is not wise for Your Majesty to stay at Estrela. You must return to Lisbon immediately and to the security of your Ribeira palace. In this rural castle, individual attacks on your person or a surprise Spanish invasion of the area are more difficult to prevent. The capture of your person would indeed be a feather in the cap of the enemy."

"And such an attempt is more likely now than previously. General Sanchez will be anxious to redeem himself in the eyes of his government, and he does possess an elite team of agents under Colonel Barbosa who can infiltrate our lines and effectively carry out such orders, as we saw in the attempted abduction of General Caro and their in-house negotiations with Paolo and who-knows-who-else," added Luke.

"Yes, I will leave. Pero da Silva has sent me a message that I am urgently required in Lisbon to handle a number of problems. I will go suddenly and secretly and will not speak to anybody here about my departure. I leave you, Roberto, in full control of this mission. How you deal initially with Alvaro, I leave to you, provided that should you have evidence that he is a murderer or a traitor, he and the evidence are to be sent to Lisbon. I want none of the summary military justice favored by Lord Ramiro and a known trademark of our English visitor. Alvaro has served me well. I will not have him murdered on mere suspicion."

The next morning, after the queen had quietly departed, Roberto, with Luke and Peter summoned, Carlos Cipriano and Alfredo Matos.

"Gentlemen, in the continuing absence of your new master, the queen has given me authority to investigate the murders associated with Estrela and the Da Costa family. I shall also be responsible for the security both of individuals and the estate. You, Carlos, will have complete control in running the household and the estates as you did under Paolo."

"I am concerned about the security of the estates. They are being worked and protected by only a third of our usual labor supply. We need to have our militia unit recalled from Magellan to protect this home area and to maintain its economic viability," advised Cipriano.

"I agree," said Ramiro. "My men and those you still have with you could probably hold the castle until help arrives, but the surrounding land could be devastated by then and the whole area bankrupted for decades."

Luke asked, "What are the arrangements being made for the dowager marchioness Micaela? Is she to remain here?"

"Before he disappeared, the new marquess said she would be remaining here for some time until he had settled in, and her position with the queen had been clarified. My wife is to be her companion as she was to the late Joana," replied Cipriano.

"Mention of the late marchioness reminds me of another issue. In the course of our investigation, we had access to the massive ring that she gave to your wife. Is it kept secure?" probed Luke.

"Not really. My wife is not one for jewelry, and that gift was an embarrassment. It is too large and bulky to be worn by women with dainty hands. Ana left her few jewels, including that golden garnet, in her bedside drawer. I suggested to her several times that it be broken up. There is a lot of gold in that ring. Why were you interested in such a monstrosity?"

Alfredo began to cough uncontrollably.

Ramiro lied. "Luke was very interested in the double-circlet base. The English have never seen such a construction."

"Nor had I. It is a Spanish practice," added the chamberlain.

Later that day, Roberto, Luke, Peter, and Ramiro met to determine the direction of their inquiry. It was decided that Luke should question Micaela. They were hoping for a confession that would open up the investigation, which had reached a stalemate. Luke was intrigued that Roberto had opted out of any interrogation of Micaela. Was this simply because of their past liaison, or were there more pressing reasons?

Luke began his questioning of Micaela gently, indicating that as matters stood, the evidence pointed to Alvaro and herself as the main suspects as both murderers and traitors. Luke once again outlined his hypothesis involving them both and pleaded with her to produce evidence that would destroy his argument.

Micaela surprised Luke by beginning to sob gently. Was this a clever aristocratic ploy, or a genuine emotional reaction to the accusation? He struggled to find a handkerchief to offer her.

Eventually, she spoke. "Up until now I believed the least you knew, the better the situation would be for Alvaro and me. Now it is clear that we must speak up to defend ourselves. My first statement will tend to confirm your suspicions and give us a motive for at least one of the murders. Alvaro and I are lovers and have been for several years."

Luke, sympathetic to his interviewee, asked, "Before Rodrigo's death, had you any plans to advance this relationship? Would you have sought an annulment or persuaded Rodrigo to do so?"

"No. Given both our close association with the queen, who would frown on such behavior, and the pressure of work, we were content to steal magic moments whenever it became possible. Given Rodrigo's age, we could wait until his death. Rodrigo was aware of the situation, which did not affect his formal relationship with me, but it created a frosty atmosphere with his brother. One of his delights in becoming marquess was that my duties as marchioness would necessitate my resignation from the court and removal from Alvaro's ambit."

"Micaela, you can see why I suspect you both. Rodrigo's murder is to your advantage."

"You always said that you thought the same person was responsible for all the murders. Yes, we have a motive to remove Rodrigo, but why would we murder Joana and Teresa?"

"Teresa became aware of your plotting, whatever that may have been, and had to be silenced. I admit, motive is not as strong as for your removal of Rodrigo."

"And you have absolutely no evidence that we are traitors!" proclaimed a now feisty Micaela.

"Again, circumstantial. Joana overheard a Spanish officer incriminate a future master of Estrela in renouncing his loyalty to the Braganzas and returning the Estrela estates to Habsburg Spain."

"Pretty thin, Luke. That conversation, even if correctly understood, was made when Paolo was marquess. There was no immediate prospect of Alvaro becoming marquess. Both Paolo and Rodrigo would have to be removed."

"Yet this did happen through two murders—Joana's to force Paolo into a monastery and Rodrigo's to open the way for Alvaro."

"None of us were aware that Paolo planned to enter a monastery if his wife predeceased him. That is a question that Roberto, Ramiro, and yourself should consider—who knew of Paolo's monastic intentions? What would either of us have to gain by renouncing our Portuguese allegiance and becoming Spaniards? Estrela is as large as most provinces and brings with it immense wealth, and Alvaro has spent the last eighteen years of his life defending the Portuguese state."

"The offer of a Spanish dukedom. Your enemies at court are ever ready to accept that the notoriously ambitious French woman would do anything to become a duchess."

"Complete rubbish!"

"How do you explain Alvaro's current trip into Spain? We are now again at war. And why is he meeting with Spain's third most powerful man, the cardinal archbishop of Toledo? To arrange the handover of his new estates to that foreign power?"

Micaela giggled and suddenly relaxed. "Luke, you have a great imagination. I know why Alvaro disappeared, although I pleaded with him to wait until the next suspension of hostilities."

34

"WHY HAS HE GONE to Toledo?" Luke asked.

"After an appropriate time of mourning, he hopes to marry me. But that is impossible at the moment. Alvaro cannot marry his brother's widow without the consent of the church. The pope continues to ignore the Portuguese bishops, and the most influential cleric on the Iberian Peninsula is the cardinal archbishop of Toledo. Alvaro is there to put his case for permission to marry me before the tribunals of Mother Church."

"Agreement should surely be a formality. It is not a major request such as an annulment," commented Luke.

"I am not sure. A Protestant does not understand the Catholic mind on such matters. Now if you add up all your evidence regarding our treacherous activity, it amounts to nothing. Alvaro, in a sense, is risking his life for love, a love of which he cannot be certain."

"What do you mean?"

"I have not consented to marry him. I pleaded with him to wait several months until I could clarify my thoughts. A lover and a husband are clearly different things."

"How much does he know of your doubts?" asked Luke gently.

"Alvaro took the fact that we sleep regularly together as an assurance that when Rodrigo died, we would marry. I have never accepted this conclusion, but like all Da Costas, he thinks that what he wants is already agreed."

"You let him embark on this dangerous enterprise, thinking you would marry him, when you have serious doubts?"

"I tried to stop him and hinted that marriage was not the inevitable outcome of our relationship, but Alvaro only hears what he wants to. The Portuguese are far too serious regarding relationships. As a French aristocrat, I would never have entertained the notion that because I slept with someone, it was an indication that I would marry them. My only excuse is that up until a month ago, I would probably have accepted Alvaro's proposal."

"Why the change of mind?"

"That, Luke, is a matter of the heart, about which I will not expound."

"Let's hope Alvaro, on hearing you reaffirm your doubts, does not run amok."

Luke left Micaela with his hypothesis partially destroyed. Her confession that they were lovers gave them a motive for at least one murder and maybe three, but real evidence seemed further away than ever. Luke's questioning of Micaela troubled him, so much so that when he retired for the night, he could not sleep.

He tossed and turned, and his mind conjured up all sorts of impossible scenarios.

He began to feel guilty that he had blackened Alvaro's name without a shred of evidence. This guilt was enhanced by an overwhelming feeling of sympathy for a man who was to be betrayed by the lover he expected to marry.

Suddenly, he jumped out of bed. He ran into the adjoining room and woke Peter.

"Are we under attack?" asked the alarmed and only half-awake captain.

"No, I have just realized I have been a fool. Alvaro could not be the murderer."

"Why not? You were so certain that he was the culprit."

"Micaela was so convincing that my certainty as to Alvaro's guilt was shattered."

"A convincing tale from Micaela is not a sufficient excuse to clear Alvaro and, for that matter, waking me up in the middle of the night."

"There is convincing evidence that Alvaro could not have been the strangler."

"Tell me before I fall asleep."

"You may have observed Alvaro always wears gloves, but when I first met him, he did not. His right hand was missing three fingers. He could not have worn the ring on his right hand. I should have realized this from the beginning. I am a fool."

"And I am tired," said Peter as he again dozed off.

The next morning, Luke informed Roberto and Ramiro of his epiphany.

"Where does that leave our inquiry? The hypothesis on which our investigation has revolved is shattered. I must tell Carlos and Alfredo," Ramiro responded.

"No! If Alvaro is not the strangler, it must be someone at Estrela. At the time of Rodrigo's murder, Carlos was the only senior person here. He could be our new suspect. Although Alfredo was at Magellan, the fewer people who become aware of our forced change of emphasis, the better," replied Luke.

"There are other possibilities in addition to Carlos," said Ramiro.

"A Spanish hit squad under Colonel Barbosa is the obvious," added Roberto.

"What possible motive would Carlos have?" asked Luke.

Ramiro was reflective. "Alvaro cannot completely be freed from suspicion regarding the murders or of treachery to the nation."

"How so?" asked Luke, now determined to protect the very man he had, only the previous day, considered the major perpetrator of the evils they confronted.

"Alvaro may have a legitimate excuse to enter Spain to seek support of the cardinal archbishop in a personal matter, but it could still cover treacherous discussions and activities. And as far as the murders are concerned, someone acting under instructions from Alvaro could be the strangler. The head of military intelligence would have many people who owed him a favor and were willing to carry out such a deed."

"I agree with Ramiro. Alvaro did not strangle the victims, but he may have ordered it," added Roberto.

"The actual strangler must have been offered a considerable inducement to kill three aristocrats," commented Luke.

"And that is the issue on which we must focus. What sort of inducement could be offered—and by whom—for the murder of those three aristocrats?" said Roberto.

"Adopting Luke's usual line, if I assume that Alvaro was behind the murders, Cipriano is the only person present in all three places able to have done the deed," concluded Ramiro.

"If I could find a motive, I suggest that Cipriano effected the killings on his own account without any request from Alvaro," muttered Luke.

"Let's try a bit of bluff. Interrogate Cipriano again and let him know that he is now our main suspect," suggested Roberto.

"Cipriano is a cold and tough customer. I cannot see him succumbing to any bluff. Do we want to alert him to our suspicions at this stage?" cautioned Luke.

"Maybe our initial approach should be through his wife," said Ramiro.

"In our past examinations of Ana, it was clear that her husband rarely discussed his activities with her. She knows little," opined Roberto.

"Perhaps we did not ask the right questions," said Luke.

Ana was pleased to see the three investigators. Since the departure of the queen, she only had Micaela for company, and it was clear that they were not relating well.

Luke took the lead in his halting Portuguese. "Baroness, we regret having to ask you a few more questions. Since our last meeting, we have cleared a number of suspects in our murder investigation, and unfortunately, we are now left with one person who looks like the probable murderer. It is your husband, Carlos."

Ana showed no emotion but dismissed the suggestion out of hand. "Absolutely impossible!"

"That is why we are interviewing you. We hope that you can show us that your husband is innocent," added Ramiro gently. "You have a small barony at one end of the Estrela estates, just as I have a lordship at the other. We are local folk uncontaminated by the corruption of the court and absolutely devoted to the area. Carlos inherited his barony at about the same time I succeeded to the lordship of Lima. I had lived on Lima all my life, succeeding my father, but if I remember rightly, Carlos and you came from elsewhere on the peninsula."

Ana remained relaxed during Ramiro's soft approach and replied to his question with enthusiasm. "Yes, we came from farther north, but as here, it was on the edge of Portuguese-speaking territory. During the period before the revolution in 1640, Carlos's activities were largely in the Spanish provinces of Estremadura and Castile-León. When he was a child, his household spoke both languages, and the Ciprianos are related to many of the Spanish gentry and nobles just across what is now the border."

"Was Carlos quick to join the revolution?"

"Our barony is subject to the marquisate of Estrela, and whatever the marquess did, the baron had to follow suit. We declared for King John and Queen Luisa at the very beginning of the revolution."

"But only because the marquess had done so?" queried Luke.

"It was more that the Spanish-born noblewoman to whom I became a companion for more than a decade, Joana, persuaded both her husband and his senior tenants that Portugal had had a proud history, and her union with Spain in 1580 had not been in her interests. As if to prove his new allegiance, Carlos manifested an ultra-Portuguese political stance, which ironically often painted Joana and her cousin the queen in a poor light."

"Could this have been a cover for a secret Spanish allegiance that is only now coming to the surface?" asked Roberto.

"No. Although Carlos speaks perfect Spanish and kept in contact with friends and family who remain on the Spanish side of the border, he sees his future as part of Portuguese Estrela."

"Was there any specific Spanish noble or official whom Carlos kept in contact with?" probed Luke.

"Yes. He is related to Federico Sanchez, the local Spanish general, and this family connection has facilitated many approved joint Spanish-Portuguese activities. Joana relied on him for many of her cross-border acts of charity and humanity."

"Was he aware that should Joana die, Paolo would renounce his titles and lands in favor of his cousin Rodrigo?" asked Luke.

"I am not sure".

"Did you know?" pressed Roberto.

Ana seemed to be losing her serenity. She hesitated for some time before giving a vague answer. "Not really."

"Explain!" demanded a growingly annoyed Luke.

"I knew that when either Joana or Paolo died, the other would leave Estrela."

"Surely, this general position must have been conveyed innocently to Carlos," continued Luke.

"Carlos's sole ambition is to remain chamberlain and castellan of Estrela for the term of his life?" asked Roberto.

"Yes!"

"Therefore, a change of marquess could seriously affect this situation," continued Roberto. "How did he react to Rodrigo's succession?"

"He was initially delighted with it and believed it would improve his situation."

"In what way?" Ramiro asked.

"Paolo was a resident marquess, and consequently, Carlos was always in his shadow and subject to the immediate oversight of both marquess and marchioness. Rodrigo and Micaela were courtiers, and Carlos did not believe they would give up the comforts, perks, and power related to the court to preside over a rural fiefdom. He would be left to run Estrela and would be the dominant local nobleman in the absence of his overlord. Consequently, the person who lost most by the death of Rodrigo is Carlos."

"Unless, having arrived at Estrela, Rodrigo made the decision to become a resident marquess. Carlos, in a fury at the change of mind, murdered him. It fits perfectly," proclaimed Luke.

"No, it doesn't! Even if Rodrigo indicated a change of mind, Carlos knew that after a few months at Estrela, he would be wanting to return to court. Why risk this probable scenario for an entirely unknown new marquess who was more likely to stay in the country? Alvaro seems to enjoy his new position, and I understand he is out of favor with the queen. He may even be on the brink of banishment from court to his new country estate. Alvaro is a much younger man and, I imagine, will take a much more hands-on approach than his much elder brother. Carlos is not a fool. He will look after his own interest but not to the extent of murdering his then marchioness and then his new marquess to put him in an even worse position. You paint him as a serial killer."

"Would the promised absence of the marquess be enough reward for Carlos to carry out these murders at the behest of another?" asked Roberto, suddenly changing the direction of his questions.

35

"ARE YOU SUGGESTING THAT Carlos murdered three people at the direction of another?"

"Possibly."

"Who could that be?"

"Alvaro da Costa," answered Ramiro.

"Surely, it has to be considered," added Luke.

"Not at all. Two of you are soldiers who do not hesitate to kill. Your reputation, General Tremayne, for summary justice goes before you, and, Lord Ramiro, you disposed of the defrocked inquisitor in a similar ruthless manner. Carlos could not do such a thing. He was a lawyer, concentrating on property matters before he succeeded to the barony. You have said nothing to convince me that Carlos is a triple murderer. Essentially, you have no convincing motive for him to act in this way, and I, married to the man for decades, know that such action would be alien to his character and experience. If he wanted someone dead, he would have another do it."

Luke was taken aback by the last sentence. After a spirited defense of her husband, Ana admitted that while he might wish to kill someone, he did not have the courage to do so himself.

Ana continued, "I know deep in my heart that Carlos would never have murdered Joana. They annoyed each other, but he knew she was my friend, and although we didn't display our affection for each other like some, he would never do anything to hurt me. And what did he have against Countess Teresa? They have never spoken to each other, and at Magellan, their paths did not cross."

"On another matter, you and the dowager marchioness Micaela are the only noblewomen in residence. How is she coping with the death of her husband?" asked Ramiro.

"Rumor has it that they were not close, and his death seems almost a relief—but she remains a deeply troubled woman," admitted Ana.

"In what way?"

"She told me she had made a momentous decision, and when she told someone affected by it, she could not predict the outcome, which could be calamitous for us all," answered Ana.

Luke remained silent, not having passed on to his comrades the devastating news that might await Alvaro on his return. Micaela was playing a very dangerous game.

Carlos was annoyed to receive another visit from the trio. He immediately tried to turn it to his advantage and sought Roberto's help.

"Count, as you have your militia tied up at Magellan as do we, could you use your influence with Caro to have both our regiments returned to us? The lack of manpower in Estrela is not only a security risk but also damaging to our rural economy."

"I believe as Caro has no immediate intention of launching a major offensive, our regiments will be returning in a week or so," replied Roberto.

Ramiro was not to be diverted. "Carlos, we are here because by a process of elimination, we have cleared most of our suspects for the murders of Joana da Costa, Teresa Pinto, and Rodrigo da Costa. You remain as the possible strangler of all three. Give us grounds to eliminate you from our list!"

"I thought, given the rumors circulating here and at Magellan, that you had linked the murders with acts of treachery by people unknown within the government. I am the chamberlain of a rural estate, and until the visit of the war council here a few weeks back, I had had no contact whatsoever with the court, the councillors, or any of the generals. The only visitor whom I had met previously was Alvaro da Costa, who came to Estrela a month or more back. I don't know why. Paolo introduced him as a cousin who was on the borders, engaged in highly secret matters of state, relevant to his position as head of military intelligence. What possible motive could I have?"

"Don't worry too much, Carlos. I may have been following the wrong path. Up until recently, I was convinced that all the murders were the work of one person who, in the end, wanted to return the allegiance of Estrela back to the Spanish Habsburgs. According to my theory, such a person had first to remove the then marquess, who had resolutely rejected any idea of returning it to Spain. Did you know that Paolo would renounce his title and estates if his wife predeceased him?" asked Luke.

"Not exactly. I had discovered from my wife that Paolo and Joana had made a pact that when one of them died, the other would also leave Estrela. I did not know that this would involve the renunciation of the title and the transfer of estates. I assumed Paolo, if the survivor, would simply have moved to Lisbon and left me to run Estrela until, on his death, an heir would succeed."

"In that case, if you did murder Joana, it may have been for reasons other than the succession," interposed the troublemaking Ramiro.

"Why would I have had any role in changing the marquess? Any new marquess may have been more difficult than his predecessor. Paolo and I had an excellent relationship."

"But you and Joana did not," Roberto emphasized.

"Only partly true. Joana was a domineering woman who constantly interfered in my running of the estate, especially with regard to the well-being of our workers. However, over the decades, we developed a workable compromise, and we often united to help our relatives, friends, and staff who still lived under Spanish rule."

"We could consider this Spanish link as evidence against you," said Ramiro provocatively.

"That's a stupid comment, Ramiro! We are both border nobles who, up until eighteen years ago, were part of an united kingdom under the current Habsburg, Felipe IV. Many of our friends and neighbors are still on the other side of the porous border. Continued contact with them cannot be construed in any way as treason. After all, our queen Luisa is in constant contact with her brother, the great Spanish grandee, the Duke of Medina-Sidonia."

"But contact with Spanish military agents may be considered inappropriate," said Luke.

"What do you mean?"

"Col. Marcos Barbosa has been welcomed here on numerous occasions. He tried to abduct Caro and probably offered several inhabitants of this castle inducements to assist him and the Spanish cause," continued Luke.

"Yes, Barbosa has been a consistent visitor to the castle. It is part of border life. He was the major conduit between the marquess and marchioness and the Spanish authorities. He brought the Spanish offer of a duchy to Paolo if he would simply transfer his allegiance from Braganza to Habsburg."

"You claimed earlier that any change of marquess was not a major priority for you, but what if it was? What if a potential heir offered you more than you were getting under Paolo? Would you assist such a person in obtaining his ends?" asked Roberto.

"And whom did you have in mind?"

"Alvaro da Costa," he responded.

"What could Alvaro offer me that would be better than what I had or what Rodrigo might offer? I have openly stated that I hoped any marquess of Estrela would remain at court and in their current roles and leave me to run Estrela. In this regard, Rodrigo suited me very well. Why would I murder him? Alvaro was too far removed from the succession at the time of Joana's and Teresa's death. I did not know that Paolo would renounce his rights, and I fully expected Micaela to produce an heir for Rodrigo who would cut Alvaro out of the succession. If the gossip of my maids is accurate, Alvaro has been very lucky. Rodrigo died only a few weeks before the birth of an heir. Micaela is pregnant."

The three investigators were astounded. She had hidden her condition extremely well.

Luke's mind raced ahead. If this child was Alvaro's, her refusal to marry him would create a major crisis. He may claim the child as his and take steps to legitimize him or her.

Roberto's mind followed a different path. If Alvaro had known of Micaela's pregnancy, then he would need to eliminate Rodrigo, before the child was born.

Ramiro was the most practical. "If Alvaro is the father and he marries Micaela in due course, then his conspiracy to obtain the marquisate of Estrela will have succeeded. If, in time, he wishes to transfer his allegiance to Spain, would it be difficult to achieve?" he asked of Cipriano.

"Put another way, if you were the master of Estrela, how would you effect a change of loyalty and the transfer of your estate back to Spain?" asked Luke.

"In the early years of the battle for independence, changes of loyalty, especially along the border areas, was commonplace. Nowadays it is unusual as most Portuguese-speaking areas have aligned with the Braganzas and most Spanish areas with the Habsburgs, and neither side seems to be interested in expanding into the other's territory. Spain has not have the forces to reconquer Portugal, and Portugal simply wants recognition as an independent state and has no territorial ambition. If I were to renounce the loyalty of Estrela to the Braganzas, I would need to ensure that Spain had enough troops available to protect me from a Portuguese counterattack. As Estrela is a mountainous area and easy to defend, it would not take many troops. Above all, I would need to ensure that the tenants and workers of Estrela were, if not in favor of change, at least not willing to physically resist it," replied a thoughtful Cipriano.

"How would you do that?" asked Luke.

"Convince them that their individual situations would not be impaired by any change of political loyalty. It would be relatively easier here than elsewhere in Portugal. This isolated mountain region has had little direct help from Lisbon, nor, unlike the far north and far south, has there been the constant intervention of the Portuguese government against Spain. In essence, this region has never been dependent on Lisbon for its existence, and there has been a much closer interaction between Spanish and Portuguese speaking neighbors. If there were ultra-Portuguese nationalists within the area, I would use our militia to enforce the decision, and I would replace these recalcitrant tenants with others, although I doubt if the importation of Spanish landlords from Estremadura would be helpful. It was a disaster for Spain in Corba."

"Did Paolo, Rodrigo, or Alvaro ever contemplate such an action?" asked Roberto.

"Paolo rejected it out of hand. I was present when he informed Colonel Barbosa of his decision. I do not know if Rodrigo or Alvaro were even aware of it, although Alvaro was here at the time."

"It is our supposition that Alvaro knew of the offer, maybe in his position as head of intelligence. He is probably the person referred to by

Joana and is, at present, in Spain finalizing his plans for such a transfer of loyalty," stated Luke, reverting to his original prejudiced views.

Ramiro suddenly said, "Carlos, show us your hands."

Carlos revealed particularly large hands that could certainly have strangled the three victims.

"Have you ever worn the so-called Guzman golden garnet ring?"

"Yes, but never in public. It is too heavy and a monstrosity."

"Has anybody over the years that your wife has possessed such a gem asked to see it?" Ramiro continued.

Carlos thought for some time. "My first reaction first reaction was to say no, but a rather strange incident has just come to mind involving the ring."

"Which was?" probed Luke.

"It was the day that the marquess delivered his reply to Colonel Barbosa. Barbosa told us that his family had always been close to the Guzmans and that he had heard that Joana had one of the famous Guzman golden garnets. He asked if he could see it. I explained that it had been gifted to my wife. Paolo intervened and asked me to put the ring on and show it to Barbosa, which I did."

"Thank you for your assistance. You have clarified a number of issues," said Roberto, suddenly bringing the interview to an end.

36

A FTER LEAVING CARLOS, RAMIRO remarked, "We must go straight to Micaela and question her regarding her pregnancy."

Roberto was clearly unhappy. He objected, "No! That is a very personal matter. A formal questioning of her by us would be in poor taste and probably counterproductive. Luke relates well with her. Leave it to him alone."

Luke sensed that Roberto had no desire to question Micaela. *Why not?*

Micaela welcomed Luke enthusiastically. She was clearly agitated—and unhappy. "I cannot stand this place any longer. I have decided to leave in the morning for Lisbon."

"Without waiting for Alvaro's return? You are going to disappear and avoid telling him that you will not marry him?"

"Yes, I need a few more weeks before I can be certain that that is the right decision."

"A decision that rests on some aspect of your pregnancy?" probed Luke.

Micaela went white. "Nobody knows about that! That is the main reason I wish to return to Lisbon, where I can conceal my condition until I deliver."

"I cannot avoid the indelicate question. Who is the father?"

This time, Micaela blushed. She began to sob. Luke was not certain that the tears were genuine. Were they produced to win him over to keeping her secret?

Luke repeated his simple question.

Finally, she responded in a whisper. "I don't know."

Luke was perplexed as to how to pursue his questioning with a modicum of decorum. Micaela solved his problem. She suddenly decided to confess.

"Over the last twelve months, I have behaved as most of the Portuguese court expects of a French courtier or, as they depict me, *courtesan*. I have slept with Alvaro, my husband Rodrigo, and another. I hope, as each of those men have distinguishing features, that the baby will be so like his father that there will be no doubt as to its paternity. If the child is clearly Alvaro's, then the option offered to me by another will be withdrawn. Please do not tell Alvaro either of my pregnancy or of any possibility that I will not marry him."

"Who will look after you in Lisbon and protect you from your detractors, especially if an enraged Alvaro comes looking for you?"

"When she hears the full story—she knows part of it—the queen will give me sanctuary," replied Micaela. "She has her own solution to my complex situation, which she will impose on me if the circumstances are right."

Luke gave Micaela a big hug—and left.

He would not impart what he had discovered to his two comrades. When they met the next day, Roberto was very anxious to hear the details of his conversation with Micaela.

"She *is* pregnant and has already left for Lisbon, where the queen will give her sanctuary until she delivers. She has put on hold all matters pertaining to her future until after the baby arrives. She told me nothing that would assist us in our inquiries."

Ramiro asked the obvious question. "Who is the father?"

"I don't know," replied Luke.

"Did you ask?" Ramiro retorted.

"Of course, but she chose not to tell me."

"Is there anything we learned yesterday that we can follow up?" asked Roberto.

"The standout piece of information was the interest shown by our Spanish colonel Barbosa in the golden garnets. But I cannot see how we could ever question that Spanish hero," said Ramiro.

"No, but we can find out more about him that could be relevant," said Luke.

"How will you do that? Visit your new friend, the Spanish general Sanchez, who is his superior officer?" teased Roberto.

"Barbosa has patrolled these borderlands on behalf of Spain for years. You have met him on numerous occasions, Ramiro, and I am sure that Father Nicodemo will know a lot about him. Can you tell us anything useful?" asked Luke.

Ramiro replied, "Yes, we have confronted each other on countless occasions. Every time I cross the frontier, I can expect Barbosa—or El Camaleón, as he is known in the borderlands—will try to track me down. He is similar to me in that he is constantly leading raids across the border. The only difference is that while I act independently, he is the effective instrument of the Spanish government. He is also like you, Luke. He is regularly trusted with key missions, often necessitating the role of a ruthless assassin."

"Why 'the Chameleon'?" Luke asked.

"He is allegedly a master of disguise, although I have no direct evidence of this ability. I think it is a cover to claim successes in actions in which he wasn't involved or advanced by victims of a Spanish outrage to highlight their fate by blaming the notorious chameleon."

"Do you know anything of his background?" asked Roberto.

"He is Andalusian, like his immediate superior Sanchez, and rumor has it that his family has been for centuries and probably still are tenants of the Duke of Medina-Sidonia, which explains his interest in the Guzman golden garnets."

"Ramiro, how would you like another intrusion across the border to question Father Nicodemo or—with a bit of luck, good or bad, depending on the outcome—an encounter with the Chameleon?" suggested Luke.

"I will remain and control the situation here until the new marquess returns. Can you leave your men here, Ramiro, in case of trouble?" asked Roberto.

"Yes, it will be easier if just Luke and I crossed the frontier, although I doubt that we will meet anybody as both sides seem intent on withdrawing forces and avoiding confrontation," answered Ramiro.

Ramiro was absolutely wrong in this prediction.

On crossing the border into Corba parish, the woods were full of people, and on entering the village, Luke and Ramiro could not believe their eyes. Father Nicodemo was richly garbed in his ecclesiastical finery, and four village lads were carrying a stature of the Virgin Mary, while four little girls dressed in white struggled to keep their long candles upright and alight. General Caro, in full military uniform with the plumes of his helmet covering most of his face, was supported by a small troop of the queen's household cavalry formed up on one side of the road. Facing him was the Spanish general Sanchez, equally resplendent in his uniform and also supported by a small troop of cavalry.

Nicodemo acknowledged the arrival of Luke and Ramiro, as did the rival generals. Nicodemo addressed the visitors and villagers who crowded into what the English would call the village green.

"We are here today to formally enact an agreement between Their Majesties, Felipe of Spain and Luisa of Portugal, to transfer the parish of Corba from Spain to Portugal. After the ceremony, we will proceed to the eastern edge of Corba Forest, which will be the new frontier."

On reaching the eastern edge of the forest, Sanchez and his Spanish troops continued back into Spain. The Portuguese returned to the village to celebrate. Caro announced that he would send a daily patrol into Corba in case some Spaniards did not readily accept the transfer. Nicodemo admitted to Luke and Ramiro that he was looking forward to visiting the Zoritas estates with a cohort of Caro's men to evict the predatory former Spanish landlord's supporters. Until further notice from the queen, Nicodemo and the Portuguese church were the new landlords.

While some of the villagers had participated in the ceremony of transfer, most of the women had been busy preparing a feast in which roasted venison and pork were the main attractions. As they were enjoying the meal, Nicodemo suddenly asked, "And what brought you two uninvited guests to this occasion?"

"Information. Tell us about Col. Marcos Barbosa," said Luke.

Nicodemo related largely what Ramiro had previously revealed.

Luke continued, "What is his relationship with the Duke of Medina-Sidonia?"

The answer shocked yet elated him. "The Chameleon hates the Duke of Medina-Sidonia and the wider Guzman family with an intensity bordering on the obsessive."

"How so? I thought his family were tenants of the duke," asked Ramiro.

"That is at the heart of the problem. Barbosa blamed an earlier duke for the death of his grandfather with the Spanish armada. The duke countermanded an order of the elder Barbosa, which eventually led to his unnecessary death. Marcos Barbosa lost his father when the current duke rose in revolt against Spain in 1640. This duke ordered a lightly armed cavalry cohort led by Barbosa Sr. to charge a large detachment of heavy Castilian cavalry. Barbosa and his men were cut to pieces."

Luke could not contain himself. "A hatred so strong that he would enter Portugal in disguise and murder a Guzman in the person of Joana da Costa?"

His enthusiasm was dampened by Nicodemo's reply. "Not likely. Barbosa has an obsessive hatred of the Guzmans, but he is a loyal, efficient, and rational officer of the Spanish state. He would not cross the border simply to murder Joana as part of a family vendetta. If it was combined with an act that would further the interests of Spain, then maybe."

"Have you seen him lately? I am surprised that he was not here with Sanchez," noted Ramiro.

Nicodemo smiled. "I saw him only a few days ago."

"Where?"

"On the road to Toledo. On my way back from seeing the cardinal archbishop, I was taking refreshments at a roadside tavern, and who should ride past with a troop of men heading for that city but Col. Marcos Barbosa."

"That would not be unusual for a man so trusted by the Spanish authorities. He was probably reporting to the cardinal archbishop or receiving new instructions. I do not think Sanchez always knows what his infamous colonel is doing," commented Ramiro.

Nicodemo began to laugh. "Gentlemen, you are the great sleuths of the moment, but if you do not ask me the right question, you may miss a most interesting fact that might assist you in your inquiries."

Luke and Ramiro tried a few questions each but did not uncover the information that Nicodemo wanted to reveal. In the end, the priest volunteered the vital information.

"On such an important day in the history of Corba—its return to Portugal—I would be remiss in not reporting a fact that may reflect on the security of the Portuguese state. Who was Colonel Barbosa escorting to Toledo?"

Luke waited for Nicodemo to answer his own question.

"None other than the one-time head of Portuguese military intelligence and now Marquess of Estrela, Alvaro da Costa."

"We know that Alvaro went to Toledo but not that he was escorted by Barbosa," replied Luke.

"You don't seem too worried about it," Nicodemo commented.

"No, his visit is on a personal matter and not political. He is seeking the cardinal archbishop's support for permission to marry his brother's widow," confided Ramiro.

It was Nicodemo's turn to be surprised. "That should not be a problem. I understand that Rodrigo da Costa and his wife may not have even slept together."

"That rumor may not be true. Micaela da Costa is pregnant," said Luke.

Nicodemo whistled. "That complicates the problem a little!"

"It may account for Alvaro's urgency to get an answer quickly—and from the highest authority on the peninsula," suggested Ramiro.

"The last we heard of Alvaro, he was a prisoner of Sanchez whom we expected would free him to pursue his journey to Toledo. He may have thought a Barbosa escort would be an appropriate safeguard."

"Do you have any other interesting information?" asked Luke, not expecting any positive response.

"Yes, there was another local I saw in the courtyard of the cardinal archbishop's palace just as I was leaving."

The two soldiers waited, knowing that Nicodemo's sense of the dramatic would delay the naming of the person.

37

N EITHER ASKED NICODEMO FOR the name, forcing the priest to ultimately declare, "It was our former landlord, Jorge Zoritas."

Luke beamed. "Yet another snippet of evidence to suggest that a conspiracy exists involving Alvaro da Costa, Marcos Barbosa, and Jorge Zoritas to achieve the marquisate of Estrela for Alvaro and for him to transfer his allegiance and his estates back to Spain and, if necessary, replace recalcitrant tenants with Zoritas's men recruited from Estremadura."

"All circumstantial!" cautioned Ramiro.

Luke asked Nicodemo, "During your time as an agent for Alvaro's intelligence unit, did you ever come across evidence that Alvaro or one of his agents conversed with Barbosa?"

"Many times. I was often that agent who passed information between the two in my role as the Black Heron, but I cannot recall any that you could consider potentially treacherous."

As the men conversed, the women of the village began cleaning up after what had become an extended meal. Marabella Gomes removed an empty platter from in front of the trio and Nicodemo commented, "You look very happy today. I did not think this political change would bring such joy."

Marabella laughed. "No, it doesn't. I am very happy because my sweetheart, who worked for the Zoritas and was paid well to move with them, just told me he will not be far way. He can visit me very easily."

"And why would that be?" asked an interested Luke.

"He said he was only moving a little farther north toward the Estrela mountains."

• 224 •

"I told you. Zoritas's men are to replace the tenants and workers on the Estrela estate who do not conform to the new marquess's change of allegiance," said a jubilant Luke.

"Not necessarily. Marabella said *toward the Estrela mountains,* not to the Estrela estate," said Ramiro.

Nicodemo smiled at Luke. "It is a pity you lack evidence. Your hypothesis certainly explains a lot of the facts."

Ramiro softened his position. "Although you have no evidence, it would be wise to take steps to prevent such a possible development. We should return to Estrela via Magellan and discuss the situation with General Caro."

On their return to Estrela, Luke and Ramiro immediately conveyed to Roberto all the information they had gathered from Nicodemo and the decisions they had made in consultation with General Caro. After discussing the state of their investigation into the three murders, Roberto summed it up.

"Joana was strangled by either Cipriano or Barbosa. Cipriano may have acted on the bidding of Alvaro, while Barbosa may have taken vengeance on a Guzman, whose family he blamed for the death of his father and grandfather. Teresa was probably murdered by the same person because she had seen or overheard something. Rodrigo was murdered to pave the way for Alvaro's succession by Cipriano or Barbosa. Did Alvaro plan it and know about it, or is he completely innocent? Is there a conspiracy to return Estrela to Spain, and again, is Alvaro guilty, or is this a major coup directed by Barbosa? Is Micaela completely innocent?"

Ramiro asked, "What next?"

"We wait until Alvaro makes a move," replied Roberto. "In the meantime, the queen should be brought up to date on what has happened. I must stay here in control of Estrela until the return of Alvaro. Luke, I am sure you would like to check on the condition of the countess Madalena and obtain any news from England. I expect you and Peter back a week today."

Ramiro added with a big smile, "Take four of my men with you. You never know you might run into a gang of brigands between here and Lisbon."

Luke's group arrived at the gate of the royal palace. After establishing his identity and mission, Luke alone was led through a labyrinth of corridors and spacious rooms until he reached an ornate door, beside which stood fully armed soldiers. His escort knocked, and the guards ceremoniously opened the double door, revealing a spacious antechamber where a youngish woman waited to receive him.

Luke was delighted—and appalled. The woman wore a patch over her left eye, and her jaw was seriously misplaced. She had only one arm, and she hobbled toward him with the aid of a stick.

It was Madalena Albuquerque.

Luke could not hold back tears as he hugged her gently. "I am overwhelmed to see you alive. I did not think you would survive."

"Several army surgeons have done their best. I lost an arm and will need support to walk, but despite the displaced jaw, which makes talking and eating a little difficult, and blindness in one eye, the blows to the head have not rendered me an idiot."

"Why are you here?"

"Diego has left me, pending the annulment of our marriage, and he went straight from Magellan to his family estates in the south. When the queen returned to Lisbon from Estrela a few days ago, she sent her carriage for me. She appointed me her senior lady-in-waiting. She feels a great amount of guilt, believing that if she had not sent me in her coach deliberately to give the impression that she was on board, it would not have been attacked, and I would not have been so badly injured."

"Has Micaela da Costa seen the queen in the last day or two?"

"Yes, she arrived yesterday and was immediately taken into the depths of the queen's private apartments. She is pregnant."

"I know, but who is the father?"

Before Madalena could answer, the door to the adjoining room opened, and the queen emerged.

"Tremayne, you have important news from Estrella and Magellan?"

Luke brought the queen up to date.

"From what you say, Viscount Delgado, Lord Ramiro, and yourself believe that Alvaro, with the aid of Cipriano or Barbosa, is our triple murderer and that he intends to transfer his allegiance from us to Spain in return for a duchy?"

"Yes, Your Majesty."

"Do you think Micaela is an accomplice or even aware of such a conspiracy?" asked the queen.

"Your Majesty is in a better position than I to judge Micaela. It appears that her future and that of Portugal depends on the paternity of her child—an issue on which she did not elaborate."

"That is quite true. That is why I have hidden Micaela deep within my palace until she gives birth, and we can assess the possible paternity of the child. Hopefully, an outcome that will save Micaela from herself and enhance the house of Braganza can be achieved."

"And how can you accomplish that?"

"I know that Micaela, in the last twelve months, slept with three men, any of whom could be the father. Two of the men are Da Costas, and should the child exhibit a large nose and tiny eyes, it is reasonable to assume the father is one of them. In that case, as her husband Rodrigo is dead, she can revert to her original plan to marry Alvaro. She can then spend the rest of her days as a rural noblewoman, far removed from the centers of power. The third man is a redhead with green eyes. If the baby has red hair, then this third man is the father."

"What if the child has no distinguishing features?" probed Luke.

"Then it is up to the third man to decide if, in those circumstances, he would marry Micaela and bring up the child as his own."

Luke suddenly became aware of what he later claimed was the obvious. "And that third man is my current comrade the viscount Roberto Delgado?"

"Yes. His regular attention to Micaela over the last year slowly won her away from Alvaro. I encouraged Micaela in this enterprise as I need Delgado's support. If Roberto marries Micaela, she will become, in a year or less, the most powerful woman in Portugal, apart from myself. She will be a duchess as Roberto will soon inherit his family's duchy, which is the wealthiest in Portugal. So in twelve months, Micaela could be a newly married marchioness in the isolated mountains of central Portugal with no political power or influence, a widowed countess who might be tempted to return to France, or the second most powerful and richest woman in Portugal."

"If she marries Delgado, will you keep her at a distance?"

"She will never return as a lady-in-waiting. That would be below the status of a duchess. I intend to place Roberto Delgado on my council of state and most likely make him my chief minister. As the wife of such a powerful man, she would not be far from the center of power. I sent a courier to Estrela yesterday, summoning Roberto back to Lisbon to take his place on the council."

"The sly old dog! He never gave the slightest hint of his interest in Micaela, although he did find excuses not to interview her on several occasions."

"Let us return to the murders. I can fully accept that Marcos Barbosa could be the murderer, at least of Joana. He hated us Guzmans. Ironically, it was Alvaro who alerted me to the porosity of our border territories and the ability of able Spanish agents such as the Chameleon to move across frontiers and complete missions against the Portuguese state with impunity. But I just received a delegation and petition yesterday that might make you and Ramiro think again and perhaps find that Carlos Cipriano is Alvaro's accomplice—or the murderer in his own cause."

"But what motive could he have?"

"Yesterday, two clergymen presented a petition to me—a novice Benedictine monk, Brother Paolo, whom both of us knew in his previous life as Paolo da Costa, Marquess of Estrela, and his abbot."

"Has he had enough of the religious life already?" asked Luke cheekily.

"No, he wants me to legitimize two of his children who are not aware of his paternity."

"Bastards? Your powers in such cases are limited."

"I think they are, and I can do little in such circumstances, but Paolo claims otherwise. Like many nobles, he got a local girl pregnant who, in this case, delivered twin boys whom he immediately distributed to childless couples on his estates. The mother died giving birth. Neither I nor the church will legitimize children born out of wedlock. Paolo knows that and has advanced an argument that the twins were born in wedlock. He claims to have married the mother just before their delivery."

"The church will have records. It should be easy to prove one way or another," commented Luke.

"Unfortunately, the priest who married them is long since dead, and the records of the local church where the union took place were destroyed when a torrent of water cascaded down the valley, obliterating the church and all its contents decades ago."

"That is strange in itself. The Da Costas of Estrela have married in the chapel of Estrela Castle for centuries. Why did Paolo go to a distant church?"

"I asked him the same question. His father opposed the marriage and threw him and his pregnant girlfriend out of the castle."

"Why does Paolo now want to recognize two children he has ignored for decades?"

"HE DOES NOT WANT the family estates to revert to the crown should Alvaro not have children. If Micaela's child is Alvaro's and they marry, then the urgency disappears, but if Alvaro is executed for murder or treason, Paolo wants one of his twins to inherit."

"If the twins are acknowledged as legitimate children born in wedlock, they obviously take precedence over cousins such as Rodrigo and Alvaro."

"Yes. That is why for the moment, I will not progress the request."

"How does this affect our inquiries into the three murders?"

The queen turned to Madalena. "My dear, would you leave us for a moment?"

After Madalena had left, the queen, in little more than a whisper, said, "Tremayne, you are the only person other than Paolo, the abbot, and myself to know that the twin boys from Paolo's alleged first marriage have been raised by neighboring tenants and are well known in the area and to yourself—Ramiro de Lima and Carlos Cipriano. You are not to divulge this information to anybody."

"Does either man have any inkling of their real paternity?"

"Paolo thinks not, but he did discuss it with his second wife, my cousin Joana. She may have said something to Ana Cipriano, her closest confidante, but Ramiro would have absolutely no idea."

"So if Cipriano was aware of his paternity, he might readily go along with Alvaro removing the interlopers in the line of succession and then, when the time was right, remove Alvaro himself."

"A possibility, surely?" suggested the queen.

"You have just complicated my inquiries. You have recalled Roberto to Lisbon, and I cannot tell my fellow investigator, Ramiro, what you have just told me. Alvaro could now be both murderer and the next victim—or totally innocent. The murders could stem from a Spanish plot to take over Estrela, or it could be a very complicated plan by an undeclared heir to succeed to the title."

"You had better return to Estrela immediately and prepare for the rampage that will occur when Alvaro returns and discovers that Micaela has gone. Do not tell him that she is here."

As Luke bowed and kissed the hand of the queen, she quietly said, "I know you were very fond of Madalena—"

Luke interrupted. "It is very gracious of you to take her in and give her a place in your service, especially as she was deserted by her husband."

"I am saddened to have to tell you that all this is very temporary. The surgeons and physician have done all they can, but they believe there is bleeding somewhere in her head, which will eventually lead to her sudden collapse and inevitable death. You shall not see her again."

"Does she know?"

"Yes."

Luke reentered the antechamber where Madalena was waiting. With tears streaming down his face, he took her in his arms. She kissed him gently, turned, and reentered the queen's chamber.

Luke hardly uttered a word as his small troop made their way back to Estrela. By the time Luke reached the castle, Roberto had already left for Lisbon in answer to the queen's summons. Cipriano was over the moon, having sent Matos back to Magellan to lead the local militia home. In the meantime, Ramiro, with several dozen men, provided the sole security for the whole region.

Luke was worried. He sensed that things were building to a climax. When the militia returned, Cipriano would have an armed force capable of effecting a change of loyalty. Alvaro was due at any time—with or without Spanish assistance. Luke hoped that Caro had taken the steps agreed upon.

Two days later, Alvaro returned. He was surprised that his castle was largely deserted and that his only guests were Ramiro, his troops, and the two English officers, Tremayne and Frost. He took immediate steps to remove Ramiro from the scene.

"I am now back and in charge of my estate. Cipriano tells me my own men will arrive within a day or two. When that happens, Ramiro, you and your men may return to your own tenancy."

The English officers were next in Alvaro's sights. "Luke, I can no longer see any purpose in you and Peter remaining here. You have completed your assessment of our military needs and can report to your government accordingly, and in regard to your secret mission, I hear you have decided that there was no traitor other than Camilla de Mota, and she has escaped our clutches by returning to her family in Spain."

Luke retorted, "We cannot leave. We are under the queen's specific orders to continue the investigation of three murders, including that of your brother and cousin. I have just returned from Lisbon with that order reaffirmed by the queen, who passed on vital information that will enable us to solve those atrocities within a few days. Then we will be gone."

Alvaro turned to Ana Cipriano, who stood beside her husband in welcoming the new marquess home. "Take me to Micaela. I have some very good news for her."

Ana hesitated.

Ramiro answered, "The lady Micaela is no longer here. She left several days ago."

Alvaro seemed stunned. "She is not here? Where is she?"

Luke lied again. "I assumed she headed for Lisbon, but she has not been seen at court."

Alvaro was genuinely alarmed. "She should have stayed in the security and comfort of the castle. She is—"

"Pregnant!" said Ramiro.

Luke tried to reduce the growing intensity. "I imagine that is why you were in a hurry to obtain permission to marry your brother's widow, and by your initial mood, you appear pleased. It was granted?"

"Yes. The cardinal archbishop told me that originally, the church had insisted that in such cases, the surviving brother had an obligation to marry the widow, but over the centuries, its position had completely reversed."

Alvaro seemed completely disoriented by the news of Micaela's absence. Luke could see anger rising in his face, which was soon red, and his veins began to bulge. "Where is the nefarious viscount Roberto Delgado? Was he not part of your investigating team after I was removed from it because of something that the marchioness Joana may or may not have heard?"

"He has been summoned back to Lisbon to become a leading member of the queen's council."

"Did he spend any time with Micaela while I was away?"

"No, Micaela kept to herself and only communicated with Ana. When we needed to question Micaela, it was left to me," Luke replied.

"She must be with him!" shouted Alvaro.

"Delgado?" asked Ramiro.

"Yes, that snake in the grass has tricked my vulnerable Micaela. He has kidnapped her."

"Only, if unlike us, he knows where she is," replied Luke. "She left here days ago. Delgado only went this morning."

"Cipriano, meet me in my apartment in an hour!" ordered a confused, emotional, and furious Alvaro.

Supper that night was tense. It was limited to Alvaro, the two Ciprianos, Ramiro, Luke, and Peter. The three guests withdrew as soon as it was possible.

The next morning, just before noon, Matos returned with the regiment of local militia that was assembled in the castle courtyard rather than being immediately demobilized and returned to their families and occupations. Luke noticed through the tower window that just after they entered the castle, a detachment of cavalry followed them. This detachment did not hide their colors. They were Spanish—and led by Barbosa.

Luke and Ramiro exchanged glances, and the latter muttered, "This is it. I hope Caro acts as planned."

A few minutes later, Spanish troops entered their room and demanded that they remain there until further notice. Fifteen minutes later, Alfredo Matos joined them. He was furious.

"The new marquess has gone mad. He is about to renounce his loyalty to Portugal and take Estrela back under Spanish rule. I refused to agree and, like you, am now a prisoner, as are all your men, Ramiro."

"Is there no way out of here?" whispered Luke.

"No, there are no secret passages. The only way out, other than through the guarded door, is out of the window. You could jump into the raging river hundreds of feet below, but I doubt if you would be rescued by Our Lady of Estrela. We will have to sit here and listen to Da Costa's address to his troops, tenants, and workers," replied Alfredo.

The four prisoners watched and listened as Alvaro announced the transfer of Estrela to Spain and his promotion to Duke of Estrela. There was absolute quietness. He then ordered his militia captains to move the troops to the edges of the Estrela estates and prepare to confront any Portuguese counter attack. The militia suddenly exploded in angry opposition to their orders. Large numbers of men simply walked away, as did many of the servants.

Alfredo was delighted. "What did Alvaro expect? The militia has been away from Estrela for weeks. When they left, Paolo was marquess. They completely missed Rodrigo's brief rule, and Alvaro disappeared a day after he became marquess. If Paolo had returned his estates to Spain, his servants and tenants would have gone along. Paolo was a popular and trusted landlord. Nobody knows Alvaro. He is a complete stranger. Several years of popular lordship, and the people may have responded favorably."

All of a sudden, the door burst opened, and a Spanish officer entered the room.

Ramiro commented, "Welcome, Colonel Barbosa. Are you here to gloat?"

"Not at all. I came to meet the English general. Federico Sanchez sings your praises, Tremayne. He has told me of your achievements over several decades. You have an impossible task here—investigating the local Portuguese noblemen. Their womenfolk are even worse. They have destroyed poor Alvaro da Costa. Sanchez and I tried to prevent the cardinal archbishop granting him a Spanish dukedom. When Paolo refused to accept our offer, that should have been the end of it. Alvaro could never succeed in these circumstances, but the cardinal saw an opportunity that required a lot of luck to have succeeded."

"What do you mean Alvaro destroyed by womenfolk?" asked Alfredo.

"When he left here after his brother's death, he had no thought of handing Estrela over to us. I understand Cipriano had mentioned the offer to him just as he was leaving. When I was escorting him to Toledo, he unburdened himself rather pathetically. At the very moment that the love of his life had become free to marry him, she was drifting away into the arms of a future duke. He told me his love, who was an ambitious woman, was blinded by the chance in time to become a Portuguese duchess. He then asked me if the offer made to Paolo could be reoffered to him. His true love would then see the advantages of being a Spanish duchess over a Portuguese."

"Did you murder Joana da Costa?" asked Luke unexpectedly.

"No. One day I will deal with the Guzman men, but I would never attack their women. If the Duke of Medina-Sidonia is assassinated, then I might be responsible. Sorry, I would love to continue this discussion, gentlemen, but I have to go. I do not have enough troops to assist Alvaro impose his will when most of his own regiment has turned against him. My role is to create problems along the border for you and then quickly disappear. My men stationed along the various entrances to the Estrela estates have seen Portuguese regiments advancing along both major roads to Estrela. You clearly foresaw what was about to happen. I release you from this prison, and half a dozen loyal militia soldiers are outside who will defend you against the apparently raving marquess. I will also free your men, Ramiro, as I leave the castle."

"What was Alvaro up to when you last saw him?" asked Alfredo.

"He and Cipriano were gathering a few faithful around them. They are blissfully unaware of the incoming Portuguese troops. I doubt if they have more than a dozen men. Most of the household servants have quietly disappeared. Good to have met you, General!"

Barbosa and his Spanish troops disappeared.

�֎ **39** ✎

R AMIRO AND MATOS GATHERED their men and deployed them carefully to defend the tower apartments of the castle should Alvaro launch a suicidal attack. They then discussed with Luke and Peter what action should be taken pending the arrival of Caro's troops. Luke suggested that they arrest Alvaro for treason before he disappeared. Ramiro agreed that Luke and Peter approach him to negotiate his surrender.

They discovered Alvaro was holed up in his apartment, protected by half a dozen armed men. They asked to see him but were kept waiting for some time.

Eventually, Cipriano emerged and ushered them into the room.

Alvaro was wild-eyed and in a highly agitated state. He screamed at Luke, "Everybody has betrayed me! Micaela has been taken by Delgado, the queen dismissed me after years of service, Matos turned my own militia against me, and now my Spanish supporters have disappeared!"

"And you have betrayed Portugal! If you come with us now, you will be guaranteed a fair trial for treason. Within hours, at least two regiments of Portuguese troops will be here. Caro will execute you on the spot," lied Luke.

"Everything I have done, I did for Micaela. I will not surrender until I find her—and talk sense into her."

"And what exactly have you done apart from declaring for Spain?" asked Luke.

Alvaro did not answer. He called for the guards outside the door to enter. "Keep the Englishmen here until the Portuguese troops near the castle. Cipriano, come with me!"

Alvaro and Cipriano left the room. Peter reasoned with the soldiers, suggesting that Alvaro's days were numbered, and if they wished to continue as servants or tenants at Estrela, they too should quietly fade away. He also threatened them with execution as traitors immediately on the arrival of Caro's troops. After half an hour, the soldiers looked at each other, nodded, and disappeared.

The rooms next to the marquess's apartment were deserted, and when Luke and Peter reached the ground level, the castle seemed to be firmly in the hands of Ramiro's men, supported by the militia loyal to Matos—and Portugal.

"Where's Alvaro?" asked Ramiro.

"I hoped you had arrested him trying to leave the castle," said Luke.

"We have not arrested him, but he could not have left the castle. I will begin a thorough search," said Alfredo.

"What about Cipriano?" asked Ramiro.

"He was with Alvaro, but I am not sure whether willingly or under some degree of coercion," answered Luke.

The four men crossed the courtyard when two shots rang out.

"The stables!" shouted Alfredo.

As they approached the stables accompanied by several soldiers, Cipriano emerged, a pistol in each hand. "He tried to kill me." He pointed to the second stall in the stable and then followed Luke and Matos, where they found Alvaro lying on the ground. Alfredo Matos bent to examine the prone body of Alvaro da Costa.

Suddenly, Alvaro stirred, jumped to his feet, and placed his dagger to the throat of Alfredo. Simultaneously, Cipriano pointed his re-primed pistol at Luke and handed the second to Alvaro.

"Call your men off! The four of us will leave here unimpeded. You two will mount this chestnut horse. I will tie you together, and if you attempt to escape, you will both be shot!" screamed a clearly disturbed Alvaro.

At that moment, Ramiro entered the stall and was confronted with the situation.

"If you wish to see your two comrades alive, open the gates and allow us to depart!" continued the raving Alvaro.

Luke nodded to Ramiro, indicating that for the time being, conformity with the demands of the marquess would be the best approach. Ramiro and Peter considered their options. Peter demanded a musket and asked Ramiro for his most proficient musketeer. With luck, they could take out both Alvaro and Cipriano before the rebels could shoot Luke and Alfredo.

Ramiro was more cautious. "No, it is too risky. Both shots would have to be accurate and fatal. One or two wounded men could still kill our friends. We will follow them and wait our opportunity."

Ramiro and Peter, with four of Ramiro's men, were soon on the trail of the fugitives and their prisoners.

Luke whispered to Alfredo, "Cipriano is struggling to ride his horse, keep a primed pistol trained on us and guide our horse by its attached rope. Ramiro is close behind. If we can cause a disturbance, it will give him a chance to act."

"What do you suggest?" asked Alfredo.

"It's risky because we do not know exactly how this horse will react. Both of us should dig our heels into the animal, hoping it will pull away, giving Ramiro and his men a clear shot."

"You will need to wait until we reach a straight stretch of the road," advised Alfredo.

Fifteen minutes later, they entered into an ideal long straight stretch that ran parallel with the raging river. Luke and Alfredo dug their heels into the horse, which reacted by pulling away from Cipriano and running very close to the river.

Several shots were heard, which panicked the horse into a wild gallop. It slipped on the wet bank and slid into the raging stream. The shots missed Alvaro and Cipriano, who galloped away, unfollowed, as their pursuers tried to save their friends who were still tied together with their hands shackled as the horse struggled to keep afloat.

Perhaps Our Lady of Estrela did act to save Luke and Alfredo. A rope bridge that had spanned the river before the recent floods had been swept away but now created a barrier just off the bank, netting the struggling horse and its two riders. Peter, attached to a rope, made his way cautiously into the river and cut Luke and Alfredo free. The horse, freed from its two riders and a heavy saddle, managed to stagger up the bank.

"Do we follow the villains downhill?" asked Luke.

"No need. I can hear the beat of a drum. Caro's men are almost here. We will stay put in case Alvaro tries to double back," said Ramiro.

"Shouldn't we send someone to warn Caro's men that Alvaro and Cipriano are fugitives?" asked Peter.

"No, Caro is well aware of Alvaro's planned treachery. We will wait," replied Ramiro.

"I doubt if they will attempt to bluff their way through. They will probably hide until the troops move through—and be completely free," bemoaned Peter.

Luke and Alfredo, shivering from the cold because of their immersion, decided to ride back to the castle immediately with horses borrowed from Ramiro's men.

Two hours later, as they looked through the tower windows toward the main gate, Luke and Alfredo could hear and see Caro's troops marching up the road. They were both surprised to see that behind the three officers leading the group—Caro, Ramiro, and Peter—there were two more riders who had been mounted back to front. There was no mistaking these disgraced riders. It was Alvaro da Costa and Carlos Cipriano.

Luke was surprised. "They must have done something very stupid, or Caro is a brilliant tactician. I never expected them to be captured so easily."

An hour later, Caro, Ramiro, Alfredo, Luke and Perter gathered to eat, drink, and discuss the evolving situation.

Luke was congratulatory. "How did you manage to capture them?"

"I took Ramiro's advice and sent small units up every possible track through the adjoining forests. They probably thought they were quite safe taking the path farthest from the river that winds ever so slowly up and down one of the neighboring mountains. My men simply turned them around in their saddles and led them back to the main force and then onto here," explained Caro.

"Where are they now?" asked Alfredo.

"Each has been confined to a single room with four of my men in the room and four guarding every exit," continued Caro.

"Where do we go from here?" asked Ramiro.

"There is no doubting Alvaro's treachery. He was caught in the act. He should be taken to Lisbon for the queen to determine his fate. Cipriano is of less importance and could be dealt with by summary military justice," declared the Portuguese general.

"Before Alvaro is sent to Lisbon and Carlos executed, Ramiro and I need to question them further regarding the three murders," explained Luke.

"Does it matter? They will both be removed from the scene in one way or another. They cannot be hanged or decapitated twice," commented Caro bluntly.

"We may even get an explanation of why Alvaro embarked on his killing spree and major act of betrayal," Luke retorted.

The next morning, Caro, Ramiro, and Luke had Alvaro, now shackled and fettered, dragged before them.

Caro asked, "Why did the head of military intelligence, a loyal servant of the Portuguese government for years, contemplate such a major betrayal?"

"Don't be a hypocrite, Caro. You and I were both born under the rule of Felipe of Spain, the current king, or his father. It was Luisa and her husband who rose in revolt against their legitimate monarch. Our families chose unwisely to side with the rebels. All I was doing was restoring part of the rebellious Portuguese province to its rightful ruler," Alvaro responded in his defense.

"Rubbish!" interrupted Ramiro. "You were a landless younger son, jealous of your brother the count and desirous to achieve the marquisate as soon as possible. The thought of a dukedom was just too much for your overweening ambition."

"I don't think that is a fair assessment of Alvaro's motives," said Luke. "He was driven and misled by a woman. He has been in love with his brother's wife Micaela for years. They were lovers and planned to marry. Everybody knows that to a French aristocrat such as Micaela, even being a marchioness is not enough. To become Duchess of Estrela would have been the perfect wedding present."

"Will I have a chance to see Micaela?" asked Alvaro, surprised at Luke's understanding comment.

"Unless she reveals her whereabouts, it will be impossible. Maybe if she hears you are imprisoned, awaiting execution, she may come to you," suggested a sympathetic Luke.

Ramiro changed tack. "When did you decide to murder your cousin's wife, Joana?"

"You have caught me red-handed acting against the house of Braganza, but I murdered no one. We all know the three victims were strangled by a man with strong hands. I have small hands and am missing three fingers on my right. There is no way I could have murdered those people—and you know it."

"No, but you could have ordered it done to ease your way to the succession at Estrela!" declaimed Caro.

"Prove it!" was the defiant reply. "In fact, I did not even think about any imminent succession until after Joana was murdered. Neither her death nor that of Teresa Pinto can, in any way, be attributed to my desire to become Marquess of Estrela. I will say no more."

Alvaro was led back to the room that served as his prison.

"LET'S BRING IN CIPRIANO," suggested Ramiro.

"Not just yet. I would like to question his wife again. Alvaro has nothing to lose. He could have confessed proudly to the murders. Instead, he denies two of them and is strangely quiet in the case of his brother."

"You accept that he had no part in the first two murders?" asked Caro.

"It's a possibility" was Luke's measured response.

Ana Cipriano was drawn and anxious. "May I see my husband?" she asked.

"After we question him later this morning, you may visit him," said Caro.

"What will happen to him?"

"Unfortunately, Ana, he will be executed as a traitor, unless you can give us any evidence that might mitigate the sentence against him," said Luke gently.

"And he is also suspected of murdering the three persons we are investigating," added Ramiro.

"There is some evidence that he was misled by Alvaro da Costa into treachery and possible murder. This is where you may be able to help him," continued the gentle, encouraging Luke.

Both Caro and Ramiro clearly admired his interrogation technique.

"When did Carlos first meet Alvaro?" Luke asked.

"At the time that Colonel Barbosa was here, suggesting to Paolo that he do exactly what Alvaro has attempted. Paolo had called Alvaro in as head of military intelligence to monitor the situation. During that visit, Alvaro and Carlos spent some time together."

"Did he mention anything of what they discussed?"

"Only that Paolo might have been rash in knocking back the offer so forcefully. If Spain made a sudden peace with its northern neighbors, it would be in a position militarily to reconquer Portugal. Carlos hinted that Paolo's successors might have a different view."

"Did Carlos make any comments that would suggest he would work toward achieving the succession for Alvaro sooner rather than later?"

"No. His only comment comparing the three Da Costas as marquess was that both Rodrigo and Alvaro, being courtiers, would probably stay in Lisbon and allow him to run the estate as if it were his own."

Luke continued, "Ana, we suspect that Carlos physically strangled both your friend the marchioness Joana and Teresa, Countess Pinto. If it were true, could there be any possible explanation?"

Luke was unprepared for the response. The usually calm, withdrawn, and sober noblewoman burst into tears, uncontrollable and edging toward the hysterical. Caro and Ramiro looked embarrassed. Luke indicated that they might temporarily leave the room and, in the process, summon one of Ana's personal maids. A girl arrived, and after much consoling and with Luke holding her hand, Ana slowly regained her composure. She began to talk very softly about her husband.

"Carlos loves women but takes to extremes the view of most aristocratic men that female servants and the wives and daughters of tenants are there for their pleasure. The marchioness Joana was aware of the problem and acted to redeem the situation. Over the years, I thought Carlos had lost his insatiable appetite, but in the weeks before her death, Joana informed me that a tenant had complained about the abuse of his daughter."

"Rape?" asked Luke.

"The inferior classes would never make that sort of accusation," Ana confided.

"Are you suggesting that if Carlos did kill anybody, it was probably related to his relationships with women?"

"Yes, but I cannot see how it could relate to any of the victims you are investigating."

Ana left. Ramiro and Caro returned. Carlos Cipriano was brought before them.

Ramiro began, "Why did you murder the marchioness Joana, the countess Teresa Pinto, and, finally, the marquess Rodrigo da Costa?"

"I did not. Why would I?"

"You are about to be decapitated for treason, so a confession of murder is not going to affect your future, but a confession or at least an explanation of your role in the killings will wash away the falsehoods that Alvaro da Costa has been telling about you," lied Luke.

Ramiro picked up the thread. "Yes. He has confessed to ordering the three murders to quicken his accession to the marquisate and that you were the willing accomplice and actually committed the murders for him. But what was your reward?"

"That is a complete fabrication! Why would Alvaro implicate himself in three murders he had no part in?" replied a suspicious Carlos.

"He has nothing to lose given his imminent execution, and we think he was trying to impress his sweetheart that he had the three killings committed so that she would become a duchess," added Luke.

"We believe you committed at least two of the murders on your own behalf to cover your continuing illegal sexual attraction to women," declared Caro.

Cipriano was silent for a time. He finally announced, "I don't want that fop Alvaro taking credit for a plan and killings that were both entirely mine. I killed Joana because she claimed I had once again broken my promise not to force my attentions on the female servants and that, as she had previously threatened, she would report it to the marquess and, this time, demand my sacking. I did not want to lose my position."

"It had nothing to do with what she thought she had heard about a successor to Paolo handing over the estate to Spain?" asked Caro.

"No. At that stage, there was no such plan."

"And Teresa Pinto?" asked Ramiro.

"As you all know, she used her charms to seduce men and bend them to her will. She invited me to her room in the queen's apartment at Magellan for such a dalliance—or so I thought. She led me on, and when I persisted, she began to scream. I had to silence her."

"And Rodrigo?"

"Saving my position. When Paolo announced the renunciation of his title and indicated that Rodrigo would succeed, I had a long talk with the incoming marquess about the future. He told me categorically that he would not be coming to Estrela. He and his wife were courtiers who would never leave Lisbon. He was open to me running the estates holding a position more elevated than just chamberlain. I said, 'Would I would be marquess in all but name?' He said yes."

"Why did you then kill the man who was going to improve your status?" asked Ramiro.

"He immediately went back on his word. On the very day that he arrived here to take up the position, he told me that his wife was desperate to become marchioness and wanted to leave court and become a rural noblewoman with a major hand in running the estate. I immediately asked where that left my future. His blunt answer was that he did not know and that his wife would make the decision."

"Clearly, none of murders had anything to do directly with the transfer of Estrela to Spain. Were you behind that?"

"Only in part. Alvaro told me that he was determined to marry his brother's widow. He wanted to give her a present that was beyond belief. I reminded him of a discussion we had had months ago around the time of Paolo's refusal of the Spanish offer. I suggested that if he delivered Estrela to Spain, he would be rewarded with a duchy. His wife would be a Spanish duchess. He told me he would leave directly for Toledo to receive permission to marry his brother's widow. I knew nothing about the actual transfer of the estate back to Spain until he returned with the Chameleon."

"Would this change of loyalty have improved your personal position?"

"Yes. Alvaro told me that as a reward for returning Estrela to Spain, he and Micaela would join the Spanish court. Micaela would be a Spanish duchess after spending years as a lowly Portuguese countess. Given this expected absence in Madrid, Alvaro would seek for me an enhanced Spanish title and the ability to lease large parts of his estate on my own behalf."

After Cipriano was taken back to his room, Luke remarked, "Well, I was absolutely wrong. I saw Alvaro as having ordered the killing of all three to conceal his plot to seize Estrela and hand over to the Spaniards. Our one-time friend has been brought undone by an ambitious woman whose role in this whole affair remains unclear."

"How will Ana Cipriano cope with all this?" asked Caro.

"Damnation!" shouted Luke as he ran from the room, followed by his comrades. He raced to the room inhabited by Cipriano and asked of the guards, "Has the baroness Cipriano visited her husband?"

"Yes."

"She has just gone in," one of them answered.

Luke burst through the door, espied the noblewoman's laden basket on the table, and immediately confiscated it.

"I am sorry, Ana. Whether you are doing this to punish Carlos because of his misdeeds or assisting your husband to escape rightful punishment, I cannot let you end his life."

Ramiro and Caro heard Luke's last utterance. "How did you know?" they both asked in unison.

"I did not know. I just felt that Ana would do something for her husband. You will probably find poison herbs or powders in this basket."

Luke sent an immediate report to the queen, and Alvaro, under heavy guard, was escorted to the royal prison in Lisbon. Cipriano was executed by firing squad at dawn the following morning.

Two days later, a courier arrived with orders for Caro and Ramiro. Luke was surprised that there was nothing for him. Caro was ordered to demobilize all existing militia and return with most of the army to Lisbon, leaving a sufficient garrison in Magellan.

Ramiro was most surprised at his royal missive. An overjoyed man sought Luke out to let him know its contents. "Meet the new Marquess of Estrela!" he announced.

Luke wondered if the queen had, against her better judgment, revealed the truth of Ramiro's paternity. "And how has that come about?" he asked.

"With Alvaro's treachery and without him leaving an heir, Estrela reverts to the crown. The queen decided to reassign the title and estates to Ramiro, Lord of Lima, for his services to the state. For the time being, I will be the royal governor of the castle and its lands until she has had time to formalize the new grant of the marquisate."

There was much celebration that night.

The next morning, another courier arrived from Lisbon with a sealed letter for Luke.

Thank you for your service to Portugal. Your time here is at an end. I have already arranged for you to take a packet back to London. Return to Lisbon immediately, and we can tidy up a few loose ends. Please bring Ana de Cipriano with you. I have offered her a place among my ladies-in-waiting as a reward for her long service to my cousin Joana.

Three days later, Luke waited in an antechamber within the queen's apartment. The queen entered the room alone and indicated to Luke to sit beside her.

"I have made a number of decisions over the last few days about which you are entitled to be informed. After conflicting advice from many sources, I decided not to send Alvaro da Costa to trial for treachery. He was my loyal intelligence chief for years, and his moment of betrayal was provoked by the disloyal behavior of the woman he loved. I have exiled him for life to India. He left yesterday morning for Goa as its military governor. He will suffer immediate execution if he ever sets foot in Portugal again."

"And what has happened to the woman he loved?"

"She delivered a red-haired baby, and her marriage to Roberto Delgado will now occur with my blessing."

"A dangerous woman!"

The queen did not comment and continued, "General, I have two pieces of bad news. Two days ago, Madalena de Albuquerque died. She suddenly collapsed and never regained consciousness. An Irish merchant has undertaken to return the body to Dublin to be buried with her family. And only this morning, the English consul informed me that your lord protector, Oliver Cromwell, has also died. I hope that whatever government emerges in England, you can convince it to honor its treaty with Portugal and supply the much-needed troops to our defense. If it does I hope you will command the English contribution." In normal circumstances Luke would have relished the opportunuty but with Cromwell's death his future was suddenly uncertain.

HISTORICAL EPILOGUE

Two years after Cromwell's death, Charles Stuart was returned to the English throne as Charles II. In 1662, he married Queen Luisa's daughter, Catherine of Braganza, and, in the following year, sent three thousand English troops to assist the Portuguese.

With this assistance and a unified army, Portugal had a number of significant victories, and in 1668, the king of Spain signed the Treaty of Lisbon, recognizing Portuguese independence.

Catherine outlived her husband, and on her return to Portugal at the beginning of the eighteenth century, she, like her mother, acted as regent.

www.ingramcontent.com/pod-product-compliance
Lightning Source LLC
Chambersburg PA
CBHW032028310726
48972CB00002B/577